Antique Mourning

Book 5 in the Alicia Trent Mystery Series

Eileen Harris

A Wings ePress, Inc.
Mystery

Wings ePress, Inc.

Edited by: Jeanne Smith
Copy Edited by: Joan C. Powell
Executive Editor: Jeanne Smith
Cover Artist: Trisha FitzGerald-Jung

All rights reserved

Wings ePress Books
www.wingsepress.com

Published In the United States Of America

Wings ePress Inc.
3000 N. Rock Road
Newton, KS 67114

Dedication

To all the wonderful teachers that make literature important.
Mine was Mr. Leonard.

One

"You want to do what?"

"Calm down, Barry, and just listen for a minute. You're making this seem bigger than it is. I'm not planning a trip to the moon."

"You might as well be. New York is almost as far away! Okay, okay, Alicia, don't give me that look. I'll listen to whatever you have to say, but I don't think you can convince me that spending a year in New York is a good idea."

"To start with, it isn't a full year. It's just the school year, so I'd be home by next summer. This little college has a great reputation in the arts. Moldering in one of their old buildings they have a large collection of antiques that one of their alumni donated years ago. They need someone to catalog the collection so they can sell it, and I'm flattered they chose me. The funds will be used to finish their new poetry building and even provide a couple of scholarships for new students."

"I'm not questioning their need or their credentials. I just don't see why you have to go all the way across the country. Don't they have anyone on the East Coast that understands antiques? There are certainly more collectibles in that part of the country than out here, so you'd think they'd have some experts a lot closer. Besides, the school's collection can't be so big that it would take a year to catalog."

I wasn't about to admit it, but his question gave me pause because I, too, had wondered why they had chosen someone so far from New York. I'd been honest when I'd said I was flattered, but I was also a wee bit concerned. Even so, whatever their reasoning, I had decided I wanted this job, so I ignored his first question and answered his second concern. "No, of course it isn't that large, but along with the job, they are offering me the chance to take a couple of classes for free. Well, not exactly free, it would be part of my salary package, but it's a great opportunity. You know I've been wanting to take some advanced art courses. I'd love to have a better background in art history."

Barry frowned. "I get the feeling I'm losing this discussion, but one last question. What do you plan to do about Eclectic Treasures while you're gone?"

"Well, as my partner, you have as much of a say in that as I do, but I thought you might hire that extra help you've been wanting. The main part of our business has always been done by appointment. Once you get the new assistant trained, let them man the shop. Then you only have to show up for the appointments. It would give you a chance to spend more time with Susan. I also think that while I'm back East, I'll be able to acquire some great inventory additions."

"Okay, you've made a very convincing argument for going. Why do I feel like there is still something you aren't telling me?"

"Probably because we've talked about reasons, not feelings. I think I need to shake up my life a little. I miss Lawrence, but it's more than that. Things just seem a little stale now. I think I need a temporary change, and this opportunity seems tailor-made for me."

"Maybe so, but what are you going to do with that brute of a cat you brought back from England? I know your neighbor always wants Watson, but that cat?"

"It seems Watson and Taboo have become a matched set. One won't go much of anywhere without the other. Since Ted and Norma aren't willing to give up time with Watson, they have had to learn to love Taboo as well. So, you can see all the details are worked out."

"You may be right. You're also right about the shop. It will be fine and we can definitely use some new inventory. I still have misgivings, and I'll miss you, of course, but over and above that, I hate to see you taking off into the unknown by yourself again."

"Ah, I guess it wouldn't do any good to tell you one more time that I can take care of myself. This time you may not have any reason to worry. The college has a great culinary department. They were hunting for a master chef, and after I told them about Laudine, they offered her the opportunity to go and train their staff. She will also have the chance to design and teach a class both of the semesters I'll be there. I've never seen her so excited. She's working out the arrangements with the restaurant for a leave."

"Oh, right! Now instead of one person that always manages to find trouble, there will be two of you! I can't tell you how relieved I am."

~ * ~

That conversation with Barry happened two weeks ago, but it kept running through my mind as Laudine and I sat on the plane headed for New York. I was excited about what the future would bring, but I hoped I wasn't making this trip in order to run away from the past. Time would answer that question. I definitely knew Laudine didn't have any doubts that she'd made the right decision. Her constant excited chatter made her feelings clear. I put my worries aside and turned to join in her excitement.

It was early morning when the plane touched down at Albany International. Laudine said, "I still have trouble understanding this country. Why is Albany the capital of New York? This small airport is nice, but New York City has huge airports. Besides, I wanted to see the big city. I've heard so much about the place."

"I can't tell you why Albany is the capital. Maybe it's so that students will be confused when they learn geography."

"Okay, don't think just because I giggled, I really think you're funny."

"Well, don't worry. You've spent time in Paris, and I'm sure it's spectacular, so you know what big cities are like. Besides, it's not like this is our last chance to get there. Hopefully we'll have time to make a trip down to the city for a visit before we go home."

We'd elected to drive the distance from Albany to the town of Canajoharie where the college was located. With little experience of the Northeast, we both wanted a chance to get a feel for the country. We chose to use the small back roads so our only view wasn't the interstate's tunnels of green. It was late August, but cool enough that we didn't need the rental's air conditioning. When we hit the first quaint small town, Laudine said, "I can't believe how beautiful all this is. When I worked for the Darnells, I never got to get out much. I love these towns and the wonderful architecture of their old buildings. It's so different from the wide-open spaces of the West. Strange each side of the same country can be so different and still so fascinating."

"I hear that. I love what little I've seen of the Northeast, but somehow, I always eventually get homesick for the West. What intrigues me most is how different it looks here in every season. Verdant green in the summer, glorious colors when the trees change in the fall, nothing but white in every direction in the winter, and fresh light green dotted with flowers in the spring. We should get to see all four seasons on this trip. I hope the reality lives up to all the pictures I've seen."

"Not to change the subject, but I'm starving. When do you plan on stopping for lunch?"

I smiled. "The cook is starving! I don't know how in the world you keep your girlish figure. If you can wait about an hour, I thought we'd eat in Amsterdam. It's a little more than halfway to the college, and June, a customer at the shop, told me about a restaurant there that she says is to die for. How does that sound?"

She'd no more than agreed before she was leaning her seat back and falling asleep. I spent the quiet hour to Amsterdam musing about what we'd find in Canajoharie.

The Raindancer Restaurant wasn't anything like I'd imagined. It wasn't one of the quaint roadside inns we'd seen here and there since we'd started driving. The building was in downtown Amsterdam and a lot more modern than I'd expected. As I drove up and parked, a sleepy Laudine said, "You're sure this is where you want to eat? It doesn't seem to have a lot of the charm typical of the region."

"It isn't exactly what I was expecting, but I feel like we should trust my friend's judgment, since she grew up around here and ought to know. According to her, this place has been around for years and is consistently great. I say we give it a try."

The inside was extremely attractive, but decidedly modern. I'd been expecting the old-world Italian decor that New York is famous for, and this was the generic decor one might find anywhere. I'd begun to wonder what June had gotten me into, when one look at the menu chased away all my doubts. There were just enough selections for anyone to find something they'd like. For starters, we made a trip to one of the most well-stocked salad bars I'd seen. After she had eaten hers, Laudine said, "Wow, that was great! I have to admit I was skeptical, but, wow! So many choices and so yummy. I could have been happy with just salad."

"When June recommended this place, she said we would get plenty of good Italian on our trip, but that this place was different and well worth a try."

"If the rest of the food here is as fresh and tasty as the salad and that heavenly bread, we're in for a treat, and we owe June a big thank you. I can't believe those wheels of cheese on the salad bar. I haven't tasted cheese that good since I left France. We certainly don't get much of that in the West."

For her main dish, Laudine had seafood en casserole. I went with the Mandarin Mahi Mahi. Both were perfectly cooked, and even Laudine couldn't find any fault with the flavor. We wanted to try some of the wonderful sounding desserts on the menu, but decided we just didn't have room. As soon as we were back in the car, Laudine began listing off the ingredients in her casserole. "I want to remember them so I can try making that dish. It was too good not to add it to my list."

I laughed, "Okay, smarty pants, you are very good at sussing out what's in a recipe, but you missed the sun-dried tomatoes."

She gave me a mock frown. "Now who's being the smarty pants?"

It wasn't long after we got back on the road that we crossed into Montgomery County and knew we had to be getting close to our destination. Laudine began leafing through a travel brochure about the area. "A lot of old towns in this part of the country have had serious fires in their history, destroying a lot that tourists would have loved. We seem to be in luck with Canajoharie, so there should still be some good architecture. They've had some fires, too, but they were very long ago.

I resisted the urge to glance at the pictures in her brochure. The winding country roads we were traveling needed all my concentration. "That's also a good thing, because it should mean there will be more antiques around that I may want to acquire for the shop."

"We'll definitely have to see the Van Alstun house." Laudine continued reading. "It's built in the Dutch Colonial style and was constructed in 1730. Your president, George Washington, even stayed there."

Here I couldn't help laughing, and Laudine demanded to know what I found funny. I said, "I don't think I've ever been to a tourist attraction in the northern part of the country that is east of the Mississippi River that doesn't boast that President Washington stayed there. It's been a joke for quite a while because no one could have stayed at all the places that claim he was there."

Laudine frowned. "Sometimes I am reminded of what a strange country this is, but never mind, there's a ton of stuff listed here that sounds worth seeing. It's interesting how many different eras are represented in the buildings. Here's something I bet you didn't know. They have one of only three dummy-lights left in the country."

"Okay, I give up. What is a 'dummy-light?'"

"It says here that they were traffic lights built around 1926. They were on a pedestal on wheels and set in the middle of the street when needed." Before I could comment, her mind jumped direction. "Hey, did you know Druthmar College is located in what used to be a convent? The brochure doesn't say how long ago that was, and there isn't a picture in here, but it sounds interesting."

"I'm ashamed to say I didn't do much research on the history of the place. I mainly checked out their academic credentials."

"Are we going to drive the extra four miles into town or turn off on the road that goes straight to the school?"

"It is getting kind of late in the day. I guess for now we'd better let the head guy know we're here and find out where we're staying. We should have lots of chances to explore the town and surrounding area another time."

"Okay, from what I can tell, we're about three miles from the turnoff."

<h1 style="text-align:center">Two</h1>

In spite of the fact that we were both watching for the turn, we almost missed it. There was an ornate metal sign naming the college and its date of inception, but it was so covered by brush and vines it was nearly impossible to see. The road was paved, but narrow and bordered so closely by forest that it, too, was almost invisible.

As I braked hard to keep from passing the entrance, Laudine said, "Ali, did you bring the bottle and the clock?"

"Don't tell me you're getting spooked already? I did bring them, but I can't imagine needing them on this trip."

I was joking and didn't glance over to see her slightly worried expression. I was too engrossed in my driving. The path—it couldn't be called a road—to the college was paved part of the way with cobblestones, more appropriate for the horse drawn carriages it had been built for than our car. In spite of the bumpy ride, I had to admit it was picturesque. The entrance road was almost a mile long and fairly steep. The college was so occluded by trees that we only got infrequent glimpses of the buildings until we rounded the final curve on our way up. I wasn't sure if people in this part of the country would call this a mountain or large hill, but to me it was a small mountain with the college sprawled down the side. For some reason, I'd been expecting very utilitarian architecture. Boy, was I wrong! As we took the final turn, Laudine said, "Talk about medieval. That building wouldn't be out of place in Tibet."

She wasn't entirely wrong. The college was a huge warren spilling down the side of the mountain. Part of it appeared to extend back into the side of the hill. If not for the more modern buildings scattered around, I could believe we'd traveled back in time. "Isn't it great? I'm going to love this place. I hope we get the chance to explore every inch and not just the section where they store donations."

"You can explore all you want. I find the place creepy. I hope the kitchen section is a little more modern."

I stopped the car on the circular drive that fronted the main building. There were doors, alcoves, and windows everywhere, but one small inconspicuous door had a large sign saying "OFFICE." We were out of the car and halfway across the brick forecourt when a short rotund man came bounding out the door.

"Hello, hello. I've been watching for you. I'm Leroy Cummings. Welcome to Druthmar! You must be Alicia and Laudine. I'm so happy you're here."

I shook hands with the college president. "It's nice to meet you. Do we call you president or professor? I know you still teach some classes."

"Leroy is just fine, for most occasions. If we have to be formal, either title is appropriate."

"Druthmar is quite a place. It's bigger than I expected. About how many students attend during the fall semester?"

"It's actually growing bigger than we'd like. We're expecting approximately forty-three hundred students when the semester begins, which barely allows us to keep our classification as a small college. We have to keep our enrollment under five thousand to keep that status. Growth is part of the reason we want to sell the antique collection. Even though our goal is to remain small, we want to be able to provide excellent facilities for our students. A couple of new buildings, beginning with a poetry building, will help us keep up."

"A poetry building? How does that help deal with the influx of students?" Laudine asked.

I cringed a little at Laudine's lack of tact, but Leroy said, "Ah, a good question. It seems like we're getting a bit of a reputation for the quality of our English Department. We have a variety of classes related to poetry. We get a lot of undergraduate as well as MFA students with an interest in that direction. We have enough funds from donations for some new classrooms, and we already have one new dorm underway, so it seemed sensible to use whatever funds the stored items bring in to enhance the poetry program.

"I shouldn't keep you standing out here. I'm sure you want to get settled in, so why don't I show you where you'll be staying while you're here? You can deal with all the paperwork tomorrow."

Laudine smiled and said, "That sounds great."

Our new boss continued. "For your stay here, I considered putting you in one of the student dorms, but decided you'd both be closer to your work if you stayed in the main building. We have some decent accommodations for visiting professors and such. If you'll follow me, I'll show you the way. I'll have one of the workers park your car and bring your things up, once you've seen the rooms."

I'd left the keys in the car, so we followed Leroy to a self-operated elevator that looked like it had been designed in the dark ages. I was about to make a comment when he said, "We're very proud of our elevator. I think it must have been designed by a genius. This building has six floors, but they aren't stacked neatly one on top the other. We call them levels. Finding the way up using the stairs is quite tricky. This elevator goes to the fourth level and then there is another to the top. Fortunately, you will be on three, but I think you will still appreciate not having to always use the stairs. All the guest quarters are on that floor, as well as a lot of unused rooms."

I said, "Along with the office and guest rooms, are there classes held in this building?"

"Yes, some of the first level and all the second contain classrooms. Oh, the kitchen and cafeteria are also on the first level. The staff members that live on campus and I are on the fourth. There are two other more modern buildings that are also classrooms. Then there is a library, and even though we don't have any intercollegiate sports, there is a small gym for physical education classes. In this building behind my office are all the business offices. I'll show you those tomorrow when we get your paperwork completed. I think that's all the buildings except for the student dorms, but I don't expect you to remember all these places. I left a copy in your rooms of the map we give new students."

I noticed he hadn't mentioned what the 5th and 6th levels were used for, but rather than ask I decided to wait and see what the map had to say. During our conversation, the elevator had creaked its way to the third floor. This section of the building seemed very old but well maintained. There were five doors off the part of the hall we could see from the elevator. Leroy led us to one in the middle. Inside was a beautiful suite of rooms with two large bedrooms, one on either side of a central sitting area. Behind that was a well-equipped modern bathroom. It all looked very livable and comfortable.

With a few words of instruction about the mechanics of the room, such as how to work the heat, he prepared to leave. Laudine and I snickered a little about being given heating instructions in August. He must have heard us, because he laughed, turned back from the door and said, "I forgot for a moment that you're from out West. Take my word that one of these nights you'll be glad you know how to work the heat. We're high enough here that it can get very chilly, even in August. In past years we've often had snow in September."

We thanked him again and he left us, promising to see us at dinner. I'd carried a padded bag up with me, so while we waited for our luggage, I pulled out the bottle and clock. I placed them on the nightstand beside what was to be my bed. As I set the bottle down, a small tendril of white curled up through the three sections and then nothing. I was glad Laudine was busy examining her own room and hadn't seen. She would have asked what the white in the bottle signified, and I had no idea. In the beginning, when I'd first found this antique in a mansion full of hoarded treasures, the three-tiered bottle had only displayed a few different colors, and I had learned what emotion each one represented from an ancient book also found among the hoard. Now those primary colors were often combined to create an infinite number of shades. Sometimes the meaning was clear and others I didn't have a clue. At least on this trip I wouldn't have to contend with the third item, a red circlet I had found at the Indian ruins on Nick's dude ranch in Arizona. My former fiancé hadn't had any idea where the necklace had come from, and he hadn't been affected by it the way I had. I still found all its capabilities unknowable, so I'd left it home locked in a metal box.

It wasn't ten minutes until there was a knock at the door. When Laudine opened it, a luggage cart rolled into the room. It took me a moment to see the small man pushing the cart. He was barely as tall as the cart handle. Neither Laudine nor I had brought a lot of luggage, but even so, I didn't see how anyone so small had the strength to push the cart. Before I could offer to help, the shortest man I'd ever met stepped out from behind the cart to introduce himself. It was a shock when his strong, deep-bass voice informed us that he was Alex Walsh, the college handyman.

After we all shook hands and introduced ourselves, he told us dinner was served at six. He offered to come back and show us the way down, but we assured him we could find the first floor. He was so genuinely helpful I knew I was going to like Mr. Walsh.

By the time we'd put our things away and changed from our travel clothes, we needed to begin finding our way down. We took a look at the map Leroy had given us. It was a layout of the whole campus showing all the buildings, not a map of this building. I was disappointed because it gave no clue about the 5th and 6th levels. We weren't worried about finding our way down. We could see the elevator from our doorway, but we decided taking the stairs would be easier than trying to figure out how to operate that antique. There was a sign pointing to our left that said "Exit." When we reached the corner, we looked both ways and then at each other. This hall extended in both directions. Rather than coming to an end, they both culminated in an intersection. We turned and walked to the other end of our hall only to find it also intersected with a long hallway. I said, "I think exploring the halls for a way down better wait for another time. We're going to have to brave the elevator after all."

Laudine whispered, "Now do you agree this place is spooky? A map of *this* building would be a lot more help than this campus one. From the look of the construction, this place has to be ancient. When the convent or monastery or whatever this place started out as was here, it must have been almost a full city. The elevator will be a breeze compared to negotiating this maze."

"You don't need to whisper. Just because the place is old and huge doesn't mean it has to be spooky. Once we figure our way around, it will feel more comfortable. I've never known you to be so uneasy."

"I'm not sure exactly what is making me jumpy. There's just something about the feel of this old place. I'm sure I'll get used to it. Let's get this elevator figured out. This cooler weather gives me quite an appetite."

I smiled to myself because Laudine's words showed how completely she had adapted to Arizona, that she now found August in upstate New York cool.

As it turned out, meals for the staff were served in a side room off the campus cafeteria. The map had indicated there were several fast-food locations around campus, but this room was adjacent to the main cafeteria. It was big but still had a cozy atmosphere, largely because of the huge fireplace that dominated one end of the room. There were several four-person tables scattered around for lunch or breakfast, but whatever staff was in residence all ate their evening meal together at one massive table. I counted twenty chairs, and they weren't crowded together. The giant table seemed to be a single slab of wood, but I didn't think it could be unless it was ancient. No trees currently alive could produce anything its size.

Tonight, there were only seven of us eating. We'd already met President Cummings and Handyman Walsh. The other three were professors who were there because they were teaching summer classes. Mr. Claude Trumain taught the classes in Renaissance art. I was hoping to take his beginning class in the fall. When I told him so, he said, "I'm always happy to have another student. It seems a lot of today's students are only interested in modern or contemporary work. It's nice to find someone interested in the classics."

He was tall and not bad looking, but he paled beside the mathematics instructor, Kenneth Flame. Even sitting down, you could tell Flame was inches taller than the other man. He was also amazingly good-looking. The only descriptive word that seemed to fit was 'beautiful.' I was sure he would be spoiled and self-centered, but when we were introduced, he didn't sound like it when he said, "I know math isn't nearly as inspiring as Rembrandt and his pals, but dare I hope one or both of you might also want to take a math class?"

"I can't speak for Laudine, but I won't be darkening your classroom door, and for that you should be very grateful, because I would definitely taint the quality of the class."

"I'm sure it can't be that bad, Miss Trent. How about you. Miss Ravanel?"

"Believe me, I am tempted, but I'm afraid I'll be too busy keeping up with the kitchen work and the classes I'll be teaching."

The last unknown at the table introduced herself as Dorothy Penn. Ms. Penn was one of the poetry instructors and seemed to also consider herself an expert on antiques. I hoped her self-taught knowledge didn't turn out to be a problem down the road. When introduced she said, "It's a pleasure to meet you, ladies. When Leroy told me they had hired Ms. Trent, I was just a little miffed. I thought they should have offered the job to me, but then he explained that I would be unusually busy getting ready for the new building and all. Still, if you need any help, just let me know."

I wasn't sure quite how to respond, so I thanked her and said, "All the Ms. and Professor titles seem a little formal. I'd be glad if all of you just called me Alicia or Ali."

Everyone agreed first names would be better. The introductions over, Laudine turned to Claude Trumain. "Your name is very French, but you don't have a French accent."

"No, my father was French, but he died when I was very young. My mom was completely English. I wish I'd taken time to learn French, but it always seemed like there were too many other things to do."

From there, the conversation slipped into a long discussion about food, so Laudine was in her element. It was great to see her seem so happy.

Three

It was barely seven the following morning when Laudine and I were up and eager to locate where we'd be working. She had it easy, since the kitchen was next to the room where we'd eaten the night before, but I needed to locate some mysterious storage place. I was just about to pick up the in-house phone to call Leroy for instruction when there was a knock on the door.

I opened the door and laughed outright when our visitor said, "Walsh for duty, madam. I am pretty sure you could both be using a guide about now."

Laudine said, "Absolutely! You are a godsend. I was pretty sure I could find the elevator, but then I'd be lost. After last night, I should know my way, but I still find this building confusing."

I said, "My sense of direction is equally hopeless. I don't even know what I'm supposed to be looking for."

"Ah, then I am a welcome sight. I thought we could all have a wee breakfast, get Laudine settled in the kitchen, and then I'll do my best to teach you how to reach the lower rooms. Oh, and Leroy asked me to have you both stop by his office right after lunch to get the necessary paperwork out of the way."

I wasn't sure I liked the sound of 'lower rooms.' I hadn't known there were rooms below. I'd suspected the storage was up in 5 or 6. Obviously I was wrong. Putting all this aside for the moment, I said, "That sounds great. Breakfast will give us a chance to pump you for information, and I'm sure Laudine is starving."

Again, the food was good and filling, but I knew in a day or so it would be better. I'd never met anyone who had Laudine's talent for making every meal an epicurean delight. Immediately after breakfast, she left us to explore her new domain.

I had a ton of questions I wanted to ask Alex about the school's old building, but before I could get going, he was already beginning his explanation of the directions I would need to get to work each day. When he finally paused for a breath, I said, "I will never know how you find your way around this place, but I hope you can teach me how to get back and forth from my room to the items I am to catalog. So far, your explanation sounds complicated."

"Don't worry, it's a fairly easy route. I'm probably making it sound worse than it is. I'm sure you will be able to find most anything once you have been here a while. For now, I'll be your guide as long as you need."

"Thank you. I wasn't kidding when I said I have a terrible sense of direction. I wish Leroy had given us a map of the building rather than the campus."

"That would have been useful, but I don't think one exists. I'm not sure there is anyone here who could draw one."

"So far I've been told about levels one through four. This morning is the first I've heard there were lower floors, and no one has said what floors five and six contain. What can you tell me?"

I was sure I saw Alex hesitate a moment before saying, "I can understand your confusion. At the moment you are mixing up floors, levels, and buildings. The construction of this place is difficult to understand, and like nothing I've ever seen. Maybe if I explain the overall layout it will help. The older part of the campus consists of three buildings that cascade down the mountain. At the top is Building Six. It and Building Five are separate, free-standing buildings, not levels. They have three floors each that aren't exactly on top of each other, so we call them levels rather than floors. The next building right below Six is Building Five. Then further down the mountain is Building Four. This is the main building where we are now. It consists of four levels. The final building is really three smaller buildings connected. The biggest part of these buildings is underground, so they are called Sub-levels A, B, and C even though they are really Buildings One, Two, Three. I don't get above Building Four very often. My trips up there are mostly when unused items need to be stored. As I've said, this part of the campus isn't like most construction. It's scattered all over the hillside and is nothing like a normal building. Building Five can only be reached by a series of halls beginning in Building Four, and to get to Six, you have to go outside and then back in. Those areas are the oldest portions of the complex, and for many years have only been used for storage, the only exception being the groundskeeper's rooms, which are in Building Five.

"You weren't kidding about confusing! I don't know how you ever keep it all straight."

"I definitely didn't understand it all overnight. Once you've been here a little while, it will all seem normal to you."

"I hope so, but right now I'll have to take your word for it. You said only the groundskeeper lives in Building Five. Surely you can't be suggesting that all the massive campus grounds are tended by one person?"

"No, of course not. They just coordinate with the company that does the work."

"Another person to remember. What is his name?"

Alex smiled. "Her name is Beth Jerome. She always has two weeks off before the fall semester, but she should be back in a few days. She can probably tell you more than anyone about the top two buildings."

"I'll look forward to meeting her."

"She's kind of moody and doesn't get along with everyone, but maybe you'll have good luck with her. Now, if you're ready, I'll show you how to find the items that need sorting. Since you can get from your room to the elevator and down here, we'll start outside the elevator and plot your route from there."

"Okay, lead on. I'll try not to get lost."

When we'd come down in the elevator for meals, we had turned right and gone around the first corner. Then the cafeteria was only three doors down. This time when we exited the elevator, Alex led me off to the left. We followed the hall to its end and made another left down one of the seemingly endless corridors. I was counting doorways on my left as we walked. When I reached nine, my guide led me to another ancient elevator on the right. So far so good. I was pretty sure I could make it back this far on my own.

Still trying to understand the sub-levels, I said, "How do the sub-levels work? You say they are three smaller buildings connected?"

"Yes. The sub-levels are three different buildings, even if their walls are connected. There is a Sub A, Sub B, and Sub C. This elevator takes you to the junction of the three and then there are halls and steps the rest of the way. When you get off the elevator, you go right for A, left for B, and C is straight ahead. What we need is in Sub C. A is just one big empty space and isn't divided into rooms. B has the same floor plan as C, but there has been some water damage in there, so until that's repaired, we aren't using it.

"So far, if I can remember what you've told me, it all makes sense. You weren't kidding when you said I'd need you as a guide."

When the elevator finally stopped, we were in a room with halls heading off in three directions. The only thing in the room was a large portrait of a stern-looking man in priest's robes. The painting was so well done it felt like the man was watching my every move. Alex led me off down the middle hall. Because the ceiling was rounded, it resembled a large concrete tunnel rather than a hallway. I was sure the construction material was something much older than concrete. This corridor veered sometimes left and sometimes right, and twice we descended six or so steps, and once we actually climbed up several steps. Finally, we came to a large, ornate iron-and-copper gate across the width of the hall. The copper was green with age. Alex opened it with a large, old-fashioned key. Beyond was another small open area with one doorway on the opposite side. Alex produced another old-fashioned key to open the door. Beyond that was a huge room.

There was some light in the room, but when my guide flipped a switch by the door, the whole place lit up. The lighting had to have been an addition, as the wires were strung visibly along the walls and ceiling. Also on the walls were sconces I felt sure had been the original lighting source. Each was fitted with a fat candle. It would be an impressive room anywhere, but the most astounding thing was the one wall that had four large windows. Windows weren't possible. I knew we had ridden the second elevator down a considerable distance. I was more than a little confused until I walked over and looked out. Then I finally understood what Alex had been trying to tell me. It was still complicated, but not as bad as I'd thought. The monastery wasn't one large building. It was more accurately six buildings. What I'd been calling levels 5 and 6 were the two uppermost buildings. They were located near the top of the incline, and parts of them were on the hillside and parts were built back into the hill. The next building down the side of the mountain had four floors that here were called levels. This was Building 4. It was the main building and the largest. It was located down the slope from 5 and 6 and was also partially built into the mountain. What they called Sub A, B, C, were three small buildings that were connected. Alex had told me that, but it hadn't made sense until now. They were lowest on the mountain and were technically Buildings 1, 2, and 3, but because of their construction, they were called sub-levels rather than buildings. These three connected buildings were slightly off to the right. The biggest portions of Sub A, B, and C were built into the mountain. The fact that so much of them was underground was why everyone called them sub-levels instead of buildings. Where I was standing looking out the window was the part of Sub C built outside the mountain. The way we'd traveled to get here was through the section inside the mountain. Anyone looking at the campus would see three very old buildings cascading down the mountain, but because Buildings 1, 2, and 3 were connected, there were actually six. To confuse matters further, since the campus had grown over the years, there were numerous newer buildings scattered around. They were much easier to understand, since they were of modern construction. It was no wonder it hadn't made sense to me when he'd originally explained it.

What made the whole complex so unique were the halls, stairs, and elevators that connected all the buildings. Now I understood the reason for the long, convoluted hallways. No wonder the air smelled fresh here. It was fresh.

The whole time I'd stood at the window looking out and thinking all this through, Alex had stood silently waiting. When I turned in his direction, he was smiling and said, "It's always something to see when a newcomer figures it out. You should have seen your face when you saw the windows."

He was so genuinely pleased with himself that I smiled back. "I'm glad you were entertained. You could have warned me. For a minute there, I thought I'd lost my mind."

He laughed. "That was my reaction my first time down here. It is mind-boggling, for sure. I have often wondered if there is anything like this place anywhere. At least you have plenty of space to sort and catalog the collection."

I didn't know if there was anywhere else similar, but what I was beginning to wonder was just how old this place was. Now I wasn't sure if the buildings had originally been built by the Catholic Church as I'd assumed. I knew I'd be doing some research to see what I could find.

He was right. There was lots of space with lots of empty tables to use for sorting. I'd been afraid the air would be dank and musty, but the opposite was true. The windows were closed, so I assumed there must be some type of ventilation to the outside. There was no dust anywhere. The only thing I found disconcerting was the way Alex's laugh had echoed into the dark corners of the huge room.

Having had his fun, Alex left me to begin organizing my work. Before going, he had shown me the in-house phone and told me to call him if I needed anything, including a guide back to the main building. He also promised to leave the doors between here and the main building unlocked during the time I was cataloging items in Sub C.

In the storage area at the back of the room, I got another surprise. I'd expected to find a room full of the haphazard jumble of someone's eclectic collection that they had donated to the college many years ago. Instead, there were several neatly stacked and labeled wooden crates. One wall had a large selection of tools labeled and hung on pegboard. So far, all my needs had been anticipated. I selected a crowbar and walked to the crates. There were two sizes. Two of them were about two feet by four feet, and four were half again as big. I wondered where the rest of the collection was. I could find out later. There was plenty here to get me started.

The top of the crate came off easily, even though the nails holding it were rusty and square like they had been made by hand. I needed to find out how long the college had been in this location and how long ago this collection had been donated. When I removed the top layer of packing material, I understood that these boxes could easily represent the whole collection. I was looking at one of several layers of jewelry, and not just any jewelry. This was an unprecedented amount of exquisite mourning jewelry, and finally I understood why this job had been offered to me. In the past, I'd cataloged several large jewelry collections and I was getting a decent reputation for my knowledge, and recently I'd written an article for a prominent antique magazine about one unusual mourning necklace I'd acquired. The quality of what I was looking at here was so much better than the necklace in my article that I was shocked. For the first time, a little self-doubt crept in. I hoped I was up to this job.

I didn't make any effort to begin work. I spent the morning opening the crates and enjoying the chance to view such exquisite items. The materials and workmanship were truly remarkable. I wondered if anyone knew or suspected such examples of mourning jewelry existed.

I opened one of the larger crates next and I was surprised again. It was filled with what I was sure were religious reliquaries. I quickly removed the tops of the remaining boxes. All four of the larger boxes contained the same type of items. Whoever had amassed this collection had chosen to surround themselves with jewelry created to mourn someone who had died, and unusual containers designed for holding relics. The relics seemed to vary from small body parts to clothing believed to be owned by departed saints. It seemed a wee bit morbid to me, but there was no doubt they had chosen items of the highest quality.

My cursory examination took me the full morning. At twelve, I decided to see if I could find my way to the dining room. I couldn't wait to tell Laudine about my discoveries, and there was paperwork to deal with.

I managed to eventually find my way back with only a couple of wrong turns. Everyone else was just sitting down when I arrived. When Alex saw me, he said, "Ah, there you are. When you didn't call, I assumed you wanted to find your own way, but I was beginning to wonder if I was going to need to organize a search party."

"I'm glad you didn't need to do that. Finding my way here wasn't quite as easy as I thought it would be, but I never got hopelessly lost."

While we ate, conversation became general. I immediately turned to Laudine and said, "You'll never believe what I discovered. The collection consists of mourning jewelry and relics of the most amazing quality."

"That's great! You should see the kitchen…"

From there she launched into a description of the equipment and workers, and I threw in a few more comments about the jewelry. Pretty quickly I realized she was as excited about what she had discovered as I was about the collection. Neither of us was hearing a word of what the other was saying.

I said, "Whoa, hang on a second. This conversation is a bit jumbled. Let's start over. You go first so I can hear all about what you've discovered, and then I'll tell you about the collection."

"Sorry, I got a little carried away there. I am really excited about the things I hope to accomplish here."

For the next hour, we took turns telling each other about our morning. There was no doubt we were both looking forward to the next few months. Laudine's description of the college kitchen was as amazing as everything else we had discovered about this unusual place. It sounded like a professional kitchen even a gourmet restaurant would envy. I was pleased for her, but also wondered where this remote, obscure college acquired all its wealth. We weren't even close to finished discussing our discoveries when lunchtime was over, but we gave up for then and headed to the president's office to deal with the necessary forms.

The outer office was dominated by a middle-aged woman sitting at a very large, very cluttered desk. She introduced herself as Marge Bailey, Leroy's secretary. She didn't spend any time on small talk, and quickly hustled us into Leroy's office. He in turn led us down the hall behind his office and turned us over to the Department of Human Resources. They were very efficient, and the paperwork was the usual things required for any job. I was soon on my way back to my workroom. I only had to backtrack twice on my way there.

Four

I decided to deal with the mourning jewelry first. Both groups of items would take some research, but I had a lot more experience with the jewelry than the reliquaries. In the past, the mourning jewelry items I had seen were typically worth somewhere between one hundred and three thousand dollars. Even with this number of items, that wouldn't be worth both my salary and a new building. The pieces in this collection were something else entirely. During the morning, I'd begun sorting them into groups of the same type, such as rings, bracelets, brooches, etc. I believed they were typically worth somewhere between three and eight thousand dollars apiece, but I suspected there were a few of the items worth considerably more. In total there were maybe six hundred pieces. This was quite a legacy for the college, and I hadn't even begun to think about the reliquaries. They should have no trouble building whatever they needed.

It turned out that Laudine and I worked well past dinnertime. I wanted to get organized quickly so I didn't feel guilty about the classes

I wanted to take, and Laudine wanted to get the kitchen and staff organized so she would have time to begin preparing her classes. We only had a short time before the majority of the students would begin arriving for the fall semester. I turned up in the kitchen looking for something to eat just as she finished for the day. We were both tired, but Laudine whipped up an omelet for our supper that would have pleased a king. To keep from being useless, I sliced some fruit and promised to do the cleanup.

I'd just put the last dish in the ultramodern dishwasher, and Laudine had long since gone off to work on her curriculum, when a woman I hadn't seen before rushed into the kitchen. Her appearance wasn't reassuring. Her hair was wind-blown in all directions and her clothes were wrinkled and not exactly clean. Before I could say a word, she said, "Where is Leroy and who are you? No one is allowed back here except school employees."

Taken by surprise, my tone was nearly as brusque as hers when I said, "I should probably ask you the same question. I'm Alicia, Alicia Trent. Is there something I can help you with?"

"No, I don't need to be wasting time with the kitchen help. I need to speak with Leroy immediately. Please go and fetch him."

I almost laughed. Almost, but something in her eyes kept me from letting the laugh escape my lips. "I'm sorry, but I don't keep tabs on the president's whereabouts. If you are in need of help, please say so. Otherwise please explain who you are."

"I gather from your tone you're not kitchen help, so you must be the new antique expert. I'm Beth Jerome. There has been an accident on campus. The police have been called and I need to talk to Leroy."

She was making an effort to contain her impatience, but her tone remained hostile and there was a cunning look in her eyes. When she finished her statement, she turned and hurried out. I didn't see any way I could help, so I gave the kitchen a last wipe-down and headed back to my room.

Laudine was in the common room when I arrived, so I told her about our unfriendly groundskeeper. She said, "She sounds awful.

Fortunately, we shouldn't need to have much contact with her while we're here. I wonder what type of accident she was talking about?"

"She certainly didn't give me any details. I guess we'll find out from Leroy in the morning. I hope it's nothing serious."

~ * ~

By morning we had both nearly forgotten the previous night's incident. We'd worked late doing research for our respective projects and had then fallen into bed and slept soundly. Once we reached the breakfast table, we were quickly reminded, as the staff was abuzz with the details.

We were barely seated before Claude coughed and said, "I expect you've already heard about last night's excitement."

"I would hardly use the word excitement to refer to what happened. The incident is frightening. Any one of us could be next," Dorothy said.

Coughing a little longer than before, Claude finally caught his breath, "Yes, of course. We are all somewhat shaken, but surely whatever happened last night has nothing to do with us."

Laudine said, "Actually we haven't heard anything since last night when Beth came running in and told Ali there had been an accident. Are you sure you're all right? Your cough sounds worse, and I know your classes will start soon."

He started to answer, but Leroy interrupted, "Beth didn't have all the information. What happened was no accident. Professor Castille died last night. He was the archaeology professor here."

"That's horrible! Since Laudine and I hadn't met him, I assume he lived off campus?"

Kenneth began speaking. I was struck again by his astounding looks, and I noticed he was looking only at Laudine when he spoke. "Actually, Albert lives here during the regular session. He doesn't teach during the summer and wasn't even supposed to be on campus for a few more weeks."

"Was he ill or was his death unexpected?" Laudine asked.

There was a pregnant pause before Leroy replied. "No, he wasn't ill. The police are investigating his death as a murder. They say Professor Castille was stabbed."

I said, "This seems like such a quiet place. It's hard to imagine a murder happening here. Do the police know who stabbed him?"

Leroy explained. "One of the summer students discovered him on a bench on the quad in front of the student union. He called the police. The first we heard was when Detective Crown showed up. He will be back this morning to question everyone."

"This gets worse and worse. What about the attacker? Did the campus police catch him? What do they know?"

Leroy looked like he might be sick. "The Canajoharie police handle the security for the college. They have two policemen that patrol the campus at night. They try to cover the main areas of campus the students frequent. Whoever did this either knew where they would be or got lucky, because neither of them saw anything. The professor was found at eleven-thirty last night, and the killer was long gone by then."

Leroy's explanation made sense, but didn't seem like it was quite right. Beth must have known what had happened when she'd come looking for Leroy. There certainly hadn't been any police around then. I said, "Surely Beth knew what had happened before the police arrived. She told me something about an accident last night when she came by the kitchen looking for you."

Leroy turned even paler. "It's possible she heard or saw something. Whatever she knew, she never found me. I was in the stockroom taking inventory to make sure we had the supplies we'll need for the arriving students. I'm sure the police will talk to her sooner or later."

Leroy's statement inspired more chatter around the table. Everyone but Laudine and I had known Professor Castille because he had been teaching at the college for three years. I didn't know if he had been close with any of them, but everyone seemed upset at his death. Even so, no one had any idea why he had been murdered, or why he was on campus without having contacted anyone. They were concerned for their own safety. I knew they would be uneasy until the police discovered the motive behind the killing.

I was sure more details would come to light as the investigation proceeded. When the hubbub slowed down, Leroy continued. "Detective Crown will be by later this morning to talk to each of you.

He'll want to know where everyone was and if you saw anything that might help. Please arrange your schedules to accommodate him."

He didn't hang around after his announcement. I noticed that the food on his plate had been moved around, but the president hadn't eaten anything. When he'd gone, the rest of us lingered a little. Some ate heartily and the rest of us picked at our food. I didn't know these people well enough yet to know who normally ate a large breakfast and who did not.

The next to leave was Claude. He was still coughing and claimed he needed to take some cough medicine before his first class. Laudine never did get an answer about his health. I was surprised classes hadn't been canceled, but I assumed the college didn't want to alarm the students and had no reason to suspect they were in any danger if classes continued.

Summer classes were so short that even one missed day represented a huge loss. Soon we all went off to our separate duties. I spent the day sorting and valuing mourning jewelry. I thought I probably wouldn't get to the reliquaries until after classes had started. As I worked, I was thinking about what had happened. It would be important for the police to determine as soon as possible whether the murder had occurred because of something in the professor's personal life, or if there was some connection to the college. Whatever was going on, I was determined not to get involved. There were real policemen working here and I had other duties.

At lunchtime, my mind was fully on my job. I wasn't hungry enough to go up for food, so I decided to take a short break and eat the orange I'd brought with me. I knew Laudine had prepared the evening menu, so the food would be excellent. I'd just sat down and begun peeling the orange when there was a knock on the frame beside the room's open door and a very large man walked in.

He was both tall and wide, but he definitely wasn't fat. Something about his manner reminded me of Nick for just a moment. I wondered how long it would be before I stopped thinking of him so often. This man didn't look much like a policeman, but he moved like a man sure of his abilities. He wasn't, well, beautiful like Flame, but I'm not sure I'd ever seen a man who exuded masculinity the way he did.

His suit was not something he'd bought off a rack, and his shoes probably cost more than I earned in a week. His clothes would never have given away the fact that he was a cop, but there was something about the way he handled himself that made me sure he was. He'd barely opened his mouth to introduce himself as Detective Jeff Crown when I knew he wasn't from this part of the country.

"I think I detect a fellow westerner," I said. "If I had to guess, I'd say you're from Los Angeles."

He gave me a very engaging smile and I responded, even though I was sure it was one of his more effective tactics for getting people to talk. "You got it right in one. I got tired of the big city and decided to try a small town. I'd think the same of you, but I understand you're just a visitor here."

"Yes, but a fairly long-term one. I've been hired to value a collection of antiques for the college, and I also plan to take some classes."

"Is this jewelry spread out all over the table the collection you're working on?"

"Well, it's half of the collection. It's mourning jewelry, and definitely the best example I've ever seen."

"I'm not much of an antique buff. What makes this jewelry only suitable to wear in the morning?"

I couldn't contain a small giggle before saying, "Not morning, as early in the day. This jewelry is used as a way of grieving for and remember someone who has died. So it's called mourning jewelry. Each piece has something like a lock of hair worked into the design."

"I see, but no fair laughing at me. I warned you I didn't know much about antiques."

He was smiling that devastating smile again, so I assumed he wasn't offended. "I wasn't really laughing at you. It's just amusing how inadequate words are sometimes."

"I've found that true myself. Suspects are masters at twisting the meaning of words. You said the jewelry was half the collection. What's the other half?"

"The rest of the collection consists of reliquaries. Very exceptional ones, too."

"Okay, that is going to take a bit more explaining. Please use words I can understand. I know they're connected to religion, but that's the extent of my knowledge, and don't think I don't know that you enjoyed dropping that word on me."

I laughed outright this time. "Well, maybe a little. Basically, a reliquary is a container. They are usually designed ornately with a religious theme and have a section made to hold a relic. Before you ask, a relic, in this context, is usually considered to be something that once belonged to a saint. It might be a piece of clothing or even a small body part like a finger bone."

He shook his head slightly. "I suppose you've noticed that whoever collected these things had a bit of a morbid streak?"

"True. I've been wondering why they chose this hobby, but the entire family has been long dead, so there isn't any one I can ask. So far I haven't found any papers or letters of explanation."

"Well, as fascinating as all this is, I'm sure you know I'm here to see what you know about the events last night. I should also tell you that I've done my research and know you have a way of getting involved in police matters wherever you go."

"Not this time, I assure you. As for last night, I was cleaning the kitchen after my friend, Laudine, and I had shared a late supper. One of the staff came in looking for Leroy, President Cummings, and said there had been an accident. I didn't find out until this morning what really happened."

"Can you tell me the name of the person who told you there had been an accident?"

"Yes, it was Beth Jerome, the college groundskeeper."

He wrote that in his notebook. "Was your friend still here with you at the time?"

"No, she'd already gone back to our suite."

"Were you or your friend acquainted with the deceased?"

"No. He wasn't due to arrive for a few more days, but he would have been living in the main building for the fall semester if he'd lived."

"Well, there isn't any way you could have seen anything from the kitchen, so that's all the questions I have at the moment. I'll let you get back to your work. I'm sure we'll run into each other again."

After he left, I realized that he hadn't been smiling when he said we'd run into each other again, and I wondered if he'd meant the comment as a warning... not to get involved.

Five

When I'd eaten my orange and was sure the policeman was long gone, I decided to take a short walk around Sub-level C to stretch my legs. The door next to the room where I was working opened onto another large room. It was almost exactly like mine except it was empty. I was about to open the next door when I heard a noise from farther down the hall. I was too new to be sure no one belonged down there, but I'd gotten the impression I was the only one working in Sub C at the moment.

I took one step in the direction of the noise I'd heard and then turned and went back to my workroom. I picked up the crowbar I'd used earlier to open crates and quietly stepped out into the hall. I was almost to the corner when the last door on the hall began to open. I jumped back against the wall and raised the crowbar ready to swing an instant before a tall, thin man wearing very expensive and well-tailored casual clothes walked through the door. I didn't lower the crowbar, but I didn't swing it either. Instead, I said, "For the moment I am assuming you have a good reason for being down here?"

Without any reaction to my surprise appearance, he said, "Yes, actually I do, and from the looks of your weapon, I'm very glad I do. I'm Tim Ashley."

After stating his name, he paused expectantly as though I would recognize it. I didn't and was preparing to quiz him further when he moved so quickly that all I saw was a blur. The next thing I knew, he was holding the crowbar and my hands were empty. I braced for a blow, but he said, "Now that I don't feel threatened, we can talk. You asked about my reason for being down here. I'm here at the request of the college board. One of the sub-levels is sinking. Not drastically, but it's still a concern. I'm a structural engineer and my company has been hired to solve the problem. That explains why I'm here. Now it's your turn."

I took a deep breath and slid down the wall until I was sitting on the floor. His claim had the ring of truth, so I took a deep breath. "I wish someone had mentioned you'd be here today! There was some trouble on campus last night, so finding you here scared me to death."

"Sorry. Leroy has been expecting me, but he didn't know I'd be arriving today. I just drove in about twenty minutes ago, so I didn't know there had been trouble. And, I still don't know who you are."

I explained who I was and why I was there. With our bonafides out of the way, Tim left to report in, and I made my way back to the workroom. I'd had enough exploring for one day. Before departing, my new acquaintance had returned my crowbar. I was pretty sure I'd never have gotten close enough to the man to have used it.

Back in what I considered the safety of my workroom, I calmed down enough to wonder why an engineer would have all the moves of a well-trained soldier. There was more to Mr. Ashley than his fancy suit indicated. I forcibly put him out of my mind for the moment and spent the rest of the afternoon sorting jewelry.

Dinner that evening was beyond anything I could have imagined. Laudine had pulled out all the stops for our first meal under her supervision. She'd chosen to serve a standing rib roast. I didn't know what she'd done to ordinary potatoes to make the scrumptious side dish she served, but that and the baby purple carrots, and a perfect tossed salad once again kept me from trying dessert. Between bites, the conversation was all about the food. Mr. Ashley, whom everyone was now calling Tim, had joined us, and Leroy had confirmed his reason for being at the college. He was staying on campus and on our floor. At least he was on the opposite side of the building. I couldn't help but wonder what he'd been doing in Sub C near my workroom, the room I'd seen him exiting.

Between food comments, I did manage to ask if there was any more information on last night's murder. There wasn't, but everyone had something to say about the policeman, Mr. Crown. I wasn't the only one who noticed his fantastic build and devastating smile. Each and every one of us had been interviewed, even Tim Ashley. I would have been interesting in watching that interview.

~ * ~

Over the next few days, Laudine and I settled into a comfortable working routine. Our resident chef rose early to get her staff started on preparing the day's meals. She started leaving more and more of the actual preparation to them and focusing her attention on her upcoming classes. She had divided their work load so that some of the staff was responsible for the staff's meals while all the rest were learning what would be needed in the cafeteria when the fall students arrived.

At seven-thirty when breakfast was served, the staff ate together. I still wasn't big on eating at that time of day, but I couldn't resist nibbling on whatever Laudine's people presented. Already some of the college employees were talking about gaining weight. I think they meant it more as a compliment than a complaint, because Laudine prided herself on serving healthy food.

We hadn't seen any more of the local police, and everyone else seemed to accept the engineer at face value. We'd heard nothing more about the murder. After the morning meal, I'd descend to my workroom to sort, catalog, and price jewelry. I seldom attended lunch. I preferred to have something light while I worked. After the workday, we'd all gather around six for the evening meal. The rest of our evenings were our own. I usually took a walk around campus after we finished eating.

Later Laudine and I sometimes streamed a movie or she'd return to the kitchen to test recipes she planned to use for teaching. The rest of my evenings were easily filled with good books I'd been wanting for ages to find the time to read. When we'd been on campus a week, I was pleased by how comfortable and at home we felt.

It was the first evening of our second week on campus. I was about to leave for my evening walk when Laudine said, "I really don't like you going for walks by yourself. Everyone seems to have forgotten a man was killed on this campus. I haven't heard about any positive action by the police, either. Have you asked the bottle about the situation here?"

"We don't really know the murder was connected to the college. The cause could easily be something from the man's personal life. It seems unlikely to be connected to the rest of the staff. What's really bothering you?"

"You're right, I do know those things. I'm not sure why I can't stop worrying. I've had a feeling about this place since our first day here, and I can't seem to shake it. If you insist on walking alone, just humor me and take one of the heavy Maglites that are scattered around everywhere. The days are getting shorter anyway, and it would make a good weapon in an emergency. You haven't consulted the bottle, have you?"

"I don't want you to worry, so I'll take the Maglite. I haven't asked the bottle because I doubt it could help. If it knew something, I think it would speak up on its own. Before you ask, I haven't gotten a prediction from the clock in ages. If there is any bad news coming, I don't want to know. I just want to relax and enjoy our time here."

"Believe me, I understand how you feel. We've been through a lot, but even so, not finding out what you can seems like sticking your head in the sand. As unsettling as it is, I think it's best to be forewarned if something is coming your way. Just think about it, will you?"

"If it will make you feel better, I promise I'll consult the clock tonight when I get back."

<h1 style="text-align:center">Six</h1>

Walking across the commons in the center of campus was one of my favorite routes. The walnuts were beginning to fall off the huge trees that spread an almost solid canopy over the grass. A few of the leaves were beginning to change. Summer was making room for fall. I wondered idly if I would be so eager to walk when winter set in and I had to trudge through the snow. I'd almost reached the center of the quad when I heard the scream.

In light of recent events, I assumed the worst and immediately began running in the direction I hoped would take me to the person in distress. I dashed through the wall of trees that surrounded the quad, turning its center into a small secluded garden enclosed by a neatly trimmed hedge, and screeched to a stop when I took in the scene before me. A young man was chasing a girl around the garden. She was squealing with what I quickly realized was delight, because just as I arrived, he caught her and began a romantic kiss. I turned and hastily retreated back through the wall of trees, embarrassed that I'd let Laudine's comments earlier spook me.

I'd no sooner slipped through the trees when another person also came through about three trees down. I backed up next to the closest tree trunk and raised the heavy Maglite. I must have been holding my breath because it escaped in a whoosh when a male voice said, "Miss Trent, I presume. Are you going to raise a weapon every time we meet?"

I lowered the flashlight slowly. "You must admit, you have a bad habit of showing up in strange ways. What are you doing out here anyway?"

"It's just possible you aren't the only one that likes an evening walk. As it happens, I heard a scream and reacted. I'm guessing you can understand that, since it seems you reacted the same way. Come, it's getting dark. I'll walk you back to the main building."

I still thought there was something off about Mr. Tim Ashley, but I didn't believe he intended me any harm, and I was glad for the company on the return walk. Safely back in our suite, I entertained Laudine with the evening's events. She laughed at all the right moments, but the worried look never left her eyes.

Alone in my room and prepared for bed, I decided to keep my promise and consult the clock before going to sleep. I'd found the clock in the same antique hoard as the bottle, but whereas I loved the three-tiered bottle and found it a useful tool, I still dreaded using the clock.

Knowing anything about future events wasn't as pleasant or helpful as I'd always imagined it would be. Especially when, so far, all the clock's messages were predictions of possible dire events. Now that it had begun speaking its predictions, they somehow seemed more ominous. The last time I had consulted the clock, the prediction had been, "On March 1, 2015, a friend has a severe problem. You can help, but your actions will determine if someone dies. You will be in grave danger."

I had worried about that prediction for months, but when the time came, the problem turned out to be something I could handle. A friend of mine, well, really more of a customer at the shop, had a serious drinking problem he'd hidden for years. He was driving Barry and me to view some items a friend of his had for sale. We were unaware of his problem until he swerved into the path of an oncoming truck. With me wrestling with the steering wheel, we managed to veer out of the way just in time. I immediately had him pull over and took the car keys. We never got to view the antiques he'd recommended because I drove him directly home. His wife put him in rehab soon after that, and as far as I knew, he was still sober. Unfortunately, not all the clock's predictions were as easy to deal with. It had been some time since there had been a prediction.

As always, when I'd turned the knobs and inserted the key, I checked to see if the date was close or far in the future before I turned the key. If whatever was going to happen was too many months away, I didn't want to know what it would say. I only listened to the predictions that were close enough to affect the near future. I was hoping for a distant date, but I was disappointed. The prediction was in the near future. There was no doubt that whatever it would tell me would happen during our first semester at the college. As soon as I turned the key, the mechanical voice said, "Around the date shown, attack number three will occur and another person may die. There will be more deaths unless you and a friend take action quickly."

This was upsetting for several reasons. First, if the clock were right that a third attack would occur, that meant there would be one more between now and then, because there couldn't be a third until a second had happened. Knowing the third victim could die was horrific, and hearing some action on my part would be necessary to prevent more deaths was instantly a heavy burden. This was also the first time the clock hadn't given an exact date. I had no idea what that might mean. I knew I would have to tell Laudine what I'd heard. I didn't keep that kind of secret from her. Whether I should tell the police was another matter. At this point, I didn't know Detective Crown well enough to know if I could make him believe me. In the past, some policemen hadn't taken kindly to my interference, and I knew I would have to see what I could find out about Crown. I would talk to Laudine the first chance I got, and then we could decide together what to do next.

I got my chance first thing the following morning. She didn't go to the kitchen to supervise because she was testing her staff to see if they could prepare the day's meals with only the written instructions she'd left for them the night before. She was still in our suite drinking coffee when I got up. When I'd told her the clock's prediction, I said, "Now that I've taken your advice and been forewarned, we'll have to take some sort of action. Do you think I should try to warn Detective Crown?"

"I have to say I feel better knowing what we may have to deal with, rather than just the vague uneasy feeling I had before. When it comes to Crown, I've only talked to him the one time when he was doing the interviews. I kind of liked him, but I'm sure if you try to warn him, his first question will be, "Where did you get that information?" I can't imagine he would be willing to accept your answer. Your clock, and the bottle, too, have to be nearly impossible for most people to accept. If I hadn't seen them be right several times, I don't think I could believe. Maybe we can think of some other way to warn him. If not, we'll have to think of something else we can do."

"So you don't think I should try enlisting his help?"

She shook her head. "The gossip in the kitchen says he was brought here for some special duty. I gather he's some kind of decorated hero. Still, he was here before the murder, so either he was brought in for something different or the gossip is just gossip. They also say his family is very wealthy, and his trust fund would make him independent if he wanted it to. I can't imagine him giving credit to a bottle or a clock."

"Well, I can hold off talking to him for a bit, but I may eventually have to try explaining my source. From the sound of the clock's prediction, it seems there is nothing we can do about a second attack. I refuse to accept that and will certainly try to prevent it, but if we really can't stop the prediction from coming true, a second attack should alert the police that the problem isn't over."

"That's true, but I don't want to believe the future is set in stone, either. I hope the police catch Professor Castille's killer quickly."

At this point, all we could do to help was keep our eyes and ears open and try to gather as much information as possible. Since my schedule was more flexible than Laudine's, I intended to have a chat with Leroy right away to see if I could discover more about whether or not he'd talked to Beth the night of the murder and, if so, why they hadn't told the police.

The office was empty, and for the first time, the president's door was closed. Marge, his secretary, was nowhere to be seen. I didn't know if the closed door meant he was gone or busy, but when I got close enough to knock, I heard what sounded like an argument coming from inside. I couldn't make out the words, but a woman's voice sounded especially angry. I was almost sure two men and a woman were arguing. Deciding to wait, I backed up to the other side of the waiting room and sat in one of the four chairs provided. I'd barely gotten seated when the woman I now knew was Beth came barreling through the door, slammed it soundly, and left without glancing in my direction. I waited, expecting the third member of the argument to come through the door, but no one exited the office. A moment later, Leroy opened his door, saw me waiting, and invited me in. He seemed perfectly calm. Still sure I'd heard three voices, I glanced around, but Leroy and I were the only ones present. I was left to wonder how the third participant of the argument had disappeared. Setting that mystery aside for the moment, I concentrated on the reason I'd come. I'd decided on the direct approach, so I asked him straight out what Beth had wanted to tell him the night of the murder.

He said, "I guess I can't blame you for wondering why we didn't talk to the police about what she said. It was silly, really, because the accident she was referring to when she saw you in the kitchen had nothing to do with the murder. I'm sure she wouldn't approve of me telling her secrets, but under the circumstances, I think it's best you know.

"Hopefully you will be able to keep what I'm about to tell you private. The night of the murder, Beth's ex-husband, Don Jerome, arrived at the school. She has been refusing to see him for a couple of years, but last night he told Beth his daughter had died recently. While they were married, Beth had helped raise the child, so naturally she was upset. The accident she was referring to the night of the murder was the car accident that killed Silvia."

"That's terrible! I know they must be devastated. Did Mr. Jerome leave or will he be in town for a while?"

"No, he didn't leave. Normally having spouses or even guests stay on campus isn't allowed, but under the circumstances, I told Beth that Don could stay a few days."

I wondered if that was what the argument I'd overheard was about and if the third participant had been Don Jerome, but I didn't ask. If he were telling the truth, Leroy had been willing to tell me what he knew, and I didn't want to do anything to give him a reason to change that policy, so I let the matter drop and soon left to return to work.

On my way out, there was still no sign of Marge. Having done all I could for the moment, I made the journey to my workroom. During the time it took to find my way, I kept trying to remember the night I'd met Beth. I was almost positive she'd said there had been an accident on campus. If so, she couldn't have been talking about her stepdaughter's accident. Since I couldn't recall her exact words, I put that worry aside until I could come up with a way to find out the truth.

The first piece of jewelry I examined on my return was a large brooch shaped like a flower. Each petal contained a large nearly perfect diamond. These gems were so intensely red they looked like there was a fire inside. At first, I thought they must be rubies, but after closer examination, I was sure they were rare diamonds. Diamonds like these mainly came from Australia from a mine I knew was due to close soon. Once the mine was closed, this piece would be worth even more. The stem was made with seven beautiful emeralds. The center of the flower was a small glass window that contained a lock of very blond hair. It wasn't the most ornate piece I'd come across, but the workmanship was so detailed and the gems of such quality, I knew it would be worth a small fortune.

I was assigning the brooch a number and writing down its description when I heard the second argument of the day. Two men were having a loud conversation somewhere in the hall outside my room. My door was open, so I would have thought they'd know I was here. When I walked out into the hall, Detective Crown and Tim Ashley immediately stopped talking and turned in my direction. When I asked if they were looking for me, both men spoke at once. The detective glared at Tim and then assured me they were just wandering around the fascinating building. They both acted like nothing had transpired and soon drifted off in separate directions. Once again, I was left wondering about the reason for a disagreement.

It had been my intention to speak with Detective Crown to see if I could find out if the police had learned anything about Professor Castille's murder, but he was gone so quickly I decided to wait for a better time.

I got my chance just as we'd finished eating our evening meal. I was about to go for my daily walk when the detective entered the dining room. He spoke briefly with Leroy and announced he was leaving for the day. I caught up with him in the hall and asked if I could speak with him for a moment. As we walked into one of the nearby empty classrooms to talk, I was once again a little intimated by how big and good-looking he was. I was determined not to let his looks bother me, so once we were seated, I said, "I got your hint when we met that you think I interfere with police matters too often, but I want to talk to you about the professor's murder."

This got me a sardonic look and a very expressive eye roll, but I pressed on.

"I don't think you can be sure Professor Castille's murder was an isolated incident, and I wanted to find out if you knew any more about why he was killed. Soon there will be a lot more kids attending classes here, and I'm sure that will make your investigation more difficult."

"You may be right, but it seems like you're asking me to give you inside information, and I'm wondering why in the world I should."

"Look, Detective, I'm not asking you to share private information, exactly. However, I spend a lot of time with the professor's coworkers. If his death had anything to do with the school, I am in a better position than you to overhear things. If nothing else, I need enough information to know what is or isn't important."

"I'll be honest with you. Using an outsider during an investigation goes against all my training, but I did some additional checking, and people I respect vouch for you. Right now, I have a policeman stationed in the main building to keep an eye on those of you who live here. His main purpose is to keep the residents safe, and you're right, they aren't going to talk about their secrets in front of him, and they might confide in you. The only deal I can make with you is that as long as it's possible the professor's death might be connected to someone at the college, I'll tell you what I can. You, in turn, need to keep me apprised of events here."

"That seems more than fair. I'd tell you anyway if I learned anything important, but knowing what is going on will help me decide what is and isn't."

"All right, Ms. Trent. It seems we have a deal of sorts. At present, the police don't really know anything you don't. The next time I come by, I'll bring a picture of the deceased. I'd be very interested to know if you'd seen him around. There has to be some reason he was here without announcing himself. Now if you'll excuse me, I am very late for a meeting."

"I don't want to make you later, but I do have a bit of information you might need to know."

Before he left, I told him about Beth's situation with her ex-husband and how Leroy had explained the situation to me. He made no comment, but he did seem interested. His visit hadn't been exactly friendly, but I hoped knowing what the police were thinking might help me prevent additional deaths. I didn't think he'd accept information from a bottle or a clock, but maybe I could slip in a bit of their knowledge as things I'd heard around.

When he came back with the picture of the professor, I already had several questions I wanted to ask him. For once I skipped my walk, since it was beginning to get dark, and, after talking to the detective, I had lost interest.

Seven

Several days passed quietly. I was making good headway with the jewelry and Laudine had nearly finished preparing her class material, so we were spending more time together. We were also worriedly waiting for what might happen next, and sincerely hoping the police would be able to prevent it. It wasn't that long until the date the clock had predicted the third murder would occur. If there was to be a second attack, it would have to come soon. I hoped that for once the clock was wrong, but I couldn't make myself believe it.

I decided to go back to walking the central area of campus. I thought I was walking now more to relieve my mounting tension than I was for exercise. I'd been walking the grounds on the hillside between the school buildings for several evenings, but the college campus was beautiful, so I liked to change my route every few walks. Tonight, for the first time, I was wearing a light jacket because the evenings were getting cooler already. It was a little later than my normal walk time, but was still just dusk. A few leaves had fallen to the ground, and I didn't think it would be long before there would be many more. Earlier in the day, I'd talked to Barry, and he'd told me the temperature in Scottsdale that day was eighty-two degrees. It was hard to reconcile the difference between that and the sixty-two here. I was paying more attention to my thoughts than my surroundings, because before I'd left for my walk, red clouds had worked their way up through the bottle. I'd tried to get it to tell me why, but there had been no response. I knew red meant danger, but nothing more.

I was about halfway through the quad at almost the exact same spot as the last time when I heard the scream. I knew it wasn't a squeal of delight this time. There was real fear in the sound. I ran, but when I broke through the hedge surrounding the garden, I was afraid I was going to be too late. Two men were fighting, one wearing a ski mask. The woman, whom I assumed had screamed, was standing nearby. As I ran, the man in the ski mask knocked the other to the ground and pushed the woman on top of him. I could see a large knife in his hand. I was terrified he would kill them both before I could get there, so I hollered for him to stop and pushed for more speed. My yell alerted him to my presence. He looked at me, and I could see him deciding whether to wait for me to arrive so he could attack, or to make a run for it. His decision was quickly made, and he darted off toward a heavily-wooded area beside one of the classroom buildings. He wasn't moving very fast and I thought his recent fight might have slowed him down. I again demanded more speed from my body and caught up as we entered the woods. I hit him several times with the heavy flashlight, but only managed to connect with his shoulder. I was surprised when he dropped down on one knee. I moved in to hit him one last time to knock him unconscious. When I got close, he reached out and yanked my legs out from under me. I didn't have time to prepare for the fall and my landing was accompanied by instant pain down my left side. I saw the attacker once again running off into the trees, so I tried to get up, but couldn't force my body to rise. I must have passed out for a moment, because the next thing I saw was the concerned face of a battered and bruised Tim Ashley bending over me. My last thought was that he must have been the one fighting with the man holding the knife. For some time, everything was a blur of confusion and pain.

When I finally felt in control again, I was lying in a hospital bed and Laudine was sitting by my side. She saw me open my eyes and said, "Don't panic. I promise you are going to be fine. Whoever knocked you down really hit you hard, because the fall dislocated your hip. I know that at the moment you aren't feeling lucky, but the doctors say you truly are because there is no secondary damage, no torn ligaments, or nerve damage. They have put your hip back in place and plan to keep you through tomorrow for observation. You'll have to avoid bending that hip as much as possible for a bit and will be on crutches for a few weeks, but they promise you'll make a full recovery."

I tried to ask if the attacker had been caught, but my throat was so dry it came out as a croak. Laudine handed me a glass of water, and after a few sips I was able to ask.

"No, the police couldn't find any sign of him. You'll have to wait for all the details, though, because I really don't know what was going on out there."

I was feeling very sleepy and knew the doctors had given me something, but I managed to ask why Tim had been in the woods, and who the girl was. Laudine looked puzzled, and I was sure she said something, but I couldn't catch her words. That was my last memory until the next time I woke and sunshine was streaming in through the window across from my bed.

Laudine was gone, but almost immediately a nurse entered my room. She was young and pretty and way too exuberantly friendly. When she saw I was awake, she informed me that Laudine had returned to the school and would be back that evening to pick me up. Evidently, I was being released later in the day. Hospitals are busy places, it seems, because she had no sooner left the room before breakfast arrived. Surprisingly, I was hungry and it was good. I'd been finished eating about ten minutes when the person who came to pick up the tray announced I had a visitor. I didn't know whom to expect, and I didn't recognize the young woman who walked in.

"Hello. I'm Lidia Tanner. I realize you don't know me, but I was in the park last night. I was walking on the commons when I stumbled on two men fighting. I think I must have screamed. If you hadn't come along, I might be dead now. I'm sorry you were hurt, and I didn't want to disturb you, but I had to stop by and say thank you."

"I'm glad you're all right, and you have nothing to thank me for. As it turns out, I underestimated the man and he got away. Do you know why the two men were fighting?"

"It was very strange. One minute they seemed to be talking and then one of the men just attacked the other. I'd never seen either of them before. The unarmed one knocked the knife out of the other's hand as they struggled. That's when we saw you running. I don't know when or how the attacker got his knife back, but when he heard you yell, it appeared in his hand, and I was sure he'd kill us. Instead, he pushed me down on the man who was on the ground and just ran away."

I think she really was telling me all she knew, but it didn't quite sit right with me. Something was missing, but I had no idea what. I only said, "I appreciate your coming by, and I'm glad you weren't hurt. Have you talked to the police?"

"Oh, yes. That handsome Detective Crown interviewed me. Earlier today, he had me sit with a sketch artist to see if I could help them get a likeness of the man. I'm afraid I wasn't very good at it. How do you describe a man wearing a mask?"

We talked a few more minutes before Lidia went downstairs to meet her mother, who'd come to pick her up. I was glad she had escaped unharmed.

Once she'd gone, I tried to remember what I'd seen of the attack. It was possible she really didn't know any more than she claimed. I'd been sure one of the men I'd seen had been Tim Ashley. Now I couldn't be sure, because my injury and time had confused my memory, and I'd still been at some distance when I'd thought I recognized him. The only way I would find out for sure was to ask him.

I seemed to be quite popular, because shortly after Lidia left, the nurse brought me some muscle relaxers to take and announced I had another visitor. This time I was surprised when Tim walked through the door. I almost thought I'd conjured him up. He looked tired and had several cuts and bruises, but his suit was immaculate. His dark hair was perfectly combed but still wet, as though he'd just showered. I didn't really trust him, but staying friendly would probably get me more information than being rude.

His sarcastic greeting didn't inspire me to trust him more. "Things are improving. This is the second time in as many days that you didn't raise a weapon when I showed up."

"Very funny! What happened last night, anyway? I'm sure it was you I saw fighting with that man. Why were you there? Why were you fighting?"

"Whoa, one question at a time. It was just bad luck that I ran into that psycho. I was taking my normal walk, which you already know I like to do, when I saw this guy sneaking around. Since the professor's murder, I have been keeping my eyes open. I approached him in the commons. When I realized he was wearing a ski mask, I became concerned. I tried questioning him, but he never said a word, just attacked. During the fight I heard a girl scream, but I never saw her arrive. We were still fighting when you arrived."

"You seem to have a knack for fortuitously showing up at strange times. I don't believe for a minute your being there was an accident. It wouldn't hurt you to be more forthcoming about what you saw!"

"It grieves me that you don't trust me. I really can't explain how I managed to have the bad luck to run into this guy. It isn't going to help boost your trust in me when I tell you that I was too busy fighting for my life to get a good look. With that and the mask he wore, he could walk in right now and I wouldn't recognize him. I was hoping you could describe him for me."

"And just what does an engineer care about getting a description?"

"All right, I understand you're suspicious, but I really am an engineer. The rest I can't tell you at the moment, but I'm hoping you will trust me enough not to share your suspicions with Detective Crown. For now, can you just accept I'm one of the good guys?"

"Honestly? I don't know if I can believe that. At the moment, I don't know enough to decide one way or the other. I do know you may have saved Lidia's life last night, and once I was down, he might not have run off if you hadn't been there, so I'll keep my suspicions to myself for now. I assume the good detective knows you were there last night?"

"Yes, he knows, and he's already questioned me. I told him the same thing I just told you. I don't know what he thinks. Detective Crown is a smart cookie, so I wouldn't be surprised if he gets it all figured out eventually. He should be careful he doesn't get himself in trouble."

I thought about his remarks after he left. I wondered if he'd told me the truth, but before I had a chance to decide one way or the other, the pills the nurse had given me put me to sleep. If it were just a muscle relaxer, I was more tired than I'd thought. This time when I woke, Laudine was again sitting beside the bed. It was late afternoon and I had been released to go home. Now that I was awake, Laudine packed my few belongings, and the nurse brought a wheelchair and a bag of pills. I didn't know what all the doctor had recommended, but he had told me there would be pain pills, if I needed them. I was already in the wheelchair ready to leave when the detective walked in. I said, "Good afternoon, Detective Crown. Have you caught the man who was running around with a knife on campus last night?"

"I'm glad to see you haven't lost your curiosity. I came by earlier, but you were sleeping. I was hoping to ask you a few questions. I'm sorry you were injured last night."

"That must mean he's still out there. Ask whatever questions you have."

"Would you like to do this privately?"

"No, anything you want to know you can ask with Laudine here."

"Okay, can you tell me if you got a good look at the man?"

His questions went on from there. He asked all the standard things. His only question that surprised me was when he asked if I knew the attacker personally. He also wanted to know how well I knew Tim Ashley, so I assumed I must not be the only one suspicious of the man. He spent about a quarter of an hour with the questions, but the only thing I got from the process was that the police didn't seem to have a clue as to the man's identity.

When he'd finished quizzing me and was about to leave, I threw out a question of my own. "Detective, do you know if the attacker last night is connected to Professor Castille's murder?"

"I wish I could answer that question. It is possible. With both events happening on campus, it even seems likely. If we ever figure out the motive for the professor's murder, we'll be able to answer a lot of those questions."

"That seems logical. Did you bring the picture of Professor Castille, and will I be able to see the drawing the police artist came up with from Tim and Lidia's description?"

"No, I didn't bring either picture. I didn't know how you'd be feeling, but I'll bring them by once you're settled at home."

He'd gone and we were safely in the elevator when Laudine said, "Well, you did manage to partially prevent what might have been the second murder. I'm not sure literally throwing yourself in harm's way was the best idea, however, but it proves the clock predicts what might be, and it's possible to change things."

"That's true. I don't remember ever being able to change a prediction. You would think that if the predictions weren't inevitable, the clock could have said, "second attempt" instead of "second murder.""

"Well, actually, it didn't mention a second attack or murder at all," Laudine said. "It just left us to assume there had to be one if there was to be a third. As usual, it's beyond me to figure out either the clock or the bottle. I'm just glad everyone is okay."

"I'll second that, for sure. Lidia, the girl who was there last night, stopped by to see me earlier. From what she said, I think she was just in the wrong place at the wrong time. It was nice of her to check on me, though."

"That was nice. Too bad she didn't see enough to identify the guy. I wish we could figure out the motive for all of this. If we knew why he killed the professor, we might be able to decide how Mr. Tim Ashley, or for that matter, the college is connected."

"So that means you think the same person was involved in both incidences. I must admit, that's the conclusion I've come to as well. This is a quiet, peaceful area. It seems unlikely to me there would be a murder, and then the attack so close together otherwise. We're beginning to get a little information, but we'll need a lot more before we can draw any conclusions."

The ride home was uncomfortable on the bumpy road, even though I was lying on the back seat. The cobblestones on the drive up to the main buildings were the worst. To take my mind off the pain, I told Laudine about Tim's visit, and anything else about this case I could think of.

Back at Druthmar, Laudine managed to get me into the wheelchair and to our rooms without encountering any of the staff. I was too tired for sympathy. For once I was grateful for the creaky elevator, and maybe a little surprised it was able to handle the extra weight of the chair.

At dinnertime, I was determined to go down. I wasn't sure if I wanted the staff to know I was still active, or if I was trying to prove something to myself. Laudine was concerned I was pushing too hard, and a little worried about what her staff might have prepared because she had been at the hospital and not there to supervise. At least, with all the other things on her mind, for a couple of weeks she wouldn't have to worry about me taking walks. The doctor had said I could use the crutches whenever I felt up to it, but I wasn't to walk without them for at least two weeks. I'd agreed to take one day off and rest in my room, but the following day I planned to make my way to my workroom with the crutches. Secretly, I had to admit I wasn't exactly looking forward to that walk.

Laudine needn't have worried, because the meal was delicious. The staff had used one of her meal plans and followed it to the letter. It was good enough that directly after eating she went to the kitchen to congratulate them. I was starved, and for once, I got all the way to the dessert. The lava cakes that boasted both hot fudge and caramel in the center were beyond wonderful.

I received all the normal sympathy for what had happened and lots of well wishing. Despite how short a time I'd known these people, it all seemed very sincere. To me, the most interesting part of the evening was the introduction of Beth's ex-husband, Don Jerome. He'd obviously once been handsome, but now he looked beaten down. My suspicious mind immediately caused me to wonder if his daughter had died under strange circumstances, but as it turned out, she had died in a car accident. He seemed devastated, but Beth hadn't seen the girl since the divorce five years previously and didn't seem all that upset. I was almost positive his was the third voice I'd heard during the argument in President Cummings' office. I knew that staff members who lived on campus weren't allowed to have a spouse live with them, and I suspected that was what they had been arguing about. Beth casually mentioned he would be with us for about a week, so I knew if the argument had been about him staying on campus, he and Beth had won.

In spite of all that had happened in the previous twenty-four hours, I slept soundly through the night without the need for any of the doctor's myriad of pills. The ones he'd prescribed to prevent infection I'd take, but the rest I hoped I would never need. When I woke, Laudine was already down with the kitchen staff, but she'd left a note telling me to call her when I was ready to get up. I thought I could probably handle getting dressed and down to the dining room on my own. Once I began, I was determined to finish, but it wasn't long until I wished I had called Laudine rather than trying to be so self-reliant. When I finally reached the breakfast table ten minutes late, I was shaky and covered with sweat. Laudine gave me a shame-on-you look, and I knew I'd hear about it later. I didn't mind, because I understood she was worried about me and wanted to keep me safe.

My late arrival and heroic effort to get there went pretty much unnoticed, because talk around the table was all about an additional attack that had happened during the previous night. This time it had resulted in the second murder. An assistant professor in the history department named James Graham had been stabbed at his home. He lived off campus by choice, because he wasn't married and could have lived on the fourth floor with the staff. Everyone seemed to be assuming all the violence was the work of one person, and though there was no proof of that so far, I tended to agree. The fact that both victims had been stabbed lent credence to the theory. I groaned inwardly as I listened to the table conversation. I had prevented one disaster, but while I was out of it in the hospital, a second murder had happened anyway. I wondered if maybe the things the clock predicted were not changeable. Maybe that's why it predicted some things and not others. Could it be possible that some things couldn't be changed and so those were the only things it revealed? At this point, I could only speculate.

I was both mad and sad that we hadn't been able to stop the killer before he could hurt anyone else, and more determined than ever to figure things out before he killed again. I was getting involved when I'd promised myself I wouldn't, but I couldn't just sit idle while people were being killed.

Everyone was inclined to linger at the table, but I tired quickly. Laudine quickly gave some last-minute instructions to her staff and then helped me back to the room and into bed. Today was the one day I planned to rest before returning to work. I was wondering whether to read or stream a movie, but we began discussing the previous night's events and what the different people had said at breakfast. When I realized this was how the conversation was going, I made an effort to keep the bottle in my line of sight. I was curious to see if it would react when hearing about the events that had taken place.

"Beth seems to have taken a liking to me," Laudine said. "It surprised me, because I didn't think she really liked anyone."

"That was my impression, too. She certainly doesn't seem to like me."

"I don't think it's you particularly. She is stand-offish with everyone. I was amazed when she started talking, but once she opened up, she couldn't seem to quit. There is something strange about her, but I did find out that she knew last night's victim. The next time I see her, I'll see if I can find out more about him. I wonder if he and Professor Castille knew each other."

From the corner of my eye, I caught a flash of yellow. The bottle was swirling pure yellow smoke. Laudine was seated where I knew she couldn't see the display. I didn't say anything, because until the bottle had some definite information, I didn't want to add to her worry.

"Those would be good things to know, but you need to be careful. We don't know who might be involved in all this."

Laudine frowned. "What about her husband? He's new, and therefore unknown around here."

I thought a moment. "Maybe, but my impression of the attacker was that he was a younger and taller man. Don Jerome must be at least fifty. I'm not sure he could run as fast as the guy I saw."

"Beth made sure to tell me that he was also staying up in Building Five, but not in her room. She didn't mind talking about him, so I can probably get her to tell me more."

"That's a good idea. At this point I don't see how we can rule anyone out, but don't be surprised if the next time you talk to Beth, she treats you completely differently. From what I hear, her actions aren't consistent."

"I've heard that as well. It will be interesting to see if she has more to say or regrets what she's already said."

"True. I'd better try to have another talk with Detective Crown. He must know when Don arrived. If he doesn't come by today, I'll track him down tomorrow."

"You don't sound very enthusiastic about that conversation. He's certainly a looker and seems interesting. I'd think he would be fun to talk to. Do you have some reason for wanting to avoid him?"

"Oh, I'm not sure. Both he and Tim Ashley are frustrating to talk to. They seem to have secrets or information, but they aren't about to say what they are. The detective has agreed to share some of what he knows, so that may help."

"I have faith in your persistence. You'll get it out of them eventually. I do know we aren't going to solve this tonight and you're about to fall asleep. All we can do is watch and listen for now, so let's see what today brings."

"I do seem to need a lot of sleep at the moment. I want to thank you for all your help. This hip thing would be a lot harder to deal with if you weren't here."

Laudine brushed off my thanks and went to her own room. In spite of knowing I should sleep, I managed to stay awake another thirty minutes, going over all the information we'd learned so far before I could no longer keep my eyes open. I'd planned to question the bottle to see if it would respond, but I was just too exhausted. I slept so soundly I must not have changed positions the entire night. I woke stiff and sore, but most of the acute pain had backed off. The sun coming through the window had woken me, and I knew from past experience it only hit the window from that angle in the late afternoon. I was trying to decide if I wanted to go through the struggle of going down for the evening meal when Laudine came through the door carrying a tray filled with different types of meats and cheeses.

"I brought these for a snack in case you woke hungry. When it's mealtime, we will either get you downstairs or I can bring you a plate of something more substantial. Your choice."

"A tray sounds tempting, but if I'm going to try and work tomorrow, I need to keep getting up and around so my muscles don't tighten up. Besides, who knows what interesting tidbits the rest of the staff may let slip at dinner?"

"Okay. I'll be back a little before six. So far, today has been pretty quiet. I for one hope it stays that way."

As soon as Laudine returned to her duties, I reached for the bottle. Now that I was awake, I wanted to know if it had anything to tell me. Before I touched it, the most beautiful lavender smoke began curling around inside. As much as I appreciated having this tool, each time it spoke I still got a shiver down my spine. This time was no exception. It said, "Crown and Ashley, huh? Interesting names for interesting men."

This certainly wasn't what I'd expected. I waited, but nothing else happened, so I said, "I'm not sure what that means, but I wanted to talk to you about the murders that have been happening on campus. The clock has said there will be a third attempt. It also says there will be more unless a friend and I can find the killer. I was hoping you could help."

The color of smoke changed to a sickly yellow-orange as the voice said, "I don't know the identity of this killer. I do know that this time, Laudine will not be the friend to help you. Your hardest task will be to decide who is your friend and who isn't. This will be a choice you have to make yourself, and your choice will affect the outcome. I am sorry about your injury. I hope it doesn't hinder you too greatly."

I didn't know which was more surprising, the information or the personal note. The bottle had never acknowledged me in that way. I suppose nothing should have surprised me anymore, because I already knew the bottle continued to evolve. Each encounter was more and more like talking to a person, except that whatever information was imparted always seemed to be either some type of riddle, or way too cryptic. Whatever I was to make of the information, I knew the bottle had given me all it would at the moment, because the smoke faded out at exactly the same time as the voice.

Almost the same moment I realized the voice was gone, there was a knock on my door. I probably should have been more cautious, but I hollered, "Come in," before I gave it any thought. Detective Crown stuck his head around the door and said, "Ah, good, you're awake. I wanted to talk with you a little more, but I didn't want to disturb you. Just before I knocked, I thought I heard you talking to someone."

He looked around the room as he spoke. I motioned him in. "You may have heard the TV. I was watching earlier. I'm glad you came by. I wanted to talk to you, too, but I wasn't quite up to hunting you down yet."

"Do you want to go first or shall I?"

I had to laugh at his comical grin. I knew he was thinking that he was the cop and I was just a civilian, but he managed not to say it except with the grin. "By all means, Officer, you go first."

"That's 'Detective' to you, lady," he laughed. "It may surprise you to know that I came to find out if you'd learned anything new. I'm sure talk around campus is full of everyone's ideas."

"True. That's part of the problem. Everyone has their own theory, and each one is different. One thing they all agree on is that our murderer is a serial offender. I don't know if three attacks technically mean he's a serial killer, but he's killed two people and I don't think he's through yet."

"That's my fear as well. We have increased the patrols on campus, but no matter how many officers we put here, we can't be everywhere. President Cummings is allowing an officer to stay on the residence floor, and we have patrolmen watching the streets in town where some of the professors live, but for all we know, this guy could start going after students."

I asked him when Beth's husband had gotten to town, and he confirmed it had been well after the first murder. I told him about my visits from Lidia and Tim. He, in turn, showed me the composite drawing of the killer, which most resembled the Pillsbury Doughboy rather than the glimpses of the man I'd chased. He'd also brought pictures of the two murdered men. I was almost afraid to look, because I was worried they'd be death photos, but I finally picked them up. Both men had been very much alive when the pictures had been taken. The photograph of Professor Castille was a shock, because I'd seen him on campus twice when I'd been out walking in the evenings. I'd never seen Professor Graham.

The detective was rising to leave when I said, "I've seen this man on campus twice before he was officially scheduled to be here. He was talking to another person outside the student union. I didn't pay much attention either time, but I think his companion was a man."

He sighed and sat back down. The look that crossed his face made it plain he was deciding whether to tell me what he knew. When he'd reached his decision, he said, "Some of what I'm about to tell you has been withheld from the news media, so I'd appreciate it if you kept the details to yourself. Other people have also admitted to seeing the professor around campus. Several thought he might have been talking to Assistant Professor Graham. Leroy tells me they weren't working on any school projects together, and I haven't been able to find any other connection. Naturally, we're still digging for information. We've searched both their houses and found nothing. So far, we haven't discovered where Professor Castille was staying here in town."

"I assume there was no evidence to suggest he was staying with Graham?"

"That is the obvious next question, but you're right...we've found nothing to indicate he was staying there."

"I see. So now there are two dead people and we still don't know much. I wish I could help more, but I've told you everything I've heard. If I hear anything new, I'll let you know."

He left, as it was getting close to the dinner hour, so I decided to see if I could get myself up, ready, and in the wheelchair by the time Laudine arrived. I managed it, but just barely.

Going down to dinner to hear the latest gossip initially seemed like a waste of time. Almost all the talk was still about last night's attack, but none of the staff seemed to have anything new to offer. As always, the food was delicious, but I was still tired, and that, along with my aching hip, killed my appetite. I was almost ready to give up and head back upstairs when Claude spoke up. Tonight, he looked as tired as I felt. He said, "Jim Graham was a friend of mine. He was quiet, but a hard worker. Recently he told me he was considering proposing to his girlfriend. I can't begin to imagine why anyone would want to hurt him. I wish I'd spent more time with him recently. Maybe I could have done something to help."

Kenneth said, "I understand how you feel. I can't say he was a friend, exactly, but we've been on a couple of committees together, and he seemed like an upfront guy. Nothing about these murders makes any sense. I can't stop thinking about how his family must feel. He was still so young and full of plans for the future. What makes it even worse is that he called me about a week ago, and I didn't return his call. I figured he was calling about some committee I didn't have time for right now. If I'd returned that call, it might have made a difference."

I noticed that even though he was still one of the best-looking men I'd ever seen, he too looked tired and worried. These killings were beginning to get to all of us. I said, "It's easy for almost everyone to find some reason to feel guilty, but the only person responsible for what happened is the attacker. The rest of us can only keep our eyes and ears open for any bit of information that might help the police catch him."

At that moment, our illustrious leader entered the room with his usual jaunty walk. "I apologize for being late. I've been consulting the police about what we might be able to do to keep the students safe. I know so far, all the attacks seem to be aimed at the staff, but we can't be sure that won't change. Even if the students aren't the intended victims, they could be injured by being in the wrong place at the wrong time. The detective didn't have any great ideas, although he did suggest a curfew. I am giving that some thought. He also said he had posted more men on campus. I know that if and when information about the attacks gets out, it is going to affect our enrollment figures. No one wants to attend an unsafe campus."

My suspicious mind wondered if he were more concerned about the college's bottom line or about student safety, but I didn't say anything. It was his job to be concerned about both. Soon after that, the conversation reverted to already-discussed information. I excused myself and maneuvered to the door. Laudine was immediately by my side offering help. I thanked her, but assured her I would be fine on my own. Before I reached the elevator, Kenneth appeared. He said, "I'm sure you can make the trip upstairs without help, but since I'm going that way, allow me to give you a hand."

I raised my hands from the wheels and said, "I'm happy to let you take over. I can't understand why a dislocated hip would make me so tired, but I seem to wear down way too quickly."

He said, "I'm no doctor, well, at least not that kind of doctor, but I would imagine your body is using all its resources to heal the damage that was done. I broke my leg once and it was a couple of months before I stopped feeling tired."

"I hope it doesn't take that long. I have work to do here, and I still want to take some classes. Speaking of tired, you look worn out yourself. I hope you aren't coming down with anything."

"No. I'm fine. I tend to stay up too late working on getting my class lectures ready when the beginning of a semester gets this close. A couple of weeks from now, I'll relax and rest up."

We'd reached my door by then, so there was no more opportunity to question him. I told him goodnight and thanked him for his help. Once inside the room, I sighed and began the task of getting myself to bed. My last thought was to wonder how, when by all accounts Kenneth was such a gifted mathematician, he had ended up teaching in such a small obscure college. The fact that he seemed visibly upset seemed to indicate he might have been closer to Instructor Graham than he'd let on. Or maybe I was just tired and seeing suspicious behavior where there was none.

Eight

The following morning, I was sure I'd passed some milestone, because I wasn't nearly as stiff and sore as the day before. Putting any weight on my hip was still painful, but not unbearably so. Even better, I felt rested and ready to face the day. I knew I'd have to use the crutches to get to the workroom, because there were too many ups and downs to use the wheelchair. I had never tried crutches, so once I was showered and dressed, I practiced a little by taking a few turns around the room. By the time I reached the dining room, I felt like an expert. One with sore shoulders and arms, but still an expert. I only stopped by long enough to tell Laudine I was off to work. As good as I felt, I still wasn't hungry.

It took me twice as long as usual, but I made it to the workroom without incident. I was examining the second piece of jewelry when Tim knocked beside the open door and walked in. When he reached my table at the back of the room, he said, "I like these weapon-free meetings. It seems you're beginning to trust me, after all. I came by this morning to see how you're doing. If you got this far from your room, you must have mastered those crutches."

"I appreciate your concern, but you're wrong. I haven't decided to trust you. Our meetings are weapons-free because you haven't taken me by surprise lately. Are you going to tell me why you really sought me out way down here?"

"There you go, being suspicious again. I honestly did want to make sure you had gotten here safely, but I also wanted to ask you a couple of questions."

I gave him an I-told-you-so smile, which he pretended to ignore. He said, "Detective Crown isn't inclined to talk to me about his case. I was wondering if you had any new information?"

"What makes you think I would be more inclined to talk to you than Crown is? For that matter, what makes you think I might know anything you don't?"

"Those are fair questions. I may have done a little research on the people here. It seems you have been involved in several police cases before. I think you somehow manage to get the police to confide in you. Pretty women are easier to trust than men that show up claiming to be engineers."

I couldn't suppress a moment of pleasure knowing he thought I was pretty, but I squelched it quickly. In the back of my mind, I could hear the bottle telling me I'd have to decide who to trust as a friend. I wasn't ready to give him details I'd heard from the police, but I didn't think it would hurt to tell him what I'd learned on my own. I explained what I knew about Beth and her husband. I didn't add what Crown had told me, as I considered it privileged information. Besides, if the detective found out I'd passed on anything he'd told me, he would quit confiding in me. Tim was good at asking the right questions, and by the time he left, he knew what I knew except what had come directly from Crown. More than ever, I was sure the engineer had an agenda of his own, but I was no closer to knowing what it was.

The rest of the morning passed smoothly, and I was making real headway with the jewelry. At a few minutes before twelve, I realized I was finally hungry. I hadn't brought any food because it would have been impossible with the crutches, and I didn't want to try and make the trip back to the kitchen. I'd resigned myself to waiting until dinner when Laudine showed up with a plate of fruit, cheese, and crackers. She even stayed for a short time and nibbled some of the cheese while I ate. When she left, I was restless. I'd been sitting all morning and needed to move around, even if it meant using the crutches.

I wasn't ready to try negotiating stairs, but I still hadn't explored the other rooms on this floor. I wandered down the hall to the right. It wasn't very exciting, because all the closed doors looked alike and I saw no sign of life anywhere. When I reached the end of my hall, I noticed that the last door before the turn was slightly ajar. I didn't know what the rooms here had been used for originally, but I got the feeling they were all about the same size. Since this one was open, I didn't feel bad about looking around inside. I'd been right about the rooms. This one was exactly the same size as the one where I worked. It was mostly empty, but there were a few pieces of furniture scattered around haphazardly. Near the back of the room there was a large, beautiful desk. It looked very old. Naturally I couldn't resist taking a look in case it was a valuable antique. The wood was a beautiful rich mahogany, and the writing surface was gilt-tooled black leather. Both were in excellent condition. It was a partner's desk, with a knee hole on each side. It had the classic nine drawers on the front side, and when I walked around to the other side, there were three drawers and two shelved cupboards. The piece had all the original handles and Hobbs locks. The key was hanging from the lock on the middle drawer. Such a gorgeous piece shouldn't be hidden away in an otherwise empty room. I opened the top right drawer to check inside. I wanted to see if the piece was marked by the maker. It was stamped John Finch, London, 1877. I was so excited by this find it took me a moment to realize the drawer was half full of papers.

By then, my hip was beginning to ache. In my excitement over the desk, I hadn't been too careful about putting weight on it. There was no chair with the desk and no place to sit except the floor. I knew if I got down there, I'd never get back up. I wanted to look through the papers in case there were any valuable old documents, but I was tempted to come back another time. I really needed to sit. I scooped up the stack, intending to take them back to my workroom where I could look through them in comfort. Before I could take a single step, I noticed the papers weren't old and the one on top had two names in bold print. One was Tim Ashley and the other was Professor Castille. Nothing was going to stop me from snooping further, and I knew I couldn't take the papers with me in case Tim came back. My hip forgotten for the moment, I began reading as quickly as I could. There was no reason I shouldn't be exploring this room, but for some reason I didn't want to be caught in there.

What I was reading explained some things, but also raised more questions. There was a letter from a Regina Castille asking for Tim's help. Evidently, they had been close friends in college and she didn't know where else to turn. She was worried about her brother, Albert, and asked that Tim check up on him. Why she considered him the man for the job, she didn't say. The letter spoke of her brother's recent strange behavior and her inability to reach him. The date on the letter indicated it had been written a few days before he had died. There was also a recent photograph of the professor, as well as his address and phone number. Both knowing more and being more confused than ever, I put the papers back as I'd found them and limped back to my office.

I did my best to concentrate on the mourning jewelry, but my mind kept wandering off to ponder the information I'd found in the desk. I'd have to decide if I was going to confront Tim with what I knew. I was wondering if I should quit work early or push on, when Dorothy Penn walked in. This was the first time we'd been alone together, but I groaned inwardly because I constantly got vibes from her that she resented me being there. Determined to be friendly, I turned and smiled.

She said, "So this is where you are hiding. They should have moved all this stuff to a more accessible part of the building. Your recent accident has to be making it difficult for you to get down here every day. I should probably ask Leroy to move the collection to the poetry department where I can give you a hand."

"I appreciate the offer, Dorothy, but all these items are exceptionally valuable and are better off here where there is less traffic. My hip is getting better every day. A little exercise keeps me from stiffening up."

"Suit yourself. Don't say I didn't offer." Here she paused briefly and looked furtively around before saying, "So, who do you think the murderer is? I'm sure you have a theory by now."

"How in the world could I even guess? There are a lot of young men on campus and many staff members that live off campus. I haven't met most of them. Even that is assuming the murderer is a man. I'm sure someone has a motive, but so far there don't seem to be any clues as to what it might be."

"Oh, come on. Surely you've realized by now the attacker has to be somebody on the staff."

"What in the world would make you think something like that?"

"It seems obvious to me. That detective keeps snooping around. It wouldn't surprise me if that guy who says he's an engineer were really some kind of cop, too, or maybe even the attacker. He showed up around the right time. The cops must know something that makes them hang around the staff rather than the students."

"I don't think they have drawn that kind of conclusion at this point. I'm sure they're just searching for information everywhere. It makes sense they would question the staff, because they travel around campus more than anyone, and they knew the victims. They are probably hoping one of the teachers will know something, or spot something suspicious."

"If you say so, but I don't intend to trust anyone until they catch this maniac."

Having stated her opinions, she turned her attention to the jewelry. I brought out some of the better pieces for her to see. I was surprised to find that she really was very knowledgeable. When the topic of conversation was poetry or antiques, she was extremely sensible and fun to talk to.

After she left, not only was my concentration shot but I was exhausted. I had done enough for my first day back. I finished packing away the things I'd been working on and was adjusting my crutches when Claude walked through the door. I wasn't up to more conversation, so I was relieved when he said, "Good, you're finishing up here. I came down to check on you and hopefully walk you back to your room."

Claude matched my slow progress to the elevator. As we walked, we talked a little about his art history course. I was more eager than ever to get started with classes. He was kind enough to promise he'd put me on the list of his students and bring me the necessary paperwork so I didn't have to go to the registration office. He explained about an assembly and reception that was a school tradition to welcome new students and returning professors. He asked if I would attend with him. I was pretty sure that had been his main purpose in coming downstairs. I agreed, as it sounded interesting, and because he was the first person I'd talked to lately who hadn't asked me what I thought the police knew. I assumed that when Claude's Art History class started, we wouldn't be breaking any rules about professors dating students.

We stepped out of the elevator on the third floor just as Leroy was walking by. I thanked Claude for the escort and invitation and asked the president if I could speak with him for a moment. I wasn't thrilled with the thought of walking to his office, but he saved me the trip by suggesting we speak in my room. I said, "I hope I didn't catch you when you're busy, but I realized earlier today I'd been remiss in leaving the mourning jewelry and reliquaries open and unguarded. There is a sizable fortune in that room, and we haven't even been locking the door. At the very least, I need a key so I can keep the door locked. We should also install a vault and, or, an alarm. If word gets out about the value of those antiques, there are lots of people that wouldn't hesitate to try and steal them."

"You're right. I've been so concerned with the attacks on campus I'm not thinking straight. Unfortunately, one key fits most of the doors on the hall where you're working. I'll have the custodian install something temporary right away. I'll also order a safe that will hold the jewelry. It would be the easiest to steal."

"Thank you. I apologize for not thinking of it sooner."

Once he'd gone, I let myself gently down on the bed, propping the crutches close by. Several hours later, Laudine came up to see if I was coming to dinner and found me fast asleep. She didn't hesitate to wake me. I opened my eyes grudgingly as she said, "Sleeping is good, but you need to eat. Besides, if you sleep too long now you won't be able to sleep tonight."

"I think that ship may have already sailed. I've been sleeping for almost three hours, but I'm glad you woke me. If I'd missed dinner, I'd have been in the kitchen hunting for food in the middle of the night. How long do I have before I need to be downstairs?"

"I thought you might need a little time to get ready. It's about half an hour until we eat."

"Perfect. I know you need to get back. I can make it down on my own. I'm getting to be an expert with these crutches. Thanks so much for waking me. Oh, when you get done this evening, I have some news to share. I made an interesting discovery today."

"If you're trying to pique my curiosity, you've succeeded. I'd stay and insist you tell me now, but I really do need to get back. I'll definitely come by later. Don't you dare fall asleep before I get here."

I'd been putting off calling Barry. I knew he'd ask questions I didn't want to answer. There was no way I could keep him in the dark, and it was only fair I tell him what was going on sooner rather than later. I wasn't eager for the lecture I knew he'd want to give me, so I decided if I called him now, he wouldn't be able to chastise me for too long, since he wouldn't want me to miss dinner. Like everyone else, he was a fan of Laudine's cooking.

I dialed his number, hoping for his voicemail. He picked up on the second ring. When I said hello, he said, "I'm glad you called. I've been wondering how you're doing, and I have a million questions about that place."

Even though I'd been reluctant to call, it was wonderful to hear his voice. I told him so and then said, "There won't be time on this call for a million questions. I only have thirty minutes before it's time for Laudine's evening meal, but I'm sure we can get some of them answered. First, I need to bring you up to date on what's going on here. I'm not about to give you the chance to say I've been keeping things from you."

"Uh-oh! This is beginning to sound like another one of your things. I don't even know what to call them. So tell me, what's going on?"

"Okay, let me give you the short version and then you can ask your questions. A professor and an instructor here at the college have been murdered. During another attack, I got there in time to run off the attacker, but in the process, I sustained a dislocated hip. The doctors assure me that I'll recover completely, and already it's much better."

"I suspected you of being involved in something, but this is worse than I thought! I don't like the thought of you being injured. I assume the guy you call an attacker is still on the loose?"

"Yes, and the bad news is that the clock predicted there will be a third victim. To anticipate your next question, no the police don't know much yet. The policeman in charge is smart and thorough, so he will figure it out eventually."

"My first instinct is to hop on the fastest plane I can get to New York, but you keep telling me that I'm too overprotective. Tell me honestly, how safe are you?"

"I live in one of the college buildings in a suite of rooms with Laudine. There are always people around. I am completely safe. There is a fairly large police presence here on campus also. I promise you I am well protected."

"All right, but you also need to promise me that if at any time you think I can help, you'll call me."

I made the requested promise, and from there we talked about other things like the jewelry and the campus and its inhabitants. I had to cut our conversation short in order to go down for dinner, but I assured Barry I would call again soon. He once more gave me his worried speech, but hopefully I'd reassured him enough so he wouldn't panic.

Every trip I made on the crutches was easier than the one before. I was getting very confident and maybe a little careless, because as I exited the elevator my left crutch caught on the edge of the door, and I fell out into the hall right into the arms of Detective Crown. He laughed and set me gently back on my feet. "I've heard of men having women throw themselves at them, but this is the first time it has happened to me."

"Very funny! I do appreciate the catch, though. It seems like I was getting a little overconfident about my ability with the crutches."

"No problem. I had to spend six weeks with crutches once, so I know they can be difficult. The trick is to learn to slow down."

He hung around and walked me in to dinner. For once, he was so pleasant I considered telling him what I'd learned about Tim, but I decided I would confront Tim directly first to see if he would tell me why he was keeping secrets.

Dinner as always was perfect, and tonight I was hungry. There was pork loin with a savory sauce, twice-baked potatoes, a delicious mix of unusual vegetables, and an apple salad. I ate at least one helping of each dish and seconds on some. I also managed a large slice of warm peach pie, but had to forgo accompanying it with a scoop of ice cream. The conversation was casual and centered around school business. It felt like everyone had forgotten the murders, but I knew they hadn't. Tim didn't show up for the meal, so I had no opportunity to ask him any questions.

I'd been back in my room about an hour when Laudine showed up. I'd been trying to decide if I should try questioning the bottle again, but I'd decided it would do me no good. If it had something new to tell me, I would have seen signs of activity.

Laudine was barely through the door of my room before she demanded, "Okay, let's hear what you've discovered."

When I'd explained what I'd seen in the papers from the desk, she said, "I hope he has a good reason for keeping his involvement a secret."

"I agree. I don't understand what possible reason there could be for secrecy. I'd think Detective Crown would be more helpful if he knew."

"Maybe, but he also might think Tim's interest was too personal and he should be kept completely out of the investigation. For all we know, this may not be the first time Tim has inserted himself into an investigation. Who knows what type of police he's encountered in the past?"

"I hadn't thought of that. Heaven knows, you and I have dealt with all kinds. I've decided I'm going to talk to Tim and admit what I know. I'm not sure it's the right decision, but if nothing else, it would give him someone to talk to. That's, of course, if he doesn't react badly to my snooping and clam up."

"It's a tough decision, but I think you've made the right choice. Honesty is often best. How he reacts is up to him, but at least now that you know why he's here, you can stop being suspicious of his actions."

"Maybe, but who knows what he's been up to since he's been here? For all I know, the police may suspect Tim. It's even possible he arrived before he made his presence known. If he confronted Castille, he might have killed him. Hopefully we'll know more once I've talked to him."

"Hopefully, but if you think there is any possibility he killed Castille, you really need to be careful."

"I don't honestly suspect him, but I have no proof either way. By now the police should have checked his story and know for sure when he arrived. I just worry about trusting anyone completely right now."

Settling down for the night felt good, but it took me longer than usual to fall asleep. When I did, I slept soundly and as far as I knew, dream free. In the morning I felt more like myself than I had since the attack. I'd promised to use the crutches, and I would yet today, but if I felt this good tomorrow, I might try going without them. I was scheduled for a return visit to the small hospital in town early the following week for an X-ray to make sure my hip was healing correctly. I knew I should use the crutches until then, but I also knew myself well enough to know I probably wouldn't.

The following morning, I stopped by the dining room long enough to hunt up a few things I could put in a bag and take with me to eat later if I got hungry. I'd discovered I could loop the bag over a crutch and carry a few things that way. There were only a couple staff members eating while I was there, and I didn't hear anything new. Hopefully I would have an uninterrupted morning of work. I wanted to make up for the time the hip injury had cost me and get a little ahead of schedule, so that when classes began, I didn't have to feel guilty about taking the time to attend. The first semester I planned to take Claude's art history class, and the second semester I would most likely take Dorothy's poetry class. I'd been undecided between Professor Castille's archaeology class and poetry, but unless there was a new professor by the second semester, my only choice would be poetry. From my brief talks with Dorothy, she seemed very knowledgeable about her subject, so either of those classes should be fun for me because I had an interest in both subjects. They might not help me in my business, but I couldn't concentrate solely on antiques.

I found my workroom door closed for the first time since my very first day on the job. Alexander was standing right outside waiting for me. Without saying a word, but looking pleased with himself, he reached up and handed me a key. The door was sporting some new and very sturdy-looking hardware. I used the key and the door opened soundlessly. I was about to thank the school's jack-of-all-trades when he motioned me inside. He had also worked his magic here. Completely surrounding the boxes of reliquaries and jewelry was a sturdy wire cage. Alex smiled and handed me another key. This one fit the huge lock keeping the cage door secure. Now that I'd seen the new additions, he said, "That should help keep things secure until the safe arrives. The one we ordered is only big enough for the jewelry, but the other boxes will be much harder to get to now. A determined thief could still get in, but it would take a lot of time to cut through that strong wire."

"This was a great idea! I knew we had to lock the door, but this is a perfect deterrent. I'll sleep a lot easier knowing these valuable items are protected. Thank you."

The cage Alex had built was probably seven feet tall and plenty big enough to hold my large table and still allow me to move the boxes around as I needed. I couldn't imagine how he'd gotten so much done so soon, but I was thankful he had. I felt much more relaxed here and the morning's work went smoothly. I got my desired interruption-free time, so I was able to make good headway.

At noon, I'd just gotten the lunch of cheese, French bread, and fruit I'd taken from the breakfast table set out to munch while I worked when Tim walked into the room. I steeled myself for the necessity of telling him the truth. At least I wouldn't have to go hunting for him. His initial anger took me by surprise when he said, "What gives you the right to go through my things? It's obvious someone riffled through my papers, and you are the only other one down here."

Even without his words, it was easy to tell he was furious. His face was red and his fists clenched. It seemed like an overreaction. I said, "You're right. Once I realized the papers weren't old like the desk, I should have left them alone. However, when you leave things lying around in rooms that aren't yours, you shouldn't be surprised when someone finds them. I planned to tell you today that I'd seen them. I'm not the one trying to keep secrets."

He made a visible effort to calm himself before saying, "Okay, you have a point. In all honesty, I am probably madder at myself than I am at you. I wasn't exactly trying to hide those papers when I put them in the desk. When I was down here the other day, I had them with me, and when I heard Detective Crown in the hall, I stuck them in the desk so I wouldn't have to explain until I was ready. I wanted to get to know him a little before deciding if I could trust him. I know how it looks, so let me explain first and then you can ask whatever you want."

"That sounds more than fair. You don't really have to explain anything to me, but I would like to know why you still haven't talked to Detective Crown."

"I want you to understand. Regina Castille was my fiancée in college. I was three years ahead of her, and when I graduated, I joined the military. During that time, we drifted apart and I didn't make any effort to find her once I finished with the service. By then, I thought she'd be better off finding someone new. I had handled some delicate situations during my service years, and it took some time before I felt able to function normally back in the states. That's all I can tell you about my military career. At least the military put me through college, and I really am an engineer. Anyway, I imagine what little she knew about my training is the reason she asked me to see what was going on with her brother. I'm not proud of the fact that once again I failed her. I got here too late to save her brother, but I'm determined to at least get justice for Albert."

"That's understandable. Especially if you still have feelings for Regina, and I suspect you do."

"Maybe, but it's way too late for anything to come of that. I can't see how she could ever forgive me for not saving her brother now, let alone for my treatment of her in the past."

"No one can protect another person completely. The only one responsible for what happened is the man who murdered him. I admire you for wanting to help bring him to justice, but I still don't know why you haven't talked to Detective Crown."

"I have two reasons. First, I'm pretty sure Crown would discount my military experience and resent me for messing in his investigation. He's going to think I only want revenge. Secondly, I've been upfront with the police a time or two in the past and it didn't turn out very well."

"I've run into that attitude myself, but I still think you need to talk to Crown. You can't blame one policeman for the behavior of another. If nothing else, it will save him wasting time investigating you. It's possible he might surprise you and even be grateful for the help. He seems like a pretty reasonable man."

We both looked up guiltily when the detective himself said, "Do I hear my name being bandied around?"

I looked over at Tim and nodded, hoping that would let him know I thought now was a good time to come clean with Crown. He coughed and then stayed quiet for so long I'd decided he wasn't going to speak. The whole time, the detective stood relaxed and silent. I needed to remember that this was a man who was good at his job. Finally, Tim coughed again and said, "Alicia has convinced me that we need to talk. There are some things I haven't told you about myself."

"Funny, that's why I'm here today. There are some things I've learned about you that I thought we should talk about."

I said, "If you gentlemen will excuse me, I'll take my lunch elsewhere and let you compare notes."

Crown said, "Nonsense. We won't run you out of your work space. Especially since I don't think you can manage the crutches and carry your lunch. We'll go downstairs to talk. Maybe if we set up close to the kitchen, that friend of yours will take pity on us and give us something to eat."

I laughed, "Her name is Laudine, and I'm sure she would like nothing better than feeding the two of you. She loves it when people enjoy what she makes."

They went off amiably enough together, and I got to eat my lunch in peace. As soon as I had finished, I went back to work. This was Friday and I wanted to reach the goal I'd set for the week. I hoped to have some free time over the weekends and use that time for sightseeing. I'd only feel justified in doing that if I got enough accomplished during the week. On Monday, students would begin arriving for a week of registration and settling in before actual classes began.

The weekend was quiet, and even though I worked a few hours each morning, it was a restful time. Unfortunately, my hip wasn't quite ready for sightseeing, but by Sunday night I was getting around fairly well without my crutches. I had to endure a lot of scolding, and not only from Laudine. Nearly everyone in residence cautioned me, but the relief of being free of the crutches was worth it.

Nine

Sunday afternoon, students had begun trickling in, but Monday morning was the mass arrival. Also a new professor, Joe Hillman, moved into the fourth floor housing. He would be the replacement for Castille in the Archaeology Department. I was surprised they'd found someone so quickly. He and a new instructor named Jenny Albright were the only additional staff members who would be living on campus this semester. The rest of the staff were either local, year-round residents, or were married and lived off-campus during the school year.

The arrival of students changed the whole atmosphere of the campus. What had seemed like a quiet retreat with beautiful grounds now made a noisy entry into the twenty-first century. Chatter, cell phones, and exuberant young people were everywhere. In a way, I resented the intrusion because the place no longer seemed mine alone, but in another way the hustle and bustle was exciting. So far there had been no third attack, so this influx of students also brought fear. I wondered if the return of the students was what the attacker had been waiting for. I couldn't imagine why it would be so, but I couldn't put it out of my mind either.

I was already registered for my class, so I had Monday free to work, and Tuesday I would make the trip into town for the checkup on my hip. Tuesday evening was the welcoming reception I was attending with Claude. My first art history class would be at two on Wednesday. My day Monday was uninterrupted, and I made good headway with the jewelry. Monday night at dinner we got to meet the two new additions to the group we'd be living and eating with for the next few months. The pictures I'd seen of Professor Castille had given me the impression that he was foreign, dark complected, and bearded. Joe Hillman was the exact opposite. He was a man in his early fifties and so pale he looked sickly, but he was very pleasant and everyone took to him immediately. I thought he seemed knowledgeable and well spoken. I could now take the archaeology class if I wanted and would soon have to make a decision between that and poetry. Our other new addition was Jenny Albright. She was a tall woman in her thirties. I thought it might take time to get to know her, because she was very quiet and seemed shy. She would be the teacher's assistant in the science department, so I wouldn't be in any of her classes.

Tuesday morning, Laudine and I got back in our rental car and drove the short distance into town. My appointment wasn't until one, but we wanted to spend time exploring Canajoharie and find an interesting place to have lunch. Laudine was armed with her trusty tourist brochures and was reading madly as I drove. She had offered to drive, but her limited experience driving in the states made me a little nervous, and I wanted to test my hip. Part of the time she would quote out loud and part of the time just her lips moved. I caught fragments like, "Wow, the Erie Canal is famous and it's right here," and "Gee, it doesn't seem like it would have taken three fires before they banned building with wood." I refrained from asking any questions. I was sure she would point out each interesting reference once we were out of the car and walking around.

I was right. The moment we were parked, my history lesson began. As with so many places in this area of New York, there was the town of Canajoharie, but within the town there were one or more villages. Today we were touring the village of Canajoharie, although Fort Plain was another interesting possibility. We began by walking down Church Street, planning to intersect with Prospect. We'd barely started when we smelled the heavenly scent of bacon in the air. Laudine, as always, was hungry, and for once I felt the same. What we'd found was one of New York's ubiquitous diners, or so we thought. We decided to give it a try. We were barely in the door before being greeted by friendly employees, and were only seated at our table a moment before hot delicious coffee appeared. We were unsure what to order so we decided to go for broke.

We asked for the house specialty: strawberry pecan pancakes. Neither of us could finish our order but it wasn't for lack of trying. The pancakes themselves were perfect, and the strawberries had to have been straight from the field. It had been years since I'd tasted anything so flavorful. I tried my heaping stack with both the homemade strawberry syrup and the local maple syrup. Both were fantastic, but the meal was best with no syrup at all. When we couldn't hold another bite, we paid a ridiculously low price for our food and continued on our tour.

We'd only walked a few blocks when we saw a sign pointing down an alley that said, "Antiques." No shop name, just a small ornate sign with the one word. This I couldn't resist. Besides, I owed Barry some new inventory. About three-fourths of the way between our street and the next was a small door. It was the only one off the skinny alley, so we were sure it had to be where we would find the antiques. I was fascinated by the location even before we entered, but once inside I was blown away. The shop contained no furniture. Looking around, the biggest thing I spotted was a table lamp, but the array of jewelry, lamps, clocks and fabulous glassware might have been the best overall quality I'd ever encountered outside of a museum. We'd only been inside a few moments when, to add to the shop's mystique, the owner appeared. He had to be six-feet-five or six and was skinny as a rail. His black suit and billowing cape brought the thought of vampires vividly to mind. In his own way, he was magnificent, and his lilting French accent was the perfect accompaniment. After his initial greeting, he didn't approach us or apply any sales pressure. He just lurked. As I browsed, I asked the strange proprietor if he carried any mourning jewelry, thinking I'd like to compare the quality to what the college owned. The man gave me a strange look and just shook his head.

While we were there, Laudine bought a bracelet she had fallen in love with and I purchased three clocks, two made by Ansonia and one by Seth Thomas, two ornate necklaces, and five unique pieces of old cloisonne. I was relieved when the shop owner agreed to ship them directly to Arizona. His fee for the service was nominal. By the time we finished shopping, it was already time to head to my appointment.

Dr. Dawhan was the same doctor who had treated me originally, but I'd only seen him once briefly. I was immediately impressed with his knowledge and bedside manner. He explained things in detail and was happy to answer questions. I liked him even better when he told me that I was healing fine, and that as long as I was a little careful, I could begin walking without the crutches. He did give me a strong warning that if I did more than I should I would pay a price. He made it very clear that over-activity would cause sore and painful muscles. I didn't mention that I had already given walking crutch-free a try, and although Laudine frowned at me, she kept silent on the subject. The doctor was happy enough with my condition that I didn't have to see him again for a full month.

Laudine wanted to get back to the school in time to be sure the staff had the evening meal prepared correctly, so we couldn't eat dinner in town, but we still had a couple of hours free to explore a little more. There were several great shops. In one, I bought a soft rose-colored over-sweater for walking on cool evenings. I was just getting worn out from hobbling around so much more than I was used to when I spotted an interesting-looking restaurant supply store across the street. Knowing she'd love it, I pointed out my discovery to Laudine. As we got closer, the outside looked more like a junk store. Inside was a different story. There were rows and rows of kitchen gadgets from antique to ultra-modern. Some were used and some new. After telling Laudine to have fun, I found a chair near the front of the store and sat down to rest. From my seat I could see several unusual-looking items, and I knew Laudine would be thrilled with the place. She would easily be able to fill the full forty-five minutes browsing the aisles before we had to leave. Every now and then she would come rushing up to my chair to show me some unusual treasure. I thought of all the antique shops I'd dragged her to and wondered if I looked then the way she did now. She might be somewhat worried about events at the school, but so far this trip seemed like just the distraction she'd needed.

My view from the window was great. This part of the old town looked like something from a Norman Rockwell painting. The architecture was quaintly ornate in a way nothing in the West ever was. Sometimes I missed the wide-open spaces of the West, but I knew there was a lot about this part of the country I would miss when I returned home.

I was staring out the window while making a mental list of the things we should visit the next time we were in town when I was sure I spotted Detective Crown hurrying down the street. His stature made him hard to miss anywhere. When he turned down the alley where the antique store we'd visited was located, I was puzzled. If I hadn't been positive it was the detective I'd seen, I'd think it must have been another large man, because that shop was the only one along the alley and I knew the detective wasn't an antique buff. I was wondering what in the world he might be up to when Laudine tapped me on the shoulder and announced she was ready to leave.

Surprisingly, she only brought one item to the counter to purchase. When I questioned her about being so frugal, she laughed. "Don't be silly. I'll be back here many times. Most of the things I intend to purchase are for home. I've located things here that I have been trying to find forever."

"Then out of all this wonderful plunder, what did you pick to purchase for the school? I certainly can't tell what it is by looking at it."

Unable to believe I was so dense, she gave me a look to see if I was kidding. When she realized I really didn't know, she said, "It's a juicer.

The one at the school is one of the new trendy ones for making healthy drinks out of vegetables. There's nothing wrong with that, but this one actually does citrus, pomegranates, and any other hard-to-make juices. Breakfasts will be much better when I can serve fresh juice."

Even though to me it looked more like a metal watermelon and an iron melted together, I only said, "Ah. Well, I'm glad you're happy with your find. I can see now you'll be running off to this place every chance you get. I certainly can't blame you, because I know I'll be visiting that antique store again. I guess right now, though, we'd better get back."

I had an hour after dinner to get ready before I had to meet Claude downstairs. We planned to walk to the reception, but he'd assured me it was sidewalk all the way. This was good news, because with my knee-length cocktail dress I could wear the new high heels I'd bought for this trip. When the time came to go, I only made it to my door on my way downstairs before I knew the shoes were a no-go. I could walk almost normally without crutches now, but not in heels. I sighed and changed into a pair of dressy flats.

I was sure the reception would be stiff and boring. Students could attend, but most didn't. The bulk of the crowd was a mixture of parents and staff. It was the moms' and dads' one chance to meet and talk to the people who would be instructing their children, and more of them than I'd expected were taking advantage of the opportunity. When I'd progressed halfway across the room and seen there was an open bar on the opposite wall, I decided the gathering might not remain this quiet all night. The evening had been catered, and there were lots of delicious-looking items to sample, but I was still way too full to try many of them. When I'd first heard it was to be catered, I was upset they hadn't asked Laudine. When I questioned her about it, she'd laughed and said, "Oh, don't worry, they did ask. I told them to find someone else because I had plenty to do already. Snacks aren't my thing, and with classes starting tomorrow, I didn't want to do a halfway job just because I was busy."

I had to admit the reception was lavish, and I knew it had to be expensive. Once again, I wondered where the school got their funds. Either they had quite a few wealthy and generous alumni, or some lucrative investments, maybe both. The early part of the evening, Claude made a great date. He only left my side when some parent dragged him away, and he made sure to introduce me to anyone he thought I might not know. I hadn't expected to see Laudine. After her refusal to cater, I assumed she wouldn't want to attend, so I was surprised when she and Kenneth walked up. It was during one of the times some parent had dragged Claude into a corner to grill him. They made an outstandingly glamorous couple, but Laudine was quick to say they'd only decided at the last minute to attend because our building seemed so empty. Maybe too quick.

Much to my surprise, the evening was fun. We'd only been there a short time before everyone was talking, dancing, and I suspect, drinking some. All the stiffness of the initial moments disappeared. I didn't think a lot of dancing was the best idea for my hip, but I did give in to my date, a couple of parents, and Kenneth. Laudine loved to dance, and I don't think she missed a single round. I'd just begged a respite due to a complaining hip and sent Claude off to find a more able partner when Detective Crown walked up and asked me to dance. When I refused, he looked strange and I thought maybe I'd hurt his feelings, so I said, "Normally I'd love to accept, but my hip is telling me to refuse or pay a stiff penalty. If you aren't busy, I'd love some company. I was just about to walk out on the patio to take a break and get a little fresh air. Would you care to join me?"

"That sounds perfect. I actually like to dance, but I am going to do something violent if one more person asks me what the police know about the murders."

He gave me his arm to lean on as we made our way outside. His arm was as rock-solid as I'd expected. As soon as we were seated on comfortable lounge chairs, I said, "What do the police know about the murders?" His head snapped around, and the look on his face was priceless until he saw my grin. He realized I was teasing him and surprised me by laughing. I like a man who can see the humor in his own behavior.

The rest of the evening was a total surprise. Except for giving in to one more dance later in the evening, I spent the rest of the reception with Detective Crown. By the time we got around to that dance, I was calling him Jeff. The surprise wasn't that we spent the evening together, although since I had arrived with a date, it did seem odd. The surprise was how much I enjoyed the evening, even though I kept expecting Claude to show up. Twice I went back to the reception room to look for him, but couldn't spot him anywhere. It seemed strange that if he'd had to leave for some reason, he hadn't told me. I explained my concern to Jeff, and he called and assigned two of his people to try and locate my missing date.

By the time the evening was winding down and people were walking to their cars or homes, Claude still hadn't been located. The area of campus around the reception hall was well lighted, but Jeff still insisted on walking me back to my building. We were barely outside the lighted area when his radio crackled and a deputy requested his presence. Unwilling to let me walk the rest of the way alone, he rerouted us to the area just outside the garden in front of the student union building. There were six or seven policemen there, and they had set up strong portable lights. Immediately I saw the focal point in the center of the artificial glow. I knew at once it was a body. My first thought was, "Oh, no, not Claude." I moved to begin running, but Jeff put a hand on my shoulder and said, "You have to stay out of the crime scene. Wait here and I'll go see if I can identify the body."

I stopped and nodded agreement. He was back in what couldn't have been more than three minutes, but I don't think I breathed the whole time he was gone. He didn't waste time on small talk. He just shook his head. "It isn't Claude."

I took an audible breath. "Do you know who it is yet?"

"Yes, President Cummings saw all the commotion and came to find out what was going on. He identified him as a brand-new replacement professor. His name is Joseph Hillman and he'd just arrived to replace Professor Castille."

"How can that be? We just met him for the first time at dinner Monday. I don't think anyone here even knew him before he arrived."

"I don't have any answers to those questions yet, Ali, but I will get them, I promise. Right now, I need you to let a deputy walk you home.

If I get any word from Professor Trumain, I'll let you know, and if you hear from him, please call me."

I didn't argue. My hip had done enough for today, and I knew I'd only be in the way at the crime scene. I was worried sick about Claude, but I kept holding on to the fact that the clock had predicted a third murder but not a fourth, not yet. I felt bad I'd been unable to tell Jeff how much I'd enjoyed spending time with him. I knew now wasn't the time, but I hoped I'd get another chance.

I was happy to see that Laudine was already in our room when I arrived. She and Kenneth had left the reception about an hour before me, and she didn't know anything about what had happened. As far as she knew, Kenneth was safely in his room. He'd said that was where he was going when he'd walked her home. I was glad to know he was safe. I took the time to bring her up to date on all that I'd seen.

"I didn't know him, but he seemed like a nice guy," Laudine commented. "It seems strange that two archaeology professors were killed. That has to mean something."

"I think so, too, but I'm too worn out to try and figure out what tonight. I wish I'd hear from Claude so I could quit worrying about him."

Laudine chuckled. "With you off snuggling up to the detective, and Claude off, heaven knows where, I just assumed the two of you had made an early night of it, because of your hip. I never saw either of you after the middle of the night."

"For your information, I wasn't snuggling up to anyone. Jeff, er Detective Crown, was just keeping me company because I couldn't dance much because of my hip."

I think she chuckled again, but it was so soft I couldn't be sure. She said, "Okay, okay. For now, let's get some sleep and see if we can make better sense of things in the morning."

Ten

The morning brought a new round of gossip and speculation. There had now been three college employees murdered, and the authorities seemed no closer to a solution than they had been after the first. I didn't know about the rest of the staff, but the professors living on campus were getting nervous. To add to the situation, the rumor was spreading that Claude Trumain had been missing since the early part of last night's reception. I listened for a time, but no one seemed to have any real information, so I made my way down to my workroom. I did stop on the way to check the date on the clock, hoping it would have some useful information, but the next date showing was eight months from now. That was too far in the future to help with the current situation, so I left it unread.

A couple of hours into my work day, Claude walked through my door. Before I could speak, he said, "I understand you were worried about me. I wanted to personally let you know that I'm fine. I'd have stopped by sooner, but I've been undergoing intense interrogation by the police. I also want to apologize for abandoning you last night. That wasn't how I wanted our night out to go."

"You don't owe me any apology, but what in the world happened to you?"

"I'll tell you what I've repeatedly explained to the police. I hope I have an easier time convincing you it's the truth. You were dancing. I think your partner was Kenneth because I was just about to ask Laudine if she'd like to dance when my cell phone rang. I was surprised anyone would call me at the reception and shocked when I realized it was our newest staff member, Professor Hillman. He told me he was on his way to his new office in the building where the archaeology classes were held and begged me to meet him there immediately. He kept saying it was an emergency. When I questioned him, he would only say it was a matter of life and death."

"He didn't explain what the problem was?"

Claude sighed. "No. He promised to explain when we met. I finally agreed to meet him. I looked around but couldn't spot you, and by then he had me good and spooked, so I ran out, intending to explain when I returned. I didn't think I'd be gone very long. When I got to the building, I immediately went up to the third floor to Professor Castille's old office. No one was there and the whole place was dark. I decided I'd wait fifteen minutes and if Joe didn't show up, I'd return to the reception. I sat on one of the chairs facing the desk. I'd been there about five minutes when I thought I heard something. I was turning to get up when someone plunged a needle into my neck. The next thing I knew, it was nine o'clock in the morning, and two policemen were standing over me repeatedly calling my name."

"Are you sure you're all right? Did you get checked out by a doctor?"

"The police had me checked out before taking me to the station for questioning. There were traces of a strong sedative still in my system and a puncture wound on my neck, but they assured me I'd be fine."

"I don't understand why Professor Hillman called you. Did you know him before he arrived here?"

"Actually, I did. I hadn't seen him in forever, but he was a freshman at Stanford when I was a senior. He pledged the fraternity where I was a member. I think he called me because he didn't know who else he could trust. He must have been killed on his way to meet me."

"You implied the police didn't seem to believe you. Why are they giving you such a hard time?"

He sighed again. "Well, in their eyes I don't have an alibi, and the call to me was the last one showing on Joe's phone. They seem to vacillate between thinking I must be the killer, to worrying that the killer may think Joe told me something and come after me next."

"What a mess. Are they doing something to protect you in case you are a target?"

"There are two policemen posted outside the main building. They also assigned a man to go with me whenever I leave this building. I'm not sure that makes me feel very safe. Hopefully it will be enough."

"I can only imagine how you must be feeling. If there is anything at all Laudine or I can do to help, call us anytime. The police need to catch this madman. I wish I knew why all this was happening. Right now, I'll walk back upstairs with you. I think I need some coffee and a moment to calm down. Of course, when I say walk, I mean use the elevator."

He smiled for the first time since he'd come into the workroom. When we walked out the door, there was a policeman waiting to accompany Claude back upstairs. Since he was only supposed to be accompanied when he left the building, such close supervision made me wonder if his escort were there to protect or to keep an eye on the person they were considering a suspect.

When Claude had gone back to work and I'd gotten my coffee, I stopped by my room to pick up a sweater. The first thing I noticed was the multiple colors swirling around in the three-tiered bottle. I wasn't sure what the mixed-up colors meant, but it seemed like a perfect representation of my own confusion. I sat on the side of the bed and put the bottle in my lap. The color cleared to the pale lavender I was used to seeing. I waited, expecting to hear the voice but nothing happened. Finally I said, "I think you know there has been another murder. Do you have any new information?"

The words came quickly. "I know you want information, but for once I am reluctant to tell you what little I know."

I said, "Surely a little information is better than none. Besides, what happens to trust if you start keeping things from me?"

"That's the only reason I have decided to speak now. It may do more harm than good, and you need to realize what I am about to tell you is only part of the story. Use it carefully."

"I'll try not to jump to any conclusions until I have more facts. I hope what you know will give me some idea where to search for those facts."

I couldn't have been more shocked when the bottle gave me its information. Whatever I was expecting, it wasn't what I heard. When I was sure there wasn't any more to hear, I put the bottle back on the nightstand and sat for a long time reeling from the shock. I could repeat the words exactly as I'd heard them. Actually, I couldn't stop them repeating over and over in my mind. I was surprised they hurt so much.

As I analyzed my feelings, I came to understand that for the first time since Lawrence had died, I was seriously attracted to a man. When I'd met Lawrence during my first cataloging job, I never expected we'd fall in love. When we did, it was beautiful, and his untimely death had brought with it an enduring grief. Now my emotions were beginning to recover, but I couldn't trust those feelings because of the bottle's words: "This is what I know. There is something illegal going on here at the college, and I suspect Leroy Cummings knows what that is. I also know the policeman in charge of investigating the recent murders is hiding something. He is not being honest about who he is and why he is here. Be careful how you deal with them both."

Eventually I made peace with my new knowledge. The bottle had warned me that her information was only partial. I wasn't happy about any of it, but I would suspend judgment until I had more facts. Almost as surprising as this new information was the fact that the bottle was able to tell me things about people it hadn't come in contact with.

Always before, it had gained knowledge by close proximity. I'd just finished taking in the new information and what seemed to be new abilities the bottle had acquired and was about to return to work when Laudine walked into the room. When she saw me, she started and said, "You surprised me. I wasn't expecting anyone to be here. What in the world is going on?"

I filled her in on what I'd learned since Claude had walked into the workroom. When I finished, she was silent for a few moments before saying, "I can understand if you're upset, but you shouldn't be, at least not yet. Your Detective Crown could have a perfectly legitimate reason for hiding things."

"I know, and I'd just come to the same conclusion when you walked in. Still, I hate the fact that I will have to be careful not to trust him too much until I find out the truth, and he isn't *my* Detective Crown."

"Methinks the lady doth protest too much." Laudine laughed. "Did you think Claude was telling the truth when he explained where he'd been? He could have murdered Joe Hillman and then injected himself."

"He could have, but I don't think so. I got the feeling he was telling the truth about that night. It does seem a little strange he didn't mention knowing Hillman the night we met him at dinner. No matter what I think, we certainly can't take him off the list of possible killers yet."

"Okay. Assuming for the moment he didn't kill Hillman or the others, do you think whatever the bottle implied is going on at the school is related to the murders?"

"Considering that all these things are happening at the same small college, you'd think they'd almost have to be connected. Even so, we can't just assume they're related until we find some proof one way or the other."

"True enough. What do you plan to do next? I think we're going to have to begin actively looking for evidence instead of waiting around."

"I think you're right. This afternoon, I'll make some calls and see if I can find out more about Jeff, er, Detective Crown. I also think I'll see if I can get Alexander to show me the way up to the fifth and sixth buildings. I have the feeling Beth Jerome knows something, and I'd like to find out what. The day I heard her arguing with Leroy, I assumed it was about her ex-husband staying at the compound. Now, I'm wondering if it might have been something else."

She was grinning when she said, "It's okay to call him Jeff. Let's both do that when we talk about him."

The grin disappeared when she continued. "Your plans sound good. I'll try to get a little chummier with some of the kitchen staff. A few of them have been here for a long time, and they live on the fourth floor with the permanent staff. They may know something. If I get the chance while Leroy is out, I may try to search his office, too. It may seem a little extreme, but I think it's time we get serious."

"I know you're right, but be really careful. Don't go near that office unless you know he'll be gone for plenty of time. We can't afford to get caught snooping."

With our plans for action made, I went back to my office. The first thing I did was call Alex and ask him to come down to the workroom when he got a chance. He thought he'd be free in about forty-five minutes and promised to come then. Next, I searched online for any information I could find about Jeffrey Crown. It was suspicious, not because of what I found, but because of what I didn't. I found exactly nothing. Even if I looked for information about my own name, a few references would come up. Something would come up about nearly everyone. Oh, there were several Jeffrey Crowns listed, but none that could be the detective. I had to conclude that either Crown wasn't his real name, or all information about him was being suppressed for some reason. So far, I had no way to determine which.

Next, I made a few phone calls to law enforcement agencies asking to confirm his identity. I got nowhere with these inquiries. I was deciding what to try next when our friendly handyman walked in.

I explained that I needed a guide to help me find the way to Buildings 5 and 6. Alex gave me a pained look, and I thought he might refuse to help.

I said, "I can see you'd rather not be my guide. If there's a problem I don't know about, I'll find someone else. Is there something I should know here?"

He hesitated so long I thought maybe he wasn't going to answer, but eventually he said, "I hesitate to tell you, because it makes me sound like an idiot. You're right, I don't like going up there, but I'll be glad to show you the way. I just don't like that part of the school. My reasons aren't logical, but I find both those old buildings spooky, almost sinister. That and the fact that Beth always makes me feel unwelcome keeps me away most of the time."

"I understand, and I really will ask someone else if you don't want to go."

"No, I'll show you. Once you're finished up there, let me know what you think of those buildings. When do you want to go?"

"I thought right after lunch. That way I don't have to come clear down here and then back up."

"Okay, I'll be in the dining room, so we can go as soon as you finish eating."

"All right, if you're sure. If you want to back out, I'll understand."

"No, it's fine. I don't want to let my imagination get the best of me. I'll see you around noon."

When he'd gone, I was more curious than ever. I could easily understand him not finding Beth easy to visit, but for him to call that part of the campus sinister seemed extreme. Alex had never appeared easy to rattle. I was eager to find out what was bothering him.

I spent what little remained of the morning working. As always, I was nearly overwhelmed by the sheer numbers of pieces the collection contained. Someone had to have been collecting for a very long time to have gathered this many rare items. Maybe more than one generation had shared the same interest in items created to remember the deceased.

Lunchtime came quickly, since I'd started work so late. As promised, Alex was in the dining room when I arrived. I was more eager to get started than hungry, but I took the time to eat some fruit and yogurt for energy. When I finished, we set off on what turned out to be more of a trek than I'd expected.

We started out by taking an elevator I'd never been on. Instead of down, this time we went up what seemed like a long way. When the elevator stopped, we exited into a tiny room much like the one on the way to my workroom. Also similar were the long halls and multiple turns. I knew I'd never remember the route, so I'd come prepared. I'd brought a piece of chalk, and I made a small mark on the wall indicating the correct direction each time we turned. I'm not sure why, but I took care to mark the way when Alex wasn't looking. The handyman seemed like a great guy, but I reminded myself that I really didn't know any of the staff here very well.

Unlike the trip to my workroom, at one point on this trip we exited the building. When we did, I could see that we were about two-thirds of the way to Building 5. When I questioned him, Alex explained that there was an underground tunnel for this part of the trip, but it had already had one cave-in. Leroy was concerned there might be more, so he had blocked it off. He grumbled that it wasn't that much of a hardship now, but he hoped they got it straightened around before winter. By the time we'd reentered the building and followed several more halls that angled always upward, my hip was beginning to complain.

The tunnel ended by opening directly into what had to be the lobby of Building 5. Immediately, I knew why Alex found the place spooky. This building had to be decades older than the parts of the complex I'd seen before. The construction was primitive but elaborate. There were crumbling statues, pillars, and faded frescoes. Here and there I saw large tapestries that were so degraded their content was unrecognizable. There were small piles of tiles from crumbling mosaics littering the floor. Without comment, Alex led me to a large door on the opposite side of the room. Here he stopped and said, "From here, you're on your own. I wouldn't be much help anyway, because I don't know my way around in here. Don't worry about finding Beth. If you wander around for a bit, I can promise she will find you. Take my keys in case Building Six is locked. It usually is because of all the things stored there. If you can't find your way back when you're ready to leave, just call me on one of the house phones and I'll come back for you."

I think he mumbled "good luck" as he turned and left. I'd come to explore, so in spite of my hip, I would explore. For nearly an hour, I wandered the first floor. All I found were a lot of rooms in about the same condition as the lobby. The only exception was one large room that looked like a sanctuary. I wondered if this had once been a seminary or nunnery and if this room had been used for services. Some of the original trappings remained. The most impressive was a carved ornate baptismal font I thought was made of marble. I wasn't an expert on antiquities older than the seventeen hundreds, but it seemed to me there were items there from many different eras. I had to wonder if the building had been in use in one capacity or another since it had been built. I still had not been able to decide when that might have been.

There didn't seem to be an elevator anywhere, but I did eventually locate a set of steps. I dragged myself up as they wound around to the next level. At least from what I could tell from the outside, this building only had three levels. It might contain underground levels, but the building's condition would make any underground rooms unsafe.

The second level was in the same condition structurally as the first, but here an effort had been made to clean up the debris. These rooms could be considered usable, and as I wandered, I found that some of them had been furnished. The third one I entered was furnished as an office, and like the other two rooms with furniture, the quality was top-of-the-line. A lot of money had been spent here. A queen would have been pleased by the opulence. Sitting on a massive chair behind the desk was Beth.

I smiled and said, "Hello, I was hoping I'd run into you while I was here. It's really quiet and peaceful up here. I can see why you'd like living here."

"I do like living here, and the peace and quiet is the main reason. What gives you the right to come snooping through my home?"

"That's strange. I was told you had two rooms on the third floor, and I haven't even been up there yet, so I don't see how my visit could be considered snooping through your home."

"How dare you! This is my building and no one comes here without my permission. Get out of my house. Get out now or I'll call for my guards!"

She was getting louder and louder. A vein in the middle of her forehead was bulging so fiercely I was worried for her health. In spite of her anger and my surprise, we both heard a quiet voice say, "Now, Beth, dear, it's time for your rest. Come upstairs with me and I'll help get you settled."

I expected her to whirl and attack the man standing on the landing, but while I stood and watched, her demeanor changed. Sounding like a little girl, she said, "Yes, Daddy. I'm coming."

Without a further glance at me, she turned and hurried up the stairs. Before turning to lead Beth to her room, the unknown man indicated I should wait. Naturally, I was curious about what was going on, so I sat behind the desk. It was the only chair in the room. I'd been waiting about five minutes and was beginning to get antsy. I didn't hear any movement from the floor above, so I began making a search of the desk. I excused my invasiveness by telling myself the desk wasn't in Beth's rooms and this area was public space.

There wasn't much to search. Besides a few pens and pencils, there was one notebook filled with a scrawling handwriting and two more of the notebooks that were blank. Working my way through the bad penmanship to read the notebook, I quickly realized it was a very poorly written work of fiction or the ramblings of a very delusional mind. I was almost half way through a story about a widowed heiress before I realized the notebook was meant to be a diary. The bulk of the story was taken up with complaints. Some of the complaints were silly things, like only being served one egg for breakfast or how difficult it was to get good servants. Others were asserting that the writer was a prisoner in her own home. I was more eager than ever for the man who'd taken Beth away to return and explain her behavior.

In a few minutes, I got my wish. He came down the stairs looking completely unruffled. I knew at once he wasn't Beth's ex-husband. He was a much younger man, maybe even a year or two younger than Beth. His posture was ramrod straight and he radiated self-confidence. He suggested we move to a close-by room where there was comfortable seating. When we were finally settled, I couldn't wait any longer. "Mr. Jerome, or whatever your name is, what in the world is going on here?"

He said, "I'm not sure if I am the one that should be explaining things to you. I'm not even sure if you're entitled to an explanation. In spite of that, I can tell you won't just let the matter drop, so I might as well tell you now."

"Tell me what? This whole situation seems very bizarre."

"That may be an understatement. Let me start at the beginning. About five years ago, Beth Cummings Jerome, who is Leroy's sister, developed a rare brain disease. Over time, she lost most of the memories of her past and replaced them with the delusional fiction that she is a rich widow and this is her estate. Occasionally she reverts to a mostly normal state, but those never last. Each year the rational moments happen less often and their duration is reduced. Beth lives in a fantasy world more and more each week."

"So everyone is under the impression Beth is staying up here with her husband, Don. You obviously aren't Don Jerome."

"This is true. When Mr. Jerome realized how severe Beth's condition really is, he decided it was best if he returned home. My name is Clint Leonard, and I'm not related to Beth. Three years ago, Leroy hired me as caretaker for his sister. In the beginning, he kept her a secret here, but she began turning up at the college in a disruptive way. My job is to keep her comfortable and out-of-sight except during her rational moments. In her delusional moments, she has decided I'm her father. This is fortunate because it gives her a reason to obey my instructions."

"How sad. It must be very difficult for Leroy. Does Beth realize what's happening to her?"

"No, I don't think she understands, but sometimes when she's herself, she finds it all confusing. Those are the times I dread the most, because there isn't anything I can do to help her."

"It can't be easy for you. Just being confined here so much of the time has to be difficult. I'm sure Leroy must be very grateful. If there is ever anything I can do to help, please don't hesitate to call me."

"I appreciate the offer. What do you plan to do now?"

"Well, right now I'm going to leave you to your work. I want to walk up to the Building Six for a quick look, and then it's back to work. If you're asking if I plan to talk about Beth's problem, the answer is no. What's happening here is a tragedy, but it's also a family matter. It was kind of you to explain the situation to me."

"Thank you for your understanding. If you'll follow me, I'll show you the door closest to Building Six. It opens right near the entrance."

Eleven

I stepped out of the elevator and did a double-take. I'd expected Building 6, which I'd assumed to be unused at this time, to be in even worse shape than 5. I was dead wrong. This section had to be the same age as building below because the design and materials were the same, but it was in great shape, well cared for, and in perfect repair inside and out. Alex had been correct when he'd told me the building was used for storage. Each room was filled with crates and boxes of all sizes, and most had a large label typed on a manual typewriter. Once in a while, I'd find a cleaner looking label I assumed was computer-generated. I wasn't sure if the things stored there were years' worth of accumulated equipment no longer used by the college or additional donations from past students. Naturally I couldn't resist browsing through and reading some of the labels. Most of the boxes were items the college owned but no longer chose to use. I found crates of blackboards with boxes of chalk, old-fashioned desks and chairs, slide projectors, and even boxes of props and costumes from long forgotten plays. Reading those labels was interesting, and I was sure some of the items had value if sold as collectibles, but eventually I tired of reading and decided to continue exploring the building. Since this building was laid out exactly like 5, I found the stairs easily.

The second level was more of the same: crates and boxes. The labels I checked here were all handwritten. Here I discovered older items like ink wells, outdated maps, and Latin textbooks. I only gave those boxes a cursory look before moving to the third and top floor. If the stored items were getting older as I went up, this floor should contain the oldest cast-outs. Again, the labels were handwritten, but the contents were fascinating enough that I spent more time reading. I was almost halfway through the last room when I came across a box marked "praxinoscopes." I knew those were made as an early attempt to create moving pictures. They were popular in the late eighteen hundreds. If I remembered correctly, a strip of pictures was placed inside a spinning cylinder. In the center was a circular mirror that reflected the images, creating cartoon-like movement. I'd seen pictures and knew some were very ornate and others simplistic. I'd never had the chance to see one in person. Those items were in a wooden box with a lid that lifted off. I couldn't see any reason not to take a peek. I tried lifting the lid, but it wouldn't budge. When I gave it an all-out tug, something inside gave way and the lid came off.

I don't know how long I just stood there staring into the container before my shock subsided enough for me to move. Before examining the contents, I looked around to assure myself that I was still alone up there. The top layer inside was all small items. They were very old and all Egyptian. I lifted out the tray. Underneath were larger items, all carefully wrapped in modern bubble wrap. I chose one at random and unwrapped it carefully. Inside was an Egyptian senet. I knew it was a type of board game. The game was so ancient that no one knew how it had originally been played. I also knew those items shouldn't be there.

The set was beautiful and in great condition. I carefully put the artifacts back as close as I could remember to how I'd found them. When I set the top tray back, I noticed a ring of very modern keys tucked between bubble-wrapped items. I debated briefly whether taking them or leaving them was the right thing to do before stuffing them hastily in my pocket. I needed to think, but I also needed out of this room before I was discovered. That one box contained a fortune. It was possible it wasn't the only box containing Egyptian antiquities. People had been murdered for much less. This fortune was double trouble, because in 1983 Egypt had passed a law that made all Egyptian antiquities the property of the state. There were stiff penalties of both jail time and fines for taking any of them out of the country. Individuals that owned this type of item before 1983 could sell what they had, but even then, they could only sell to buyers in Egypt. I didn't think these artifacts had been here since 1983. If the college had proof of ownership, it should have been the first item in the box. Even if they had been here that long, Egypt would still want them back. Their discovery would require whoever claimed to own them to provide proof. I would have to tell someone what I'd seen, and as I thought about that, I could almost hear the bottle telling me that I would have to decide who to trust.

I trusted Laudine completely, but like the bottle had said, this time she wasn't the one who could help me. I couldn't confide in Leroy, because it had also said he was up to something and that something might well be selling illegal antiques. The only two possibilities of help were Tim and Jeff. I didn't completely trust either of them, and I had no reliable way to choose between them.

The elevator opened on the bottom floor lobby. I spotted one of the house phones and called Alex. After I explained that I wasn't sure I could find my way back to the main building, he agreed to meet me just below Building 5. He was waiting at the arranged spot when I arrived. I said, "Thanks for coming. I'm sure I would never have found my way back by dinnertime."

"Exploring make you hungry, did it? You're in luck, because Laudine stuffed and is baking these huge fish. I know because I asked what the heavenly smell was. I was surprised 'cause it was the first time I ever thought fish smelled good."

I laughed. "Yes, exploring did make me hungry, but even if I weren't, I would still get lost. You amaze me by how well you know your way around. Buildings Five and Six are fascinating. Both seem to be quite a bit older than the rest of the complex."

"Yes, they were the original two buildings. I think one was used for priests and the other for nuns. I've heard they were a very old-fashioned order and practiced some unusual rituals. You know, maintaining silence with very strict rules of conduct, maybe even practiced exorcism and the like. When the church decided to modernize and combine the order with a school, the rest of the buildings were added."

"Building Six was in a lot better shape than Building Five. I guess they have to keep Six repaired to protect all the stuff stored there."

"I'm sure that's the reason. I asked Beth once why she didn't move into Six. It seemed like a logical question since Five seemed to be crumbling around her, but she told me to mind my own business and walked off."

"That sounds like Beth. I ran into her while I was up there, and she made it obvious she resented the intrusion into what she considers her domain. I hope you weren't the one that had to carry all the stuff stored up there."

Now he laughed. "No. That isn't my problem. I may take small items up now and then, but when they load up outdated materials and want them stored, they call a moving company. There is a road of sorts that goes all the way up. I'm not sure why they bother, since they never bring anything back down, or at least I don't think they do. I see trucks up there now and then, but I've never seen anything come back down to the college."

"With all the things you have to do, I'm glad you aren't stuck with that duty as well. Do they store anything up there besides the outdated material?"

I thought he might balk at this line of questioning. After all, it was really none of my business, but it didn't seem to bother him.

"From time to time, people donate things to the school. Some of those things get stored in Building Six. Sometimes I do take those things up. I use the tunnels, which is why I hope they get the one that had the cave-in repaired before the snow starts. I don't know if the antiques you're working with now were ever stored up there. They appeared in the workroom about a week before you arrived. I never thought to ask how they got there."

I had other questions I would have loved to ask as part of what Alex considered idle conversation, but then we were back in the main building. It was five minutes till six, so I had no option but to agree to going in to dinner. We went our separate ways to wash up. I wasn't disappointed when I saw the big fish Alex had promised we were having.

I was sitting next to Claude. While the food was being brought to the table, he said, "So, tomorrow is your first day of class. Are you prepared to start studying?"

"What? I have to study? I thought surely you were planning to give me an automatic A."

He looked worried until he realized I was kidding. Actually, with all that was going on, I'd completely forgotten about class, but I had my book and supplies, so I was ready.

"Very funny. Just for that, I'll have to grade your work more closely than the rest."

The entire dinner continued in the same spirit of friendly banter, and for once no one mentioned murder. The fish were large, and there was a separate one for each person at the table. They were stuffed with a crab meat dressing. I thought it was possible Laudine had created the perfect meal. As so often happened, I couldn't begin to think about dessert. When everyone had finished, I helped carry dishes to the kitchen, and when I got the chance, I let Laudine know I'd like her to stop by my room when she finished for the night. She gave me a searching look but just nodded.

It seemed like the day had been a long one, and as I made my way to my room, I was looking forward to lying down. I almost groaned out loud when I stepped off the elevator and came face to face with Dorothy Penn. I knew before she spoke that she was looking for me, and I'd barely gotten the word "hello" out of my mouth before she confirmed it.

"I see you get around pretty well for someone still recovering. I hear you were poking around in the two oldest buildings earlier today. You are braver than I am."

"Oh, why is that?"

"What? You must know what I mean. I tried going up there once or twice, but that Beth person practically threw me out. Then she has that big assistant guy living up there. At least I think he must live there because he always seems to be around. Doesn't all that seem a little fishy to you? I complained to Leroy more than once about those two, but he never does anything. That seems a little off to me as well."

"I can tell you're worried about what goes on up there. I guess if they're doing their jobs and there's no proof they're hurting anyone, it's probably not a dangerous situation."

"Well, that sounds all prim and proper, Miss La De Da, but you're forgetting that people are getting murdered around here. I think we need to be worrying about anything that seems strange, but I can see I'm not going to get any help from you."

Having said what she came to say, she whirled around and marched off. I watched her go and then tiredly made my way to my room. In a way she wasn't wrong in thinking we needed to be suspicious of anything strange, but I wasn't sure her reasons for saying so were because of the murders or if it was just that she was a busybody. Either way, it wasn't my place to tell her what was really going on in Buildings 5 and 6. I wasn't going to tell her Leroy's secret about his sister, and I wasn't sure myself what to think of the artifacts I'd found in Building 6.

It wasn't long until Laudine knocked on my door before walking in. She was carrying a large platter, which turned out to hold six or seven kinds of small cakes. Even before she spoke, I knew what she would say, and I was right. "No excuses, my friend. You passed up dessert earlier, but I know you can handle at least one of these now. You've lost some weight since you were injured. I won't allow Barry a chance to say I let you fade away while we were here."

"You win, and besides, they look delicious, but I'm not unhappy about losing a few pounds. I hope not to gain them back. Hmm, I think I'll start with the lemon one."

As expected, the beautiful little cake bites were delicious, and we munched away while I told her what I had discovered. By the time I was finished, there were only two lonely desserts left on the plate. Laudine said, "Oh, boy. Now the decision the bottle promised would come is here. You'll have to tell someone about the Egyptian antiquities. Have you decided who you can trust?"

"I wish I could say yes, but truthfully, I'm still not sure, but I have decided who I'm going to talk to."

"Well, don't keep me in suspense. Who's the lucky man?"

"Very funny. I think I have to talk to Jeff, Detective Crown. I have two reasons, but neither of them is great. First, he is the law here and should have a better idea what needs to be done than anyone else. Second, I think I have to have faith in my judgment, and I believe he is an honest man."

"Those really aren't bad reasons. I think you've made the sensible choice. When will you talk to him?"

"I've decided to get it over with first thing in the morning. If he isn't here at the college, I'll call the station and ask if he'll stop by."

"Sounds good. Not to change the subject, but since both the professors killed were archaeologists and they are probably trained in things like Egyptian artifacts, do you think this may have something to do with why they were murdered?"

"The thought has crossed my mind. So far, I can't figure out how, though. If the college is involved in selling illegal or stolen items, it seems like Leroy would have to be involved. I guess I could accept that, but somehow he doesn't seem capable of murder."

"I know what you mean, but I guess you can't really tell that by looking at someone. Also, he may have accomplices. Like always, we need more information before we can come to any conclusions. Hopefully your detective can figure this out."

"I don't suppose it would help to say he isn't my detective."

She was laughing as she went to her own room for the night.

Twelve

I woke up dreading the fact that I would have to meet with Jeff. My class started at one, so I would have to track the detective down before noon. I knew I was worried he might not turn out to be the person I hoped. The bottle had said I would have to decide where to place my trust. I had to do it now, and at this moment the only thing I had to go on was character judgment. I had to trust my own instincts. Normally that would have been okay with me, but I knew I liked this man more than a little. I hoped that fact wasn't clouding my ability to see clearly. As I showered and dressed for the day, I put those thoughts aside. My choice had been made, so there was no use second guessing myself now.

The detective was already there when I walked into the dining room. I smiled inwardly because Jeff had been showing up early most mornings lately, and I knew Laudine had made another convert to her cooking. I'd heard her tell him to stop by for meals anytime he was in the area. She liked nothing better than feeding a crowd. He was definitely taking her up on her offer. As I walked to an empty seat, I leaned down as I passed Jeff and let him know I needed to talk to him when he got a chance. The food looked wonderful as always, and I couldn't resist eating half a grapefruit and a slice of the raisin cinnamon French toast with fresh maple syrup. As soon as I finished, I made my way down to the workroom. The once difficult and confusing route was routine now. When I was about halfway there, I thought I heard someone in the hall ahead of me, but I was thinking about other things and dismissed it as just old building noise.

I became aware of two things at once when I opened the door. I reached for the light switch and realized the lights were already on and simultaneously heard a loud banging noise begin. Quickly looking around, I saw a shape by the protective cage Alex had built. Wanting to find out what was going on but not wanting to be spotted, I ducked behind a bookshelf and worked my way a little closer. As I moved, I grabbed a broom leaning against the wall. If worse came to worse, the sturdy handle might afford me some protection. A subtle sound or movement must have alerted the intruder to my presence, because before I got close enough to identify who was using a hammer to try and break the cage lock, they swung around and rushed directly at me. I could tell it was a man, but his face was averted and he was moving so fast I couldn't tell if it was someone familiar or not. When he was close enough to touch, I struck out with the broom. I knew I connected because I heard a grunt on impact, but it didn't slow him much. The man gave me a strong shove, and I went down in a tangle of arms, legs, and broom. I did my best to avoid falling on my sore hip. I was getting up slowly when Jeff walked through the door and called my name. I called back and in a moment he was by my side. "What in the world is going on in here? As I came down the hall, I heard something crashing and then what sounded like running. Are you all right?"

"Yes, I'm fine, but someone was trying to break into the cage where we keep the jewelry collection. They must have run by you on your way here. Who did you see?"

"Ali, no one came by me. I didn't see a single other person. I did hear running, but it sounded like they ran down the hall in the opposite direction. You didn't recognize the intruder?"

"No. I'm sure it was a man, but I didn't see any features. It didn't register at the time, but I'm wondering now if he was wearing a dark mask. Whoever it was has to still be here, or there is a way out on this floor I don't know about."

"If you're sure you aren't hurt, I'll go check around and see what I can find. They've probably figured out a way to escape by now, but it's worth a look."

I didn't want him to go, but I knew it was the right thing. At least when I walked back and unlocked the cage door, nothing hurt. Thank goodness this time a shove wasn't going to send me to the hospital.

It was almost an hour before he returned. I had locked the cage door behind me, so I had to get up from my work to let him in. When the door was open, he said, "Look, I need to ask you some questions about what happened, and there was something you wanted to talk to me about. Let's go upstairs, get some coffee, and talk."

I smiled and followed him to the elevator. He was right, I needed the break, but I couldn't resist saying, "You can't fool me. I know you're hoping Laudine has a cake ready."

He gave me a mock frown, but refrained from saying anything.

We found coffee, and Jeff, the cake I had joked about. He began his list of questions as soon as we were seated. His first one wasn't what I expected. "Why would someone try to steal mourning jewelry? Oh, I know it's valuable, but beating the cage open with a hammer in the middle of the day seems like a strange way to go about things. Is there an easy way to sell this type of jewelry?"

"Well, yes and no. If you have proof of ownership and the right connections, it isn't that hard to approach museums, private collectors, or even auctions that draw anyone interested. I suppose there are fences that will take anything, but most wouldn't want to take items with the high dollar amount of this jewelry without proof of ownership."

"That's kind of what I thought. That's why I don't understand the reason for today's attempted theft. Do you have some type of inventory listing all the items in the collection?"

"Yes, I have the original list the donor provided with the collection itself. I haven't checked it yet because all the items are listed in groups by what type of jewelry they are. For instance, all the necklaces are listed together, all the bracelets, etc. Sorting them by category is what I've been doing so far. That, and sorting them by approximate value within each group. I've almost finished with that part of the job, so matching them to the inventory comes next."

He looked thoughtful for a moment. "Anyone familiar with antiques or anyone that has been in here enough to observe you would know this?"

"Probably. It's a pretty standard way to handle large collections. Why?"

"Maybe no reason, but since today's attempted robbery doesn't make sense, I'm trying to figure out why it happened. It's possible that if someone has already stolen items from the collection and they know you're getting close to discovering the theft, they may have tried to either steal the whole thing or at least mix all the items together again to cover their tracks."

"That makes sense, but how would you prove such a thing?"

"Ah, there lies the rub, of course. I couldn't prove it unless the thief confessed, or was caught with stolen merchandise, but it could be useful in helping me investigate different types of suspects. At least the theft attempt was unsuccessful. Even so, you need to stop confronting the bad guys. I'm glad this time you weren't hurt."

I told him all I'd seen or heard. He said, "That's all I think we need to discuss about the attempted robbery for now. It's your turn. What did you want to talk to me about?"

Before I told him about Leroy's sister, I made him promise to keep the information to himself unless it had some connection to the murders. Once he'd promised, I told him about my visit to 5 and 6. He had a lot of questions about the handling of Egyptian antiquities.

I answered what I could and agreed to find out more. When he was satisfied he'd gotten all the details about my discoveries, he said, "Do you think you could find your way back to Building Six without Alex as a guide?"

I ran the route through my head for a moment before answering. Finally I said, "Yes. I marked the way with chalk, so I am ninety-nine percent sure I could, but to go the way I went would require going through Building Five. That's almost impossible to do without being discovered. Alex says there is a road of sorts going all the way up there. That might be the best way to keep anyone from knowing what you're up to. The big problem would be getting a key. Building Six is normally kept locked."

"I hate to ask, but would you be willing to go back there with me? You're the only one who knows where the box of antiquities is located, and from what you've told me, there are hundreds of boxes. We don't have to worry about keys. I had Alex give me copies of all his keys when the investigation began."

"I'd be happy to show you where it is, but it depends when you want to go. I have my first class this afternoon. Beside the fact that I don't want to miss it, there would be lots of questions if I didn't show up."

"That's not a problem. I thought we'd go just after supper tonight. It will be almost dark, but not quite. It should be hard for anyone to spot us. If you're sure you're okay with going, I'll meet you outside the kitchen door at seven."

I readily agreed and hurried off to put in a couple hours' work before class began. I did do some work, but also spent time thinking about how Egyptian antiquities, mourning jewelry, and murder could be connected. It all meant something, but I didn't have enough information to know what yet. I did decide that my first priority would be to match the jewelry to the inventory as quickly as possible.

Thirteen

I managed to make it to my first class about five minutes before it began. I was glad I'd allotted plenty of time, because finding the right classroom took some doing. The Language and Arts Building was at the back of the campus. It was the last one before the woods took over, and finding my way around felt like negotiating a maze. I hoped that would end when it became more familiar. I was a little disappointed in the first class. Claude wasn't a very animated speaker, and the entire time was devoted to explaining what the future classes would consist of. I told myself that was probably normal, and I needed to withhold judgment until the actual lectures began.

By dinnertime I was too nervous about the return trip to Building 6 to eat much. I'd told Laudine where we were going because I thought someone should know. Jeff would probably disapprove, but I knew she would keep the information to herself. When everyone else was finally eating dessert, I excused myself and made my way unseen to where Jeff and I had agreed to meet.

I'd only been waiting about a minute when a shape came around the corner of the building. From his size I knew it had to be Jeff, and I moved quietly in his direction. As he'd predicted, it was dusk. The lengthening shadows and dying sunlight made it hard to see clearly in the distance. When I got close, he said, "Follow me. I've located what has to be the start of the road. It's pretty rough but I think we can manage it."

He wasn't exactly whispering, but he was speaking quietly. The unnatural tone sent a little shiver along my spine because it reminded me it was important we weren't noticed by the wrong person. Someone here was a killer, and they might also be involved with the antiquities. I nodded my acceptance of his request and followed him through the edge of the woods to the road. It was only moments until we stepped out of the trees onto a narrow track. I wouldn't want to drive a car up this trail, but it was no problem for walking. Until we were a good distance from the main building, neither of us said anything. When Jeff finally spoke, it was in his normal voice, and that went a long way toward helping me calm down. He said, "I'm glad we don't have to make this climb in a foot of snow. I don't think they could bring much up here during the winter."

"I've heard they do a lot of snowmobiling in this area. Maybe they use those to haul boxes up here in the winter."

He nodded. For a time, we didn't say much as we concentrated on the uphill climb. As we passed Building 5, we moved off the track and out into the trees. We were taking no chance that someone would accidentally see us from a window. Once we were inside Building 6, we remained cautious, but we knew it was less likely we'd run into anyone. Under normal circumstances, no one would be there at this time of the evening. For all we knew at this point, the antiquities might legitimately belong to the college. Jeff just wanted to get a look at them and check around for anything else suspicious before he talked to Leroy.

I had no trouble finding the way up to the third floor, and I remembered exactly where the box we were interested in was located. When we reached the spot, however, there was nothing except some scuff marks where something heavy had been moved. It was obvious from the even rows of remaining boxes that this open spot shouldn't be there. I looked at Jeff and stated the obvious, "It's gone! Someone knew I'd been up here and was taking no chance I might have discovered their secret."

"It seems that way. From what you said yesterday, Beth, her caretaker, Alex, and Laudine are the only ones who knew about your visit. Any one of them could have moved the box, or someone else might have observed your activities. Let's scout around and see if we can spot any other spaces where something might have been moved."

I said, "Well, yes, those people would know, but any one of them could have told someone else. The way news spreads around here, there could be any number of suspects."

We walked the entire room, discovering two additional places that could have contained boxes that were no longer there. We checked the remaining rooms on the third floor and did some spot checking on the second, but the empty spaces were only in the room where I'd seen the Egyptian antiquities. When we could think of nothing else helpful to do at the moment, we quietly made our way back out onto the trail. This time when we left the cleared area to bypass Building 5, Jeff said, "Wait here a moment. I want to scout the woods around Building Six. I won't be long."

I wasn't thrilled about being left alone in the woods, especially now that it was pitch black, but I didn't argue. I was pretty sure he was keeping an eye on me and knew I would be safe while he took a quick look around alone. At least the trip to Building 6 hadn't bothered my hip. The ten or so minutes he was gone seemed a lot longer, and several times I thought I heard footsteps or twigs snapping in the opposite direction from the way he'd taken, but I didn't see any signs indicating someone else was out there. Now and then Jeff's light bobbed into view up near the building. I waited for the light to begin coming closer signaling his return, but at some point it went out. Not long after that, he returned, stepping out of the dark woods next to where I was waiting. I nearly jumped out of my skin, but also breathed a sigh of relief, happy to be finished with this adventure. He surprised me again when, rather than starting off back down the small road, he pulled me toward the woods onto what might have been an overgrown footpath and said, "Follow me for a moment. I discovered something over here I want you to see."

I followed with only curiosity about what he'd found and not even a shadow of fear. I may not have had the best of reasons to trust Jeff, but I did. The woods were inky black and Jeff wasn't using his light. I don't know how he managed it, but he never missed a step. He was holding my hand to make sure I didn't get lost, and his grip was warm and comforting. I only stumbled once and he kept me upright with little effort. I'm not sure how far we walked, maybe the distance of a football field. When he stopped, even though the moon was coming up, it took me a few minutes to make out an even darker shadow among the trees. It was some sort of structure, but I couldn't tell anything about its makeup or size. My eyes were just beginning to adjust when Jeff led me up four steps and inside out of the cooling night air. He checked the room with his flashlight and then leaned over and flipped a light switch before saying, "It looks lived in, don't you think? The electricity works, and there isn't a sign of dust anywhere."

I said, "In that case, isn't this breaking and entering? Someone might call the police."

"Very funny. It might be entering, but there was no breaking. The door was unlocked when I discovered the place."

"That sounds pretty iffy to me, but now that we're here, we might as well check the place out. There's another room over here."

I opened the door to the second room revealing a small bedroom with an attached bathroom, and one additional door I assumed was a closet. I was poking around the bathroom and had just discovered shaving equipment leading me to believe the cabin's occupant was a man, when Jeff pulled a shirt from the closet that could only belong to one person. At the same time, the door opened and Alex said, "Maybe you'd like to tell me why you feel you can snoop through my house?"

We both whirled toward the door to see him standing there holding a baseball bat. Jeff said, "You might as well put down the bat. I doubt you can take us both. Let's all sit down and we'll explain how we ended up here."

We moved back to the main room and settled around a small table. I was curious to see if Jeff was going to tell Alex what we'd discovered. I had trusted the handyman from the beginning, but I didn't know if Jeff would, since neither of us knew him very well. I was pleased when he told him the whole story, beginning with when Alex had dropped me off at the upper buildings the day before. He only left out the part about Leroy's sister, since I had promised to keep that to myself. When he finished, Alex said, "So, when you spotted my cabin here in the woods, you thought the killer might be hiding out here. That makes sense. What I don't understand is why you've decided to trust me so quickly."

Jeff smiled. "I trusted you even before I met you. I've done my research on the people here. I know about your past service to your government. Besides, I know it wasn't you who knocked Ali down yesterday, because I passed you downstairs just before I took the elevator up."

I said, "I don't have such logical reasons for trusting you. Since I've been here, we've become friends and trust goes along with that."

"Well, I appreciate the vote of confidence. I knew Ali was up to something when we came up here yesterday, but I had no idea what."

"That makes sense, because even though I didn't have any special goal in mind, I was curious about Buildings Five and Six. Everyone I've talked to about this part of the complex has been less than forthcoming, so I thought I'd see for myself what was going on up there. Now I almost wish I'd stayed away, because I've only created more questions rather than finding any answers."

Alex looked at Jeff and said, "What will you do now? If the box Ali saw is gone, you can't confront anyone, with no proof it ever existed."

"That's true, but I think I'll talk to Leroy anyway. I may be able to tell if he's involved by his reaction when we talk. If the Egyptian antiquities are somehow legal, he would know. For now, except for Leroy, I'd like to keep our conversation tonight just between us."

I said, "I'd like to apologize for invading your space. I never suspected you didn't live on the fourth floor with the rest of the staff. In fact, I always wondered why you didn't eat with us very often. I'd decided your schedule must be the reason. I never suspected you were going home to eat. Even so, we should have checked to find out who lived here before we just barged in."

Jeff said, "Add my apology to Ali's. I should know better."

Alex laughed. "I appreciate the apologies, but it's okay. I understand how it happened, and under the same circumstances, I'd probably have jumped to the same conclusion. You're also right about me not usually eating in the staff cafeteria. I like coming home for meals and I like my own cooking, but I have to admit that now that Laudine is preparing the staff meals, I often bring her food home to eat here."

We thanked Alex for being so understanding and took our leave. We wanted to get back before we were missed. While we'd been inside, the moon had moved behind a bank of clouds. I could barely see my hand in front of my face. Jeff switched on his trusty flashlight and led us back toward the trail down. About halfway back to the trail, he turned off the flashlight and said, "There is just one more thing I have to do before we return. Whatever you do, don't scream." Instinctively I knew what was going to happen. When he reached for me and his hands wrapped around my shoulders, I jumped, but not because I had any desire to scream. I leaned forward into his embrace as he bent down and kissed me. It wasn't a casual kiss, and when he turned the flashlight back on and started walking again as though nothing had happened, my legs were a bit unsteady as I followed. That kiss wasn't something I was likely to forget, but for the moment I tried to concentrate on the other events of the night.

We reached the main building safely. I was chilled and still trying to figure out if the things we'd seen had given us any useful knowledge. I knew I wasn't ready to retire for the night. Jeff said,

"I'll walk you to your room. That way I'll know for certain I got you through the night's activities safely."

"I appreciate the thought, but I don't think I'm ready to go up yet. I'm going to make a stop in the kitchen for some hot chocolate."

"In that case, would you mind if I join you? I have a couple of questions, and hot chocolate sounds great."

I grinned and said, "You're welcome to come along, but I hope you realize Laudine won't still be there to ply you with goodies."

He muttered something under his breath and marched off toward the kitchen. I had to hurry to keep up with his long strides. I noticed happily that even after our long walk, my hip still wasn't giving me a single twinge as I hustled after the man. At the door, he waited until I was by his side and then pushed it open for me to enter. Unexpectedly, the room was brightly lit, and I'd been wrong when I'd said Laudine wouldn't still be there. She and Leroy were sitting at the worktable eating pieces of pie and chatting happily. The room was wonderfully warm and still filled with delicious smells from the day's cooking. Before they noticed us, I heard Leroy say something about a recipe being his grandmother's favorite. I said, "This is a surprise. I thought we'd find a cold dark room. We came to find some hot chocolate. Will we be bothering you if we make a pot?"

Laudine jumped up and said, "Not at all. Sit and let me fix it for you."

"Absolutely not! You've worked all day. I'm sure we can find what we need."

"That works for me, but at least bring some plates and forks with you so you can taste this. I'm trying out some pumpkin pie recipes. I think this one is my favorite so far."

I turned and grinned at Jeff before gathering up the things we needed for the hot chocolate. The man had the audacity to wink at me before checking the cupboards for the necessary plates.

For a time, we joined their discussion of favorite recipes and wonderful restaurants from the past, but when there was a lull in the conversation, Jeff said, "Leroy, I hate to interject a serious note into the evening, but there are a couple of things I need to talk to you about."

"Then let's get to it. Now is as good a time as any."

Jeff began by asking Leroy if he wanted to be alone for the discussion, but he seemed perfectly comfortable with Laudine and me remaining. With that settled, he told Leroy all about my trip to Building 6 the day before. For now, he skipped over my encounter in Building 5. When he finished, Leroy said, "That's impossible! Any items that go up there are checked and approved by me. I have a complete inventory that includes everything ever stored there since I've been here, as well as what was already there when I arrived."

"So, are you telling me you deny any knowledge about the Egyptian artifacts in question?"

"Emphatically! First thing in the morning, we need to go up there and figure out what's going on. Something like this could cause a great deal of trouble for the college."

"Before we discuss that, I have another part of the story to tell you."

He explained all the details of our visit to Building 6 tonight. Leroy was quiet for a moment before saying, "Now I'm really confused. How are we going to make this right if we can't find the evidence?"

Jeff said, "It does make things difficult. My next question is going to be about your sister. I'll ask you again if you would prefer we talk alone?"

"No, it's all right, really. I noticed earlier that you skipped over any mention of Building Five. It stands to reason Ali would have stopped at Five on her way to Six, so my secret is probably already out of the bag. Go ahead and ask what you need to."

"I appreciate your cooperation, and I hate to bring up what should only be a family matter, but under the circumstances, I do need to ask a few questions. First let me say I am not making any judgment about your decision to keep Beth here, and I'm not accusing her of anything. Like I've said before, I've done my research on the people here, and it's my opinion that at this time Beth isn't capable of organizing any type of theft or sale of stolen items."

That statement surprised me, because it indicated that Jeff had already had some knowledge of Beth's condition even before I'd told him what I'd learned. He had never given any indication he knew. I suppose he would consider that police business and not something he should share. I needed to remember there was a lot about this man I didn't know.

Jeff continued. "My questions are about her caregiver. Since he's been so careful to always stay out of sight, I haven't had enough information to check his background. Right now, I think everyone believes her ex-husband is still up there. I need whatever information you have about him. Things like where he comes from and whatever references he gave you. Also, the details on how you found him originally would be helpful."

Leroy said, "I'll be glad to get all that information for you. He seems so involved in his profession, I can't imagine him trafficking in stolen items, but I know it makes sense to check."

I had one important question, so before this meeting broke up, I said, "Leroy, I hate to ask, but under the circumstances I hope you'll understand. Are you positive the mourning jewelry and reliquaries are really the property of the college?"

"I understand why you might be concerned. This type of doubt is why we have to get this mess cleared up quickly before it really hurts the college's reputation. I'm glad to be able to assure you that the collection you're working with is completely legitimate. I have a copy of the will leaving it to the college and all the documents that go along with that up to and including the trucking company's delivery notice. I'd be glad to show them to you if you'd like."

"Thank you for understanding. I have no doubt all is in order as you say. However, I would like to see the documentation when it's convenient. I've been more than a little curious about the collectors of such unusual items and would be interested to see if the will sheds any light on them."

"You can come by my office anytime. The collection was donated since I've been president here. I think it came during my second year. That doesn't help much, though, because the person I dealt with was the grandson of the actual collector. He was ninety-one when he died. He donated the collection to the college in his will. The lawyer who handled the will didn't have many details about the original collector. The only information the college ever received was the paperwork the lawyer sent along with the items."

Jeff said, "As fascinating as all this is, I have work to do. I need Leroy to come with me to his office so I can get that information on Mr. Madison."

The men left, but Laudine and I decided on one more cup of hot chocolate. It wasn't really late and we wanted to discuss all we'd heard. Since I only had class two days a week and tomorrow wasn't one of them, I didn't have to get up early to make up for the time I had taken off to attend class.

We hadn't heard a lot of new information, but we tended to agree that Leroy probably wasn't involved in any wrongdoing. He had seemed very forthright when questioned, but I was sure Jeff would withhold judgment, and I knew we should, too, in light of what the bottle had said. We needed proof rather than going with our feelings. When we had exhausted that subject, I told Laudine about Jeff's kiss. She must have been able to tell I wasn't ready to discuss my feelings yet, because she let the matter drop with only a smile.

In spite of not having to get up early, I had a little trouble getting out of bed in the morning. When I woke, the room was chilly, and it was a dark and gloomy day outside. I wanted to roll over and sleep for an hour or so more, but instead I got up and into a hot shower to stay warm. I could have used the heat that Leroy had explained to us the day we arrived, but I had to admit I'd long since forgotten the instructions. A quick stop by the dining room assured me there were no new rumors yet today. All was quiet in my workshop during the morning, so I worked steadily until noon. I decided to have a quick lunch and then check to see if Leroy had time to show me the records we'd discussed.

I found him in his office poring over papers. When I said hello, he started visibly and said, "Sorry, I'm reading up on different care homes in case I have to resort to that for my sister. I guess I'm feeling a little guilty. Marge must be at lunch, since she didn't announce you."

"She may be, because she wasn't at her desk. You know, you're just trying to do what's best for your sister. You can't beat yourself up for that. She's lucky to have you."

"I appreciate your saying so. Maybe eventually I'll even come to believe it. What can I do for you this morning?"

"I stopped by to see if you had time to show me the papers relating to the collection I'm working on. If you're busy, it isn't a problem. I can come back another time."

"No, no, now is fine. It will give me a good excuse to quit depressing myself with these brochures. I dug it all out of my files earlier this morning so it would be ready when you came by. Have a seat in the conference room next door and I'll bring in what I have."

There was no way into the conference room from Leroy's office, so I was starting for the door when he said, "You don't have to go back out into the waiting room. Just push on the right side of the bookcase there. It's a hidden door of sorts. It goes right into the room next door. I don't know why it was originally built, but it's handy for meetings and such."

I thanked him and used the clever door. While I waited for him to bring the papers, I thought that at least that solved one mystery. I now knew how the third person had exited the day I had heard the argument in his office.

The information about the antique collection wasn't a folder with a few documents. It was a file box overflowing with unfiled papers. I looked at the box in dismay. Leroy said, "It does look like a disaster, doesn't it? I meant to get around to organizing it all but I never did. If you have the time, why don't you take the documents down to your workroom? You can sort them whenever you want. When you've finished with them, you can bring them back."

"That sounds like a plan. It may take me a couple of weeks, though, because classes have started and I don't want things to cut into my work time."

"Don't worry about that. Take all the time you need. That box has been locked up and unused for several years. I'll just be grateful to get the papers back in some sort of order."

When I left, lugging the box with me, Marge was back at her desk typing furiously. I said hello, but she only grunted in return. I didn't know if she objected to me personally or was just extremely busy and/or unfriendly.

I'd only been back at work a short time when four men came in rolling a large safe, with an exuberant Alex bouncing along behind them. He was obviously pleased with himself and he shouted the obvious. "It has arrived!" The four men were all very red in the face, and I didn't want to speculate on how they had gotten anything so heavy all the way down there. With some maneuvering and Alex directing, they got it inside the cage and placed where it needed to be. The timing of its arrival was great, because now I would have somewhere to keep the authentication documents when I wasn't using them. I thanked them for their hard work, and they departed with Alex chatting happily, trotting by their side.

At the end of the workday, I was tempted to stay and begin looking through the file box of papers, but I was hungry and knew Laudine would have something wonderful prepared. I decided to go up for supper and then come back later to begin looking through the things Leroy had given me.

I was correct about the evening meal. Laudine and her staff had prepared a full Mexican meal of carne asada, enchiladas, and refried beans. The tortillas were homemade, warm, and perfect. Dessert was peach empanadas. It was all very authentic and everyone seemed to enjoy it as much as I did. Teasing her a little I said, "You never stop surprising me. What will it be next, Chinese food?"

Without even cracking a smile, she said, "No, I'm thinking I need to try Thai food."

From her look it was obvious she was completely serious. I knew I would look forward to that night's meal.

When I'd eaten all I could hold, I let Laudine know I was going back to work and headed down to my work space.

Fourteen

The trip through the dimly-lit tunnel-like halls was a lot spookier at night. I had to keep a tight rein on my imagination to prevent every shadow from being a monster, and every groaning noise the old building made someone following me. When I finally reached the brightly-lit safety of my cage, I could laugh at my suggestibility. It took me two tries to get the combination on the new safe right. I brought out the box of documents, and I was tempted to dump its entire contents on my work table and sort them before trying to read anything. If it had been morning, I might have, but I didn't want to work that late, so I dug through until I found the Last Will and Testament of one Euclid Madison. I expected it to be a page or two long, but it was a large packet containing fifteen pages.

I soon discovered Euclid had died at age eighty-eight. Having no children of his own, he chose to donate the inherited collection to his alma mater, Druthmar College. The will indicated that both his father and grandfather had added to the collection over the years, but he himself had never taken an interest and it had remained in storage since he had received it. He'd been unable to assign a dollar value to the jewelry or the reliquaries, but had bequeathed both in their entirety to the school. From the will, I'd learned that Druthmar did own the collection unencumbered, the approximate dates when it had been amassed, and the collectors now had names. That didn't help satisfy my curiosity about why someone would choose to collect only items connected with grief. I'd done what I could tonight, but as I packed the papers away and stored them in the safe, I was hoping the remaining paperwork would tell me more. I regretted that between work and class I would have no free time tomorrow until after supper. I knew I would be back then, because even though I couldn't be sure anything in the file box would be informative, my curiosity was such that I'd have to check. I wanted to know if this family had some reason for collecting items related to death, or if they had just found this type of item easily available and believed they would have future value. I'd dealt with a lot of antiques in the past, but I'd always known where they came from and usually why they'd been collected.

As I was closing the safe door, I was sure I heard noises in the hall. I took notice because of recent events, but decided I was once again letting my imagination turn the normal noises in a building this old into something more. I finished putting my work space in order for the night and was preparing to leave the cage when I once again heard something. This time I was sure it wasn't my imagination. Someone was down here with me.

I hate movies where women go running into danger totally unprepared, so I picked up my trusty crowbar and quietly made my way to the door to peek out. My caution was justified, because in the dim light of the hall I could see someone hugging the shadows and moving quietly in my direction. If I stayed where I was, a confrontation seemed inevitable. I hoped to avoid that, so I picked up a stapler and stepped into the hall. Pointing it at the intruder and praying the shadows prevented a clear view of my "gun," I said, "You can stop skulking out there. I have a gun and if you don't raise your hands and kneel on the floor immediately, I won't hesitate to fire."

I was pleased that my voice didn't shake, but my stern tone didn't produce the reaction I was hoping for. I'd barely finished the sentence when the figure whirled and ran in the opposite direction. It took me a moment to realize they were fleeing, but when I did, I dropped the stapler, renewed my grip on the crowbar, and sprinted after them. I was afraid that when I got to the end where the hall branched both directions, I wouldn't know which way to turn, but when I reached the end, I saw a brief flash of movement off to my right. I also heard a noise I thought sounded like off-key music notes or maybe a cough, but I couldn't be sure. I turned in that direction and tried to increase my pace. I ran until the hall came to a dead end. I had encountered no one.

I turned and walked back the way I'd come, trying each door on both sides of the hall. Most of them made enough noise when I opened them that I would have heard it if the intruder had gone through them. The two that opened silently seemed empty. I decided to search those two rooms anyway. My intruder had to have gone somewhere. The first room was easy. All the walls were white and solid and the room contained no furniture. The second was a different story. Here the walls were paneled and lined with empty bookshelves. The floor space contained two long tables with matching chairs. I had no idea when or why, but at some point in the past, this room must have been used as a library. The bookcases were ornately carved and beautiful, even under their present coating of dust. Footprints on the equally dusty floor assured me someone had been in the room recently, but there were so many and were so confusing I couldn't tell where they went. I began examining the shelves for any area where the dust might be disturbed. I was convinced there was a way out of this room beside the one visible door.

The dust on the bookshelves was disturbed in many places as if someone had been looking for something, but one set of shelves showed much more activity than the rest. I concentrated my efforts on that bookcase. The shelves were built solidly, and there was nothing that could be used to trigger a door mechanism other than the ornate carving. The shelves went all the way to the ceiling. The only way to reach the upper ones was the attached rolling ladder. It was positioned on a different wall, so I was convinced the intruder hadn't needed it. I started at the bottom and worked my way up, fingering every bit of the carved areas. I was stretching to reach well above my head when I decided this couldn't be the answer. I began tapping the walls behind the shelves, and I was positive the wall behind this set of shelves sounded different from the rest. I was at a loss about what to try next. I sighed and leaned back against the shelves to think. As I did, I was sure I felt something move against my back. I straightened and spun around, expecting to see the shelves swing open, slide back into the wall, or at least somehow reveal an opening.

I looked carefully, but there was nothing. Both the wall and bookcase appeared exactly as before. I began attacking the carved areas with renewed vigor. When I grabbed one particular section, I could swear there was a small amount of give. I pushed and pulled with all my might but nothing happened. Finally, I pushed that section up rather than back and instantly and quietly the shelves slid into the wall, and I was staring into a pitch-black tunnel. I remembered the Maglight Laudine had me carrying and ran back to the workroom. I'd completely forgotten I'd recently had a hip injury, but as I walked back with the flashlight in hand, I realized I was limping slightly. The smart thing to do would probably be to go for help to explore the tunnel, but my curiosity drew me forward. A part of me knew this was a lot like the movie behavior I'd always considered unrealistic, but I told myself the intruder was long gone by then and I was only exploring an empty tunnel.

The walls there were old, mostly dirt. Random sections were smeared with something that resembled concrete. At least the passageway seemed dry and vermin-free. Occasionally I'd have to maneuver around a support beam planted in the middle of the walk space. I tried shining my flashlight as far as possible into the distance but could see no end. This didn't mean much, as my light wasn't very helpful with distance viewing. At one time, this underground passage must have been used extensively, because the dirt on the floor was packed rock-hard solid. Here and there were small piles of decaying books littering the floor. Other places I spotted broken bits of plaster. The clutter led me to suspect that at some time in the distant past, a hurried exodus had occurred. My imagination conjured up all kinds of things the inhabitants might have been fleeing from. Sooner than I had expected, I came to a wall I assumed was the end of the tunnel. Here was a perfectly ordinary latch that could be used to slide the wall into the next section. I had explored one just like it on the inside of the bookcase wall to be sure I could get out if I needed to. When I pushed the handle sideways, the wall slid silently out of sight and I walked out into the hall directly in front of the dining area. There was no hope of discovering who the intruder had been because, as I'd suspected, they were long gone, but I now knew there was at least one additional way up from the sub-levels. It had seemed shorter than the way I normally used. All was quiet on the main floor as I made my way to the elevator that would take me to my room.

Laudine was in bed when I arrived, so I decided on an early night. I slept straight through till morning, but my dreams were filled with shadowy halls and hidden doors. When I woke, Laudine had already left for work. Today she was holding her first class. I was eager to hear how she liked teaching. Later in the semester when she had gotten comfortable with her new job, I hoped to sit in on at least one of her lectures. I had skipped breakfast and eaten a piece of fruit in the workroom for lunch, so I hadn't had a chance to tell anyone about my previous night's discovery. I worked until one and then returned to my room and gathered up my books for class.

I was pleased that this session was much more interesting. Claude still wasn't a very exciting speaker, but he knew his material intimately and presented it in an easily-understood way. His cough hadn't left him completely, but it didn't detract from the material he presented. It reminded me of the noise I'd heard last night, but I didn't think it seemed quite the same. This class and the next two were to be dedicated to the time frame of the thirteen and fourteen hundreds. He would tell us about the types of art produced during that time, as well as a little about the major painters. From them, he had picked three to discuss in depth. The first was Paolo Uccello, who lived from 1347 to 1475. This Italian artist had left a large body of work, but was best known for his painting of Saint George and the Dragon. The other two painters we would discuss were Leonardo da Vinci and Jan Van Eyck. I found the class fascinating and was sorry when it came to a close. Claude suggested we have coffee after class. I was tempted to accept and tell him about the hidden passageway, but I didn't feel comfortable taking any more time off work, and I remembered that sound in the tunnel that might have been a cough, so I went straight back to work, but I had to force myself to concentrate on my task. Now more than ever, I hoped Laudine and I would be able to make a trip to New York City. I wanted to visit art museums.

At dinner, which was another wonderful meal, I again let Jeff know I needed to talk to him. I wanted to show him the tunnel and get his opinion about my would-be intruder. I'd made the decision he was the friend I would trust, and I needed to stick to that decision.

I finished eating first, so I waited outside in the hall for him to join me. I was marveling at how impossible the hidden door was to see, even knowing it was there, when he joined me. We decided that if he accompanied me on my evening walk, we could be assured our conversation wouldn't be overheard. Instead of my usual routes, Jeff stuck to the main drive. About halfway down to the road was a bench and a small table. We stopped there and I told him what had happened the previous night. He said, "I'm not surprised this old place has hidden passages. I think most religious orders felt a safe escape was a good idea. There have been a lot of fanatical factions throughout history. What worries me is that someone appears to be targeting you or your work. We need to know why. We can't convict Claude on the sound you heard, but I can promise you that I will keep a close eye on him and do a little more digging into his past."

"He doesn't seem like a murderer, but I guess people often think that about killers when they are discovered. I refuse to make any judgment based on what I heard, but keeping an eye on him can't hurt."

"One thing I can do is investigate your passageway and try to find out if there are any others. If there are hidden rooms as well as tunnels, whoever the killer is could be hiding there. I'll get some men out here tomorrow and we'll do a thorough search to see what we can find."

"That may help. I certainly don't like the idea that thieves and murderers can roam around at will. It makes us too vulnerable. I'll need to show you the passage I discovered so you can tell your men what to look for. Are you going to make your search public knowledge?"

"I don't think so. I don't want to have everyone exploring and possibly getting into trouble. I'll spread the word that we're going to search the building from top to bottom. I'll come up with some type of logical explanation for the search that doesn't mention hidden passageways. We've already done a room search, of course, but most of the residents don't know that. Let's go see what you've found. I have to admit I'm curious."

We started from the opening across from the dining room. Jeff paid close attention to the door and how it worked. We traveled the whole length of the tunnel. We didn't encounter anyone or find anything changed since the night before. Once he'd explored thoroughly, Jeff left to arrange the search for the following day. I returned to my room, hoping Laudine would be there so I could tell her my news.

On entering our suite, I found her practically hopping up and down waiting for me. She was obviously bursting at the seams with something she wanted to share. I was eager to tell her about the hidden passage but decided to let her give her news first. I was surprised when she grabbed my arm and insisted I follow her down to the main floor. When she led me to the back of the kitchen, I was completely confused. One side of the large rear wall opened into a pantry. She walked up next to the pantry and began pressing on the wall. Almost immediately a section opened to reveal another underground tunnel. I would need to catch Jeff in the morning and make him aware of this new discovery. I'd barely finished that thought when Laudine was handing me one of the many Maglites stashed around the building and stepping into the tunnel. I pulled back and said, "Hang on a second. I need to tell you my news before we decide to go in there."

She looked startled, but said, "Okay, what's up?"

We moved over to the work table and sat. I told her all about the other tunnel. When I'd finished, she laughed. "Here I thought I had the biggest news, but I didn't encounter any intruders. This place must have other secrets if we both discovered hidden tunnels the same day. You still need to come into this one, because it isn't just a tunnel. There's at least one room in there, and you're going to love it. I only saw the one, but I couldn't spend very long inside without the staff wondering where I'd gone."

I wasn't surprised that Laudine had also explored the tunnel she had found without worrying about danger. Her curiosity was equal to mine. She led the way. With both of us using bright flashlights, the tunnel was nearly daylight bright. We'd only gone a short way before Laudine stopped and showed me a mark on the wall. When she pressed down on it, a door I hadn't even suspected was there slid into the adjoining wall. Inside was the room she'd discovered, but it wasn't empty. Stacked haphazardly, as though it had been done hurriedly, were piles and piles of books. I was sure she had discovered the contents that had once been housed in the library on Sub-level C. In addition to the books there were several religious statues, a baptismal font, and to my surprise, a very large reliquary. Many of the books were suffering from lack of proper care, but I knew some of them would be valuable. I wasn't an expert on religious antiques, so I couldn't evaluate the rest of the items. I wondered if the college would decide to sell what Laudine had discovered or if they would keep at least the books for their library. We'd only given the room's contents a cursory exam when I said, "This really is an amazing discovery. I'd bet money these things were taken from the library on C and hidden here for protection. Unless there are records somewhere, we may never know what they were afraid of."

"That makes sense. Do you want to explore the rest of the tunnel tonight to see what else we can find?"

"It has to be getting late. We may not be able to do a thorough job tonight, but let's at least walk the full length. Tomorrow when Jeff's people do their search, we'll lose the opportunity to be the first to see what's here."

"That works for me. This room is as far as I got today, so I'm eager to see if there's anything else interesting hidden away."

We left the book room behind and continued on down the tunnel. For a time, we walked in silence. Eventually Laudine said, "Does it feel like it's getting colder to you? I think the passageway is getting narrower, too."

"Now that you mention it, I can feel the temperature change. This passage feels more like a tunnel than a hall. I'm beginning to wonder if it leads to the outside. Let's keep going a little further and see what we find."

I'd barely finished the sentence when Laudine, who was in the lead, tripped and fell against the wall. She reached out to brace herself and managed to keep from going all the way down. I was about to say that maybe we should give up our exploration and let the police take over, but the words were whisked away when the section of wall next to Laudine collapsed. I managed to yank her back away from the falling dirt. When the dust cloud cleared, we could see a space behind the pile of debris from the cave-in, but at the moment I was more interested in checking the walls around the opening. I was afraid we were in danger of the whole tunnel coming down on top of us. After careful inspection, I discovered the walls around the new opening were solid. Next, I examined the pile of dirt at our feet. It didn't take an expert to realize it was different. Someone, at some point in time, had chiseled out this opening in the wall and then filled it back. The filling had degraded, whereas the original walls hadn't.

While I was checking all this, Laudine had gingerly made her way over the unstable mound of rubble and was peering into the opening. Our flashlights were beginning to dim and I knew it was time to leave. The batteries would soon be too dim to be of much use or would go out completely. I had started to explain this to Laudine when she made a strange noise and said, "I think you need to come here. I hope I'm not seeing what I think I am."

There was unusual tension in her voice, so I scrambled over the debris to her side. Her light was even fainter than mine, but when both lights were aimed into the newly exposed space, it was obvious what we were seeing was human remains. I had no idea how old they were, but they weren't recent, because all that was left was a skeleton. One arm was detached and down by the feet, or I should say foot, because the left foot was missing. Otherwise, the body seemed to be intact.

I said, "Our lights are about done, so we need to get out of here as quickly as possible. Do you want to go forward in the hope we can get outside, or turn around and go back?"

She thought a moment. "I'd really like to know if this tunnel leads to the school grounds, but to be on the safe side, we'd better turn around. If we're headed back the way we came, we can find our way out even if these flashlights fail completely."

Never mentioning what we'd found, we hurried back. The tunnel seemed ominous in our waning light, and I wasn't sure if I'd imagined the sound I heard behind us, or if it had been real. It had sounded like a faint cough.

It wasn't until we were safely back in the well-lighted kitchen with cups of hot coffee in front of us that we were ready to discuss what we'd found. I began by saying, "I guess our discovery can't wait until the police arrive in the morning. Shall I call them now?"

"Normally I'd say we have no choice, but that skeleton has been there for a long time already. I don't see how waiting until morning can hurt. The police will be swarming all over this place tomorrow anyway, because of the tunnels we've found."

"That makes sense, I guess. I wonder if what we saw has anything to do with the current murders? Somebody obviously walled that body into that space to hide it. You know, all the discoveries we make just enhance the mystery, but don't seem to solve anything. I wish we'd discover some answers."

"Me, too. Answers would be nice. At the moment I can't help wondering if that person was alive when he or she was walled in."

"That's a ghoulish thought, but I have to admit I've been wondering, too. I'm beginning to agree with your original opinion that this place is creepy."

"Maybe we should use what Lawrence taught us and go over all the details we've learned so far? Let's make a list of what we know and what we need to find out. Then let's try to get a little sleep and start in again tomorrow."

"He was so good at putting events in order and it seems like a good idea, but let's also add a maybe column."

Laudine got a tablet and pen. We thought a moment before I said, "I guess we should make the first murder item number one."

It only took us about thirty minutes to complete all three lists. The first were the things that had happened and the things we'd discovered. The maybe list was shorter and included information we'd gained from the bottle as well as things like the times I'd thought I'd heard a cough. The final list of the things we needed to know was the longest, and as we headed off to bed, I was feeling daunted by our lack of useful information. I hoped a good night's sleep would improve my negative attitude.

Fifteen

Detective Crown came into the dining room about halfway through breakfast. I'd seen him arrive earlier with at least eight other men. I was sure he had them combing the building for additional hidden areas, as well as searching the tunnels we'd already found. The moment he finished eating, I pulled him aside and asked him to follow me into the kitchen. With Laudine's help, I explained about our latest discovery and the body inside. He quickly rounded up two of his men and went to find the skeleton. I went down to work, hoping he'd come by later to let me know what they had found.

As it turned out, before I heard anything, my workday was over and I was back in my room reading over the material to be covered in tomorrow's class.

I heard our suite door open, so I walked out into the sitting area between our bedrooms. I'd expected to find Laudine, but was surprised to see she'd brought Jeff and Leroy along. Laudine said, "Oh good, you're here. I was afraid I'd have to wake you. These guys wouldn't tell me anything until we were all together, and I'm dying to know what they've found."

I smiled at the men. "I have to admit, I've been waiting to hear, too. What can—"

Jeff interrupted, "I know you have a million questions. Let me just explain what we know and then you can ask any other questions you have."

Laudine and I nodded our agreement, and he began. "We did the search of the buildings we discussed yesterday. We only found one additional tunnel. It runs from Building Six down to Five and then down to the grounds just behind this building. This one is just a tunnel with no rooms anywhere along its length. Obviously, we can't guarantee there aren't any others, but we tried to be thorough. I've shown Leroy all the tunnels we've found. I thought he needed to know.

"We also found the skeleton you guys discovered last night. It's been removed for a closer examination, but so far, we know it's the remains of a woman, probably in her thirties. Until all the tests are complete, we can't be sure how long it's been there, but the medical examiner was guessing more than a hundred years. At this point, I can't see how it could be connected to our current murders, and we'll probably never know why she was killed. It's pretty definite she was murdered, though. The examiner found a large wound at the back of her skull."

Here Leroy took over the narrative. "The books you found are wonderful! Most of them are in fairly decent condition, too. The constant temperature and dryness down there helped preserve them. I don't know what the college board will decide to do with them, but I'm hoping we can keep them for the library here. They have already authorized me to have them examined and to have any necessary repairs done. I'd be very surprised if we don't find some rare or even unknown editions in that collection."

"All that's great, but I'm assuming you didn't find anything to solve our current murders or anything identifying the intruder I spotted in the basement?"

Jeff said, "Unfortunately, no. As far as the current investigation goes, we didn't get answers to any of our questions. The only thing that may be helpful is knowing about the tunnels. Now we can watch them and either catch anyone using them or at least prevent the killer from moving around secretly."

"I have to admit I'm disappointed. I was hoping for more. Do we know whether Claude could have made the sound I heard last night?"

"He has an alibi of sorts. He told me his sister was visiting for the day. We were able to verify that they did have dinner together at one of the local restaurants. She could have lied about being with him later, but we have no reason to suspect her. She was in Albany for a conference and drove over for the one day. She left this morning to catch her plane back to Maine."

The men left soon after that, and Laudine and I were so disappointed there were no new clues to follow we skipped our usual discussion time and went to bed.

In the morning, my normal optimism had returned. I knew we'd have to keep digging until we discovered the truth. Also, my love of books kept me thinking about the treasures in the tunnel Laudine had found. It wasn't my area of expertise exactly, but I did have enough experience with old collections that I wanted to take a closer look at what was down there. I decided to skip breakfast and go indulge my curiosity.

To be on the safe side, I told Laudine where I was going, grabbed a flashlight with fresh batteries, and headed into the darkness. Now that I was slightly familiar with the tunnel, it didn't take any time at all to arrive at the door to the hidden room. Once inside, I sat on the floor next to the first pile of books and picked one up at random. In moments I knew there were real treasures here. The first book I picked up was *Antonio and Mellida* by John Marston. It was a play written in the sixteen hundreds. As I glanced at the books one after another, I came across *The Spanish Moois Tragedy* by Thomas Decker, also from the sixteen hundreds. Even older was the *Moiny Psalter*, and older still I found handwritten books in languages I didn't recognize.

All this I discovered from picking just a few at random from possibly a hundred or more. I knew for sure that someone with a whole lot more knowledge about rare books than I had would be needed to deal with this find.

I could have spent the entire day right there, but I had work to do and needed to get back down to the jewelry. I had started back through the tunnel when it occurred to me that I'd seen a few moldering books along the other passage. Also, the library where the books had once been housed was off that tunnel. Knowing those things, it didn't make sense that the books had been found in a room off a completely different tunnel. There might be several possible explanations, but I was sure the most logical one was that the two tunnels were connected somewhere. Rather than going immediately back to work, I began looking for anything that might indicate another doorway. It took some effort, but I finally saw a tiny marking on the wall that resembled the one that had marked the door to the room with the books. When I got to the door, I was sure the dark tunnel facing me was going to lead to the one I'd originally discovered from the library. I turned on my flashlight and walked in. This tunnel was cruder and smaller than the others and contained nothing of interest, but did eventually connect the two passageways. Something else I would need to report to Jeff, but not before I put in a few hours of work.

~ * ~

By noon I was ready to begin comparing the sorted items to the inventory list. I would make that my afternoon task, but for once I was hungry enough to make the trip upstairs for lunch.

On the creaky elevator ride up to the dining room, I decided I'd make it known during lunch that I was comparing the jewelry I was sorting with the total inventory list. If any pieces were missing and any one there knew about it, my announcement might spark some action. I should be safe enough, since I worked in a cage and was with other people most of the rest of the time. My thought was that the guilty party might make a try for the list.

Lunch was light sandwiches and hearty soup. I managed to effortlessly slip my information into the general conversation. I hadn't warned Laudine in advance about what I planned to do, and she looked none too happy as I spoke. As soon as I'd finished eating, she motioned me into the kitchen. "What in the world are you thinking? If anyone here has been involved in stealing from the college, they will go to great lengths to prevent you from completing the inventory. If any of them is the killer, those lengths could mean attempted murder. You might as well pin a target on your back! Oh, never mind, I don't want to hear your reasons. I have a class to teach. We can talk about it tonight."

With that she turned and walked off. I was still standing there with my mouth open, amazed that she was so angry, when Jeff grabbed my arm and practically dragged me out of the kitchen and down the hall away from the people in the dining room. Before I had a chance to object, he said, "What in the hell is the matter with you? Are you trying to get yourself killed?"

"Just hold on right there. I'm not stupid, so I am aware there's risk involved. However, it seems pretty minimal. I spend my working hours locked in a cage and there are always police around. At this point, we have no proof that any jewelry has been stolen, and if it has, there's no evidence the thief is also a murderer."

Here he tried to say something, but I wasn't having it. "I'm not finished yet. There have already been three murders and could be more at any time. So far, the police have nothing. Something needs to be done, and if my inventory check brings us closer to a solution, it will be well worth it. I haven't done anything illegal, so back off."

I knew I was partially taking the fact that Laudine had upset me out on Jeff. There might even be a small voice in the back of my head saying that perhaps I'd acted a little too quickly, but I wasn't about to back down. Although, when I finished speaking, I admit I was holding my breath waiting to see what would happen next.

"Fine! Consider me backed off, but from now on, a policeman will be outside the door of your and Laudine's room, will walk with you to your classes, and will be in the room where you work. If you go anywhere else, that policeman will go there, too."

I didn't say anything else. He wasn't in the mood for explanations, and I wasn't calm enough to soothe ruffled feathers yet anyway. Jeff would do what he wanted and I had work to do. I returned downstairs and began comparing the items to the list. The afternoon went smoothly, but I hadn't been at my task more than five minutes when a policeman entered the big room. He didn't try to enter the cage, so I said, "Hello," and kept working. He stayed at his post until I locked up and headed up to supper. He followed me out. Suspecting this was going to be a daily occurrence, once we reached the elevator I said, "I get the feeling we may be seeing a lot of each other. My name is Ali. I'm sorry you got stuck with this duty."

He smiled wryly and said, "I'm Tom, Tom Tanner. You definitely got the chief riled up, but I don't mind the duty. Tomorrow I'm bringing a chair, though, and maybe a book."

I laughed. His friendly manner went a long way toward restoring my good humor. "That's probably a good idea. Also tomorrow is a class day, so we'll get to go for a walk."

I didn't know when he got to eat, but he remained outside the dining room door the whole time I was there. Then he followed me upstairs, where another policeman took over. He gave me a friendly salute as he left. Once I'd introduced myself to my second keeper, I went inside to wait for Laudine.

She arrived earlier than most nights, so I assumed she was eager to pick up where she'd left off at lunch. I wanted to head her off, so I started to speak, but she said, "No, let me go first. I need to apologize for being so angry earlier. I overreacted. After I had a chance to think it through, I began to realize why you did what you did. I still can't be happy about your decision because I won't be able to stop worrying about you, but I do understand."

"No need to apologize. I should have warned you before I made my announcement. If I'm honest, I probably should have thought things through a little better before acting. Besides, your lecture didn't hold a candle to Jeff's reaction. I now have a policeman as a bodyguard. Everyone may be worrying for nothing, you know. At this point, we don't know that anyone has stolen any of the jewelry. I worked on the inventory some this afternoon, and so far, I've been able to match jewelry to each item on the list."

"You should have seen Detective Crown this afternoon. He was a positive thundercloud. After he'd barked at nearly everyone, even his own men were avoiding him. I can only imagine the lecture he must have given you."

I chuckled at her description. "We did have a bit of a fight. I don't know if he was just worried about me or ticked off because he considered me interfering in his investigation. It may have been some of both."

Laudine smiled. "Oh, methinks the man is smitten, but I approve of you being watched. In case your plan works, you may be glad of the protection. Besides, an extra pair of eyes never hurts."

Sixteen

The following morning, my original shadow was back. "Good morning, Tom. Have you eaten already or would you like some breakfast?"

"Morning, Ali. I'm scheduled to eat before I go on duty, but I got a late start today."

"Then let's go down and eat together. You can't be accused of shirking your duty if you're sitting right beside me."

It took a little more persuading, but he finally agreed. He managed to eat a full breakfast while I ate one of Laudine's perfect cinnamon rolls.

The morning went smoothly. I was able to forget I was being watched and got a lot done. I was almost ready to go downstairs for a little lunch when I discovered two items on the inventory I couldn't find. I made a thorough search, but two necklaces encrusted with rare gems were not among the items I'd been given. I knew I couldn't keep this information quiet until I'd done a full inventory. I'd have to alert Jeff to the fact that there was going to be a discrepancy. I put the items I'd been working with back in the safe and made my way to the cafeteria, with Tom right behind me. Jeff wasn't at the table when we arrived, so Tom and I sat down to eat. I'd just filled my plate when I heard the detective's voice talking to Laudine in the kitchen. I told Tom he could keep eating since I was only going into the kitchen to speak to my friend, Laudine. He considered a moment and then agreed. In the kitchen, I discovered Jeff and Laudine deep in conversation with Leroy and two more policemen. Kenneth and Claude were there also. When I walked up, Laudine explained by saying, "You missed all the excitement. About five minutes ago, our two friendly professors came running out the entrance to the kitchen tunnel. Claude was carrying several books."

Kenneth said, "That explanation makes our actions sound very suspicious. The truth is that we discovered the tunnel from the end that opens to the grounds and came through to find out where it led. We intended to tell the police immediately. Claude had the books to show the cops what was down there. We were quite proud of ourselves for finding what might possibly be a useful clue. Now everyone is looking at us like we're Jack the Ripper."

I burst out laughing. They all turned toward me like I was nuts. "Look, Detective Crown, Laudine and I discovered two tunnels, and might have looked just as suspicious when we did. I don't think you can arrest these guys for the same thing. Besides, if Claude wanted to steal books, he could have chosen better. There are some real gems down there, but the two he's holding are nearly worthless."

Once more Jeff's reaction impressed me. He grinned. "It's nice you want to save your friends from prison, but I wasn't planning to arrest them. I only wanted to know how they discovered the tunnel. If it's too easy to find, lots of people may know about it. Later today, we're going to close off the outside entrance, just in case."

Now Laudine laughed. "I didn't mean to make them sound like criminals. I was just trying to give you a quick explanation of what was going on."

When the kitchen settled back down and most everyone had gone back to their work, I caught up with Jeff. When I'd explained about the missing items, he said, "Damn! Now I have the real worry that someone will come after you. I wish I knew if the thefts are connected to the murders. Things keep getting more and more confusing. Is your watchdog keeping you close?"

"You have nothing to worry about...he's taking his duty seriously. You know, since I was hired to work for the college, I am responsible to Leroy. Do you have a problem with me telling him about the missing jewelry? I need to keep him informed."

"No, telling him shouldn't matter. If he's involved, he already knows some things are missing, and if he's not involved, you should keep him up-to-date."

Just before Jeff left, I remembered to tell him about the connecting tunnel I'd discovered. I didn't think it was important, but I didn't want to keep any information to myself. When I finished lunch, I went straight to the president's office to tell him what I knew. His wonderful secretary was as rude as ever, but she eventually let me talk to Leroy. He didn't seem surprised, just deeply concerned. From there, I returned to the workroom. I worked straight through until time for class. My buddy walked me to class and back, but no problems presented themselves. After class I went back to work, eager to get the inventory completed. I only took a short break for supper, intending to spend my evening sorting through more of the items I'd received with the will. In spite of everything else that was going on, I was still curious about the origin of the fabulous collection. Tom, my ever-present companion, must have been tired of following me around by then, but he didn't complain.

I was about halfway through the box and so far had only found legal papers concerning the transfer of the collection from one relative to another and then to the college. The next item I pulled out was a fat spiral notebook with solid cardboard covers. When I opened it, my hopes took a big jump, because I was holding the diary of the man who had originally begun the collection. I had just started the first page when there was a noise in the hall. It sounded like something heavy was being dragged by my door. Tom jumped up and flung open the door. After sticking his head outside, he turned to me and said, "I saw the flash of someone rounding the corner down the hall. I'm going to take a quick look. Don't go anywhere. I'll be right back."

He was no sooner out of sight than I thought he'd returned, because I caught a glimpse as I worked of someone coming through the open door. It wasn't until a voice said, "Good evening, Miss Trent," that I realized I was alone with Beth's caregiver. I saw the gun in his hand even before his name registered.

"Hello, Mr. Leonard. I must admit I'm disappointed that you're the thief and murderer."

"You're making a big assumption. I've been a lot of things in my life, but never a murderer. I've come for the inventory list you claim to have, and even if I have to shoot you to get it, I promise to try not to kill you."

"Just how do you plan to get the list when it and I are locked in here, and you are out there?"

"I assume you will hand it to me, since you'd rather not get shot. Stop stalling. I know you're thinking your watchdog will return any minute, but he won't, so hand over the list."

I pretended to sort through the papers on my desk looking for the list, but as he'd said, I was hoping Tom would return. When I couldn't delay any longer, I picked up the list, preparing to hand it over. I was upset that my plan had worked enough to bring out the thief, but was going to allow him to get away. I wasn't worried about the list. I could give it to him with no worries as I had made several copies before I ever announced I was checking it against the inventory. I was madly trying to think up some new way to stall a little longer when he raised the gun enough so that it was pointed directly at me. All he said was, "Now."

I rose to do as he'd requested when there was a blur of motion in the doorway and someone tackled Clint from behind. The gun discharged as they hit the ground, but I knew no one had been hurt because I heard the bullet slam harmlessly into the wall on the opposite side of the room. When both people got to their feet, Clint's hands were cuffed behind his back and Jeff was holding Clint's gun. He shoved it in his pocket and asked, "Are you okay, Ali?"

"I'm fine. How did you know you were needed down here?"

He looked at Clint. "Our thief here wasn't as clever as he thought. His accomplice managed to give Tom a blow to the head and escape, but Tom was still conscious enough to call me on the radio we all carry. When I got the call, I was already about halfway here because I was coming to see you."

"Who was his accomplice?"

"Tom didn't get a good look, but I have a pretty good idea. I'm sure Mr. Leonard here will tell me what I need to know very soon."

About that time, Tom came sheepishly through the door. He was white as a sheet and there was a thin stream of blood trickling down his forehead. Jeff said, "Go get yourself checked out. I doubt if you have a concussion, but we want to be sure. We'll talk later about your decisions tonight."

As he turned to obey Jeff, he looked worse than when he'd entered. I could hardly blame him, because the detective's voice had been steely.

I felt sorry for him and couldn't help saying, "Don't be too hard on him. He really was trying his best to keep me safe."

"You can be sure I won't be any harder on him than necessary. He will be lucky to remain a policeman. You might have been killed tonight because he made the choice to leave you alone."

I knew this wasn't the time to talk to him about Tom. He was still angry. I let the matter drop for the moment. After assuring himself again that I was fine, he took his prisoner and returned to the station. I hoped the whole story about the jewelry theft would come out. The sooner the better. In any case, I'd had enough for tonight, so I locked up the papers I'd been reading and headed back upstairs. I found Laudine in the kitchen and explained all that happened.

"I've been worried sick that something like this would happen ever since you made it known you were comparing the jewelry to the inventory. Thank God it's over and you're all right."

"Mostly over, I guess, but not completely. The accomplice is still out there, but Jeff seems pretty confident Clint will talk. I hope he's right. That may settle the matter of the jewelry thefts, but it doesn't tell us anything about the murders. The caregiver is claiming he hasn't ever murdered anyone. We'll have to wait to see how that plays out. Maybe Jeff will be able to determine the truth one way or another."

"All that's true, but for the moment, I'm just going to be happy that you're okay. I'll begin worrying about all the rest again tomorrow."

"Makes sense to me. We have to relax now and then. You're not going to believe it, but I'm starving. Are there any leftovers around?"

"Not leftovers exactly, but some test dishes I've been working on."

She pulled out her test dishes for the promised Thai food meal, and we spent an hour before bed happily talking and munching on pad thai and prik king. They were both delicious and spicy hot. I didn't see how she could improve either one.

Seventeen

I was leaving the dining room after breakfast when one of the policemen I'd seen several times patrolling the grounds told me I was wanted in Leroy's office. His unfriendly secretary was nowhere to be seen in the outer office. When I knocked on the door, Jeff's voice said, "Come in."

I knew Jeff preferred to tell us what he knew before we began asking questions, so I took a seat and contained my curiosity. I'd barely gotten seated when Laudine knocked and entered the room. She must have drawn the same conclusions I had, because she quietly took a seat. Jeff, Leroy, Tim, and Alex were already in the room.

Jeff said, "I have asked you to be here because you all have been involved in the discoveries we've made so far. We finally have a few answers, and I wanted to bring you up to date.

"I can now say I'm convinced the jewelry thefts and the murders are not connected. For some time, Clint Leonard, the registered nurse living in Building Five, has been stealing items of value from the college and selling them. And he hasn't been working alone—Leroy's secretary has been his accomplice the whole time. He says she is his wife. Her real name is Tammy Leonard. When we arrested Clint, she disappeared, and the police are looking for her now. I don't think she will get far. We've also arrested the fence the two have been using. It's possible we'll be able to get back some of the stolen items. Some are probably lost forever. Ali, when you finish matching the jewelry to your list of items, I'll need a list of what's missing. Leroy and his staff will go through the hundreds of pages listing the inventory stored in Building Six and try to check to see if the most valuable items are there. It would be nearly impossible to check every box in the entire storage area. The time and manpower it would take would never be cost effective. I'm sure that's what the thieves were counting on. If it hadn't been for the jewelry being more easily inventoried, they might never have been caught. That's all I know so far, and I'm not taking any questions at the moment."

It was very clear that Jeff was serious about not answering any questions, so we all stood to leave, but Leroy said, "Ali, could you and Laudine stay for just a minute longer?"

We glanced at each other and then sat back down. Jeff stayed as well.

The others were safely out of earshot when Leroy said, "I thought you might be wondering what part my sister played in all this. I was extremely relieved when the police told me those two didn't include her in their plans. She was just Clint's way of getting access to college property."

Laudine said, "Thank goodness they didn't use her condition to involve her."

"I agree, but I owe you all an apology. None of this would have happened if I'd put my sister in a facility where she could get the proper care she needed. Because of that, the college has lost valuable property and Ali's life was threatened. Soon I will be reporting all this to the college board and I will abide by what they decide. In the meantime, I've moved Beth to a private hospital where she will be safe and cared for."

I said, "Well, my life wasn't exactly threatened. He said he would shoot me, but try not to kill me."

Jeff gave me a horrified look and I couldn't help but grin at him. Then I turned to Leroy. "I'm glad Beth will be where they can take the best care of her. I hope you won't be too hard on yourself over all this. You may have made some honest mistakes, but you didn't set out to do anything wrong."

Leroy gave me a strange look as everyone murmured their agreement, and as we filed out of the office, I wondered what he was thinking, and also couldn't help wondering how my situation would be affected if he were fired.

I'm not sure where the others went from there, but Laudine and I headed for the kitchen to have coffee and, since it was already late morning, maybe a leftover donut from breakfast.

Our snack ended up being a bowl of fresh fruit and two of Laudine's tasty donuts, When I went back to work, I knew there would be no need to take a lunch break. I worked straight through until five with no interruptions. It took every minute of the time, but I managed to finish matching the jewelry to the inventory. I found eight more discrepancies. I made a list of what was missing for Jeff, a copy for Leroy, and called it a day. After the previous night's adventure, I decided to take the diary I'd found among the papers Leroy had given me with me to my room to read after dinner. It felt kind of like closing the barn door after the horse had been stolen, but at the moment I didn't want to be alone down there at night. Before going to dinner, I stored the diary in my nightstand. It meant an extra trip up and then back downstairs, but my hip seemed back to normal, and the creaky old elevator and I were getting to be good friends.

Dinner discussion was all about Clint's arrest. Everyone just seemed to accept that Clint had been a member of the landscaping staff. They had been informed that Beth was also gone, but assumed she had quit because of all the hubbub. I couldn't think of any good reason to tell them otherwise. Nothing new came to light. Laudine must have still been perfecting her Thai recipes, because tonight the meal was completely Italian. We started with antipasto, and after both spaghetti and lasagna, she served cannoli. Once again, I was too full to try the dessert.

Back in my room, the first thing I saw was the mixture of colors swirling in the bottle. I had no idea what they represented, but each color was bright and distinct as they swirled around each other up through the three tiers of glass. Not long after I crawled in bed and removed the journal from the nightstand, the colors dimmed, and I wondered if the display had been a reaction to the old diary.

I barely noticed time passing as I read the whole first half of the diary. I wanted to continue, but it was late and I knew I'd be in no shape for work in the morning if I didn't get some sleep. The diary was detailed. Its author wrote well, and I could see pictures in my head as the man's life unfolded. I put the book away in my dresser well away from the nightstand holding the bottle. The glass was empty, and in case the reaction had been to the book I didn't want to rekindle it. I finally managed to fall asleep, but I had confusing dreams about Ezra Madison and his collection.

In the morning, Laudine was making coffee when I woke. I got out two cups and said, "I've been reading the journal written by the man who began the mourning jewelry and reliquary collections. I was so happy when I found it because I wanted to know why someone would choose those things to collect. Now I almost wish I'd never found it."

"Why would you wish that? Does it explain his thinking?"

"Yes, but it's very depressing. The poor man had the worst luck. His name was Ezra. He married when he was thirty and not long after, his wife delivered a son. Next, she had twin daughters. His wife died in childbirth when the girls were born. When the son, Wilton, was ten, he threw one of the girls off the stair landing and killed her. Six months later, the other daughter killed herself. Euclid was convinced Wilton must have talked her into it before he was taken away to a juvenile correction facility. I don't know why he thought that, since that would have been six months before she killed herself. They found her dead at the bottom of the stairs exactly where her sister had died, but with no note, they could never know why she had done it. That's when the poor man began collecting. He started out collecting any and all items he could find on the subject of death, but soon settled on the two types I'm working with."

"Wow, what a horrible tragedy! The son must have had some sort of life after the murder, though, since it was a grandson that donated the collection to the college."

"Yes, the grandson of Ezra. His name was Euclid. It seems that, since Wilton was so young when he killed his sister, when he turned twenty-one, they decided he was rehabilitated and let him go free."

"Well, I guess that sort of makes sense. He was only ten."

"True. When he got out, Euclid moved back in with his father. I can't imagine how Ezra must have felt, but I guess for a time, things went pretty well. Wilton shared his father's interest in items of mourning and helped his father with the collection. The diary doesn't mention any problems during that time. Then when he was twenty-six, he got married and got a place of his own. A year later they had a son and Wilton's wife also died in childbirth. Wilton once again moved back in with his father, and this time he brought his son with him."

"How did that work out for them?"

"I don't know yet. That's the point where I decided I better get some sleep, but there is still half the diary left, so there may have been more drama."

"When you've read the rest, let me know how it turns out. It's horrible, but since it happened so long ago, it's kind of like reading a horror novel."

"I'm ashamed to say I felt the same. Since even the grandson Euclid is now deceased, it does seem more like a story than something real. It certainly holds a person's interest. Partly because the old man writes really well. His description is so good I can see the house and people in my mind. I'll probably read the rest tonight, so I'll let you know tomorrow what happens. When I'm finished, if you'd like to read it for yourself, you may."

After dinner I finished reading the diary. The second half was even more compelling than the first, and I knew Laudine would find it as interesting as I had. I'd tell her all about it the first chance I got.

The following morning, I got very close to finishing the evaluation on the jewelry.

For once I was starving by lunchtime and went up to eat with the staff. I saw Laudine long enough to let her know I had finished the diary and would tell her all about it that night. Late that afternoon, I took the time to take a close look at a few of the reliquaries. They were beautifully made and very ornate, but they made me a little sad. Each one represented someone grieving for a person they loved who had died. Seeing them also made me realize there was no way I could do them justice on my own. If I didn't see Leroy tonight, I'd have to talk to him in the morning. I wanted to get permission to hire someone to help me evaluate them. If I had to take a pay cut, so be it. The items were too high quality for me not to bring in a true expert. Jewelry I could handle, even mourning jewelry, but not the reliquaries. I knew who I wanted to hire, but before I approached Leroy, I'd check around to be sure the man I had in mind was still considered the foremost expert on religious antiques.

I got my chance to talk to Leroy just before dinner. I'd come up to the kitchen a little early. I had finished assigning a value to the jewelry collection and had decided to wait until the following day to begin writing up the catalog entries for each one. When I walked in, Leroy was the only one in the dining room. He was standing by the drink counter. As I walked through the door he said, "Hello, Ali. How are things going with the cataloging?"

"The work is moving along great, but I do have a question for you. Is now a good time?"

"Sure, I was with the board most of the day. It looks like I'm not going to lose my position over the mistakes I've made, but I am on probation and will be closely watched. Anymore screwups and I'll be fired immediately. I was just trying to decide if that was a good reason to have a cocktail to celebrate."

"I'm glad they're going to keep you, but sorry to hear about the restrictions. Still, it seems like a reason to celebrate. I can talk while you mix the drink."

"Well, it could have been much worse. I think under the circumstances the board was very fair. Let's hear your questions."

"No, not questions. Just one question. I've taken a cursory look at the reliquaries in the collection, and they are truly special. I'd like to bring in an expert to help evaluate them. I feel confident handling the jewelry on my own, but the reliquaries are a specialized item. I think we need an expert on religious antiques."

"That sounds like an excellent idea to me. I'll leave it to you to decide on the right person. We can pay them whatever they normally charge. Even though the college will pay them, they need to report to you. You're the only one who will know if we're getting good advice."

"Thank you. I do have a man in mind. I'll contact him first thing in the morning and see if he's available. If this is going to be a financial hardship for the college, I can take a pay cut to help cover the cost."

"No, no, the salary won't be a problem, but I appreciate your offering. The college just received large dividends on two of our investments, so the timing is good. Some of our alumni are very wealthy and have given us some very good investments, as well as tips on others. We're lucky to be in such good shape financially while other small colleges struggle. Hire your person as soon as possible. I'll look forward to meeting them.

"Oh, I almost forgot, I wanted to let you know that the board decided to hire an expert to take a look at the books you and Laudine found in the tunnel before they decide what to do with them. Alex Walsh will be supervising a crew later in the week to bring them from the tunnel to the empty library room on your floor. It's the same crew we use to move things to Building Six, so we know they are reliable."

"That's fantastic! Hopefully the expert will be able to make some recommendations on how to best preserve their condition until the board makes a decision."

"That's part of the reason he's being hired so quickly. His name is Danford Loomis, maybe you have heard of him?"

"Actually, I have heard the name. He has a very good reputation, but I've never met him. I hope I get the chance while he's here."

While we were eating, I realized that even though I'd only asked one question, Leroy had inadvertently answered several. I'd been wondering why this college seemed not to ever have to worry about money. If Leroy were telling the truth, I had my answer. Now I could put that worry aside. I considered it very good news that the antique books were going to be handled properly. I was sure that enough of them were irreplaceable that taking proper care of them was essential.

The meal was excellent as always, but I was tired and went straight to my room when I'd finished. When Laudine came in for the night, she found me sitting on the couch but sound asleep. She woke me to send me to bed, but after my nap I was wide awake. It seemed like the best time to tell her about the diary. I asked if she wanted to hear about it rather than going straight to bed, and she insisted I tell her what the second half contained.

We decided to have hot chocolate to go with the story. We could fix that in the room and wouldn't have to go all the way back down to the kitchen.

"I think we left off where Old Man Madison let his son Wilton move home and bring his baby Euclid with him. The diary skips a few years at that point. There was no explanation why. When it picks back up, Euclid is four. It's already evident he has an interest in music and has a great deal of talent. Even at that young age, he wanted nothing to do with the things his father and grandfather collected."

"Did the men mind his lack of interest?"

"I'm not sure, since the diary didn't say, but it was around this same time that Ezra began noticing strange changes in his son. At one point, he caught Wilton taking apart some reliquaries and removing the sacred items. Later he found a cache of them under Euclid's mattress. When he questioned Wilton about it, he calmly explained that he was protecting his son from evil spirits."

"Wow, that must have scared the old man!"

"The diary confirms it did and that he began watching his son more closely. He claims to have discovered many incidents of strange behavior. He doesn't explain most of them, but he does say that one night he caught Wilton releasing dozens of spiders into the boy's bedroom. Then next he describes the night he finds Wilton on the stair landing holding little Euclid. The boy's father claims to have been carrying his son up to bed, but the grandfather was sure he was lying."

"I can't even begin to imagine what he must have been thinking, let alone what he would decide to do. He'd lost so much already."

"It would have been a tough call, but I think he should have called the authorities. Obviously, his son had gone off the rails again. He didn't, though. Instead, two days later he called the police to tell them his son was hurt. When they got to the house, they discovered Wilton's body at the bottom of the infamous stairs. Ezra convinced the authorities his son was suffering from depression because of his wife's death and must have decided to kill himself. No one questioned this because of Wilton's strange past."

"Tell me that isn't the end. The diary must have had more to say about what happened."

"You're right about that. The night before Wilton died, Ezra had again found him on the landing carrying Euclid. This time the boy was crying. He somehow convinced Wilton to hand him the boy and when Euclid was safe, Ezra pushed his son over the railing. He claimed in the diary that he didn't know what else to do. Insane asylums were horrible places in those days, so he didn't want his son sent back there, but he also knew it was impossible to keep him at home with the boy."

"It's horrible to say, but I can almost see his point—not quite, but almost."

"Well, a person can't condone what he did, but I understand what you mean. It must have been a terrible choice for him, and his options weren't good."

Laudine thought a moment before saying, "How badly was the child affected by what happened?"

"He had a rough beginning, but Euclid seems to have grown up and done all right. The grandfather must have done the best job he could raising him. As an adult, he was a very accomplished musician. He played for years with the Philharmonic Orchestra. He never married or had children, but according to the last entries in the journal, he had a happy and satisfying life. If you'd like to read the whole story for yourself, I'd be glad to lend it to you."

"No, that's okay. I got the gist of it, and that was depressing enough. I don't want to read the details."

We talked a little longer before heading off to bed. I told her about my plan to invite Father Timmon to help with setting a value for the reliquaries.

First thing in the morning, I placed my call to the priest. I'd met Jonathan Timmon twice at conferences I'd attended. Both times I'd been impressed, and the antique community considered him one of the top experts on religious antiques. If he weren't already on a job, he would be perfect for what I needed, and as it turned out, the timing worked out great. He would be free in two weeks and would come straight to the college. He was intrigued by the reliquary collection and seemed eager to do the job. I thought I could be done or close to done with a first draft of the catalog entries by then and could be free to help and learn from Father Timmon. I'd offered to pick him up at the airport, but he preferred to rent a car and drive. I spent the rest of the afternoon writing the forward for the final catalog. That only left the job of writing the individual entries. Most of the information I would need for that would come from the descriptions I'd written as I valued the items. After a light breakfast, I got started on the job.

Mid-afternoon, Claude came down to the workroom and told me that he, Laudine, and Kenneth had decided to attend a concert being held on campus that night and asked if I'd like to go with them. I readily accepted, thinking it would be nice to think of something other than work for once.

The concert started at eight-thirty, so immediately after dinner we met in the lobby. Since the auditorium was all the way around on the other side of the campus, we decided to drive. That way if we decided to go into town for a drink afterward, we wouldn't have to walk all the way back to the main building for a car.

Everyone must have been as happy as I was to be doing something other than work, for we were all in high spirits as we piled into the car. I noticed Claude still had his cough, but it seemed much better. I wondered briefly if he could possibly be connected to the crimes on campus. I just couldn't picture any of my new friends here as murderers. I decided to put those thoughts out of my mind for tonight. Kenneth was parking the car when I heard a sound very like the "cough" I'd been hearing when trouble was around. I was shocked when Kenneth said, "Oh, excuse me for just a second. That's my phone and I need to take this call."

He made the conversation short, but it was long enough for me to realized his ring tone could have been the sound I'd been hearing. I also knew that, if it were common, it could be on anyone's phone. I'd tell Jeff what I'd discovered, but I didn't think it would be a lot of help. Still, I knew from past experience that most clues didn't mean much by themselves, but when you got enough of them, they painted a picture.

The concert was good. It reminded me of Euclid playing with his orchestra, and I hoped he'd had a good life. Afterward we did drive to town for a drink and a little dancing. The evening's tone was that of a group of friends spending some time together, and I think we all enjoyed it.

Eighteen

Almost a week had gone by since the concert. During that time there were no more attacks, and Laudine and I both got a lot of work done. Our schedules were mostly routine, and the initial stress of getting established was gone. I was learning a lot, as well as enjoying my classes, and Laudine seemed to enjoy teaching. It seemed like a good time for me to sit in on one of her lectures. I cleared the idea with her, and she seemed genuinely happy that I was interested. Since her lectures were from ten-thirty until twelve, I worked a few hours before heading over to the building where the culinary classes were being held. I was shocked when I walked in and discovered she had over a hundred students. She motioned me down to the front where she had saved a seat.

Her lecture wasn't like anything I'd ever seen. She worked from a slightly elevated platform, and it contained a complete kitchen. If anyone from the *Food Network* had been there, they would have offered her a job on the spot. She was both informative and entertaining. She had the rapt attention of everyone in the room. For today's class, she crafted a complex souffle as she gave step-by-step instruction for every move she made. She seemed in her element here, just as much as she always had in the kitchen, and I was so proud of all that my friend had accomplished.

After Laudine's class, I grabbed a couple of tacos from one of the fast-food restaurants on campus and spent some time just exploring before going to my art history class. I couldn't help thinking that Claude could use a little of Laudine's charisma, but in spite of his limitations, I was very happy with all the information I was gaining.

After Art History ended, I had started to walk back to the main building when I noticed the archaeology building nearby. I couldn't believe I hadn't noticed it before. I decided to take a look at the office that had been Professor Castille's and then Professor Hillman's. It had long since stopped being a crime scene, but was still unused, as so far no new archaeology professor had been hired. I didn't go expecting to find anything at this late date. The police had scoured the office after each death. I just wanted to satisfy my curiosity and see if I could get a feel for Professor Castille as a person. Professor Hillman hadn't been there long enough to make many changes, so I hoped some evidence of Castille's personality might remain. Even this long after his death, no one knew why he had been on campus before he was supposed to arrive, and no one had discovered any reason for why he'd been killed.

The building was alive with normal daytime activity, but the office I wanted was empty. Once inside, I sat behind the desk and stared around the room. There were lots of books on the shelves, papers scattered on the credenza, and class notes on the desk. There wasn't a lot of decoration except for a few pictures and artifacts from a dig the professor had been on in Africa years before. Maybe his home was more personalized, but his office seemed devoid of personality. It was possible Professor Hillman had removed more than I thought, but looking around, I found no evidence the second professor had ever been there. He definitely hadn't spent any time making the office his.

I idly poked through the desk drawers while scanning the office. They were nearly full of stockpiled office supplies. Someone had been determined not to run out of things like paperclips, post-it notes, or staples. On top of a package of notebook paper was a picture frame turned face down. When I turned it over, a woman's face was looking up at me. Neither of the men had been married at the time of their death, but this might be a girlfriend or sister. Since it wasn't being displayed, I assumed it had probably been Castille's and Tillman had stuck it in a drawer when he took over. The woman wasn't young, but she was very attractive. I reached to pick up the picture, but the corner of the frame hit the edge of the desktop and caused me to drop it. When I bent to retrieve it, I found the glass had broken and a piece of the jagged glass had torn the picture near the right edge. I was glad to see the face had not been damaged. Surely someone would eventually claim the professor's belongings. I'd have to tell Jeff what I'd done. I picked up the loose shards of glass, but as I went to put the frame back in the drawer, I saw that where the picture had torn there seemed to be another picture behind the first. Now that I'd already made a mess, I decided to open the back and see if there were additional pictures. Maybe the first picture would be labeled with the woman's name. It wasn't, but behind it was another picture. This one was of Professor Castille standing alone in front of a pyramid in Egypt. It might not mean anything, but my mind immediately leaped to the box of Egyptian artifacts I'd discovered in Building 6. Behind that picture was a list of seven numbers. I had to no idea if they were significant, but the fact that they had been hidden made me suspicious. Now I didn't feel so comfortable in the office of two men that had been killed. I quickly made my way back to what I felt was the safety of the main building.

I was relieved when I passed through the door into the familiarity of the main building. I stopped in the middle of the hall because I wasn't sure what I wanted to do next. I should go down and work an hour or so before dinner, but I wanted to talk to Jeff about what I'd found in Castille's office. Before I could make a decision, the detective himself rounded a corner and walked into the hall. I was happy to see he had Tom with him. They were talking amicably, so I assumed my one-time protector had kept his job. I was glad. The officer was young but seemed like a good man. When they saw me standing there, they walked over.

"Hey, Ali, you look a little worried. Why am I finding you standing in the middle of the hall?"

I greeted them both, but then when I went to answer Jeff's question, I didn't know what to say. Face to face with the man, the picture I'd found seemed insignificant. I felt silly running to the detective. He looked at me, sent Tom off on an errand, and then took my arm and led me to the dining room. Once he had me settled with a cup of coffee he said, "Okay, what's going on? You look confused, and that isn't something I've seen before. Talk to me."

I didn't have much choice at that point, so I took a sip of coffee and told him the whole story, beginning when I'd decided to go by the professor's office. When I finished, he said, "I'm surprised you could get in. I'm sure my men locked it up when they were done. They told me about the picture when they went through the office after Castille was killed. We identified her as a colleague from the company where he worked before coming to the college. I even called her at the time. She was saddened to hear about his death, but assured me she hadn't talked to him in years. There is no excuse for the officers' failure to check behind the picture, but it's obvious they didn't. Let me see the other picture and the numbers."

I stared at him a moment before saying, "I didn't take them. I didn't want to be accused of tampering with evidence, and I wasn't even sure you'd be interested. There is nothing suspicious about them other than the fact that they were kind of hidden."

It was his turn to stare at me a moment. "Okay, I'm going to go get them now. You actually made the right decision. If they do turn out to be pertinent, it's better I get them and log them into evidence. While I'm there, I can check with the department and see if they unlocked the room for any reason."

A second later, he was out the dining room door. I once again was left with a choice of what to do next. I decided to blow off work for the rest of the day. I had one more week before my expert arrived, and by then I could easily have the jewelry part of the collection nearly ready for the college to sell.

I walked into the kitchen to see what Laudine was up to. The staff was already busy with preparation for the evening meal. Even so, she spotted me almost immediately and walked over. "Hey, I'm glad you stopped by. I wanted to let you know Kenneth and I are going to a foreign film at the auditorium tonight, so I might be a little late getting back to our room. Also, I wanted to find out what time we're leaving in the morning."

I stood there just looking at her, and I'm sure my face was as blank as my mind. She shook her head and said, "I can see you have completely forgotten that your one-month followup appointment with Dr. Dawhan is tomorrow."

"Yikes, guilty as charged. I even put it on the Google calendar and still forgot. It just doesn't seem possible that a month has passed already. I guess since our calendars are linked, that's how you knew. It may be the last time I have to see him, but one last checkup seems like a good idea. What time is the appointment?"

She laughed. "It's at three, but I was hoping we could go early to do a little shopping and maybe have lunch."

"That works for me. I have the jewelry nearly finished and not a lot to do until Father Timmon arrives. You want to leave around nine? That should give you plenty of time at the kitchen store."

"Nine sounds fine, but I'm sure the kitchen store won't be our only stop. I doubt you'll want to miss that mysterious antique store, and this time I want to look in some of the local clothing stores. I have the staff all set to handle dinner here, so we can stay as long as we want this time."

Laudine and I always seemed to be ready early any time we had to go somewhere. Today was no exception, and we were in the car and on our way out of the driveway at ten to nine. I hadn't realized the college had begun to feel oppressive, but as we drove through the gate, it was like a weight had been lifted off my shoulders. Laudine must have been feeling something similar because she said, "It feels good to have a free day ahead of us. It will be nice to put all the mysteries aside and just do something fun."

Only a month had passed since we'd made this same drive, but the scenery was already changing and the air was noticeably cooler. All the greenery was bigger and darker, and I knew it wouldn't be long until color began to permeate the green. Fall was coming.

To pass the time, I asked her how her date with Kenneth had gone. She smiled. "It wasn't a date, exactly. We do enjoy spending time together and like a lot of the same things, but I don't think this is going to develop into anything serious."

"Is that a good or bad thing?"

"A little of both, I guess. I do want to fall in love one of these days, but I'm not sure I'm ready right now."

"I can certainly understand that. You have a lot going on with your career. Still, you have to admit he is beautiful."

She laughed, but things got quiet until we got close to town. I was sure we were both thinking about the past.

Our first stop was the kitchen store, since it was closest to where we parked. With my hip no longer bothering me, I wandered through the aisles. I even found a couple of antique items that were so unique and in such good shape that I purchased them for the shop. Eventually, Laudine emerged pushing a cart piled high with purchases she was having shipped home to Scottsdale. I was pretty sure I knew what every third item in the cart was for, but the rest were a complete mystery. My friend was grinning from ear to ear, so I assumed she was happy with the treasures she'd discovered.

From there, we cut across the street intending to make the antique store our next stop, but on the way, we discovered a section with three or four clothing shops that were too interesting to pass by. We paused to check them out It wasn't long until we were loaded down with packages, and it was almost time for lunch. I suggested we take our purchases to the car and then move it closer to the antique store. We'd just completed the move and walked to the beginning of the small side street that housed the antiques shop when I saw Jeff walking our way. He hadn't seen us, and I quickly pulled Laudine into a nearby shop to give him time to move on. Once I'd explained to Laudine about seeing him there on both our visits, we were very curious what business he could possibly have in the antique store. He was barely out of sight when Laudine said, "It's already twelve. Why don't we find a place to eat lunch and come back here after? We should have plenty of time before your doctor's visit."

"Food sounds great to me. Do you have someplace in mind?"

"I didn't have, but while we were hiding from Jeff, I spotted what might either be interesting or terrible. It would be a definite gamble."

"We weren't exactly hiding. We were making a tactical retreat. Anyway, I'm up for a gamble. What do you have in mind?"

Outside the shop, Laudine stopped me and pointed across the street. "See that green door over there? It just says restaurant. I saw someone open it, and the only thing inside is a staircase. Evidently the restaurant is upstairs. Wanta give it a try?"

"Sure. Let's go see what's behind that door. It's not like we know how good anything else we tried would be either."

The second we stepped through the door, we both knew the type of food that was being served upstairs. We grinned at each other, because the smell of Mexican food was unexpected but more than welcome. We had both been missing salsa, refried beans, and all the rest. Mexican food restaurants were few and far between in this part of the country. Laudine said, "Smells yummy," as we trudged determinedly up the steep and narrow stairs.

At the top of the steps was a hostess station. We were promptly led to a booth by a window that overlooked the street below. The restaurant itself was fantastic. The decor was tasteful and authentic. The room wasn't huge, but it wasn't tiny either. The booths were artfully arranged to give each one a semblance of privacy. We hadn't been seated more than a minute or two before water, menus, and chips and salsa appeared. I couldn't wait a moment longer to try a chip. Laudine and I both reached out at the same time, laughed, and scooped up some salsa with a still-warm chip. I sighed with delight at the feel of the spicy hot and delicious sauce as it touched my tongue.

For me, a good salsa is paramount in Mexican food. I was pretty sure we were in for a treat.

We both ordered the combination platter, and it was huge. We did our best to eat it all. We were disappointed that we had no room left for sopapillas, but we were stuffed, and every bite had been delicious. I don't think we actually waddled on the way out, but we decided to walk around the block before tackling the antique store.

Nothing in the shop had changed. I could swear the owner was wearing the same exotic outfit. There was no doubt the store's merchandise was exquisite, but there was something odd about the place, something besides the owner. There was no dust on anything and no disorder to the items. The inventory was arranged as if it had all been placed at once in a preplanned, organized fashion. All the antique stores I'd been in before were somewhat disorganized, because the items were acquired over time and displayed wherever space could be found. This felt more like a movie set than a real shop. Even with my growing suspicions, the merchandise was too good to ignore. I spent at least an hour looking at all the wonderful treasures and wishing I could afford more than the six or so items I bought for the shop. I paid for my finds and arranged to have them shipped directly to Eclectic Treasures. Before giving myself time to change my mind, I quickly said, "I have several customers at home that are looking for Egyptian antiques. I was wondering if you ever get in any type of Egyptian artifacts?"

On the off chance this man was the fence for the treasures I'd seen in Building 6, I also said, "They have fairly large collections and also have some items for sale. If you're interested, I could have them contact you."

In spite of my belief that something was off about the shop, I was surprised when the owner immediately expressed interest in buying additional inventory. He also told me he got in the type of thing I was interested in from time to time and requested my contact information so we could arrange a time for him to learn more about the items my clients had for sale. I asked for a couple of days to contact them for email pictures, got his number instead of giving him mine, and hustled Laudine out of the shop.

Outside and back on a main street, I pulled Laudine up next to a building and told her what I'd done. She said, "Surely you don't suspect Jeff of having illegal dealings with this man? Even if the owner of the shop does fence stolen goods, and we don't know that for sure yet, it doesn't mean Jeff is involved."

"Of course, you're right. Still, the furtive way I've seen him coming and going, coupled with the way the shop owner reacted when I mentioned Egyptian artifacts, has to mean something is going on."

"You may be right. What do you plan to do?"

"I guess my best option is to follow up with the antique shop owner. See if I can get him to buy something that is obviously not legal. If he goes for it, then he definitely isn't on the up and up. If not, then I am probably way off base."

"There are a lot of 'what ifs' about that plan. Even so, it may be the best place for you to start. I would bet Jeff isn't involved in this mess, but I understand you have to know for sure.

"Right now, though, you have to get to the doctor's office if you don't want to be late for your appointment."

The visit went as expected. The doctor released me with orders to come in immediately if I had any future problems. When it was over, we still weren't ready to give up on our day. We walked aimlessly around town, stopping at all the shops that looked interesting. By the time we got back to the college, it was nearly seven. We were worn out but relaxed and happy. By eight, I'd had a sandwich and I was ready for a bath and an early night. Laudine was already reading in her room. I nearly jumped out of my skin when there was a loud booming knock on the door to our suite. I was almost to the door when Laudine rushed into our sitting room and said, "What in the world is going on? I thought the building was coming down."

"Someone's at the door, and they seem very determined to get our attention."

Laudine looked dubious but didn't say anything, so I opened the door. Jeff pushed by me into the room looking like a thundercloud.

Before I could say anything, he was yelling. I caught very few of his words, but the fact that he was furious was obvious. Laudine said, "I'll just go back to my reading. I don't think I'll be needed for this conversation."

Her door closed quietly behind her and I turned to Jeff. "I think you'd better sit and start at the beginning. Obviously, something is up."

He didn't sit, but I did. He made a visible effort to calm himself as he paced back and forth. Finally he said, "You just can't help but meddle when you shouldn't, can you? If Frank had been a real thief or fence, you could have gotten in serious trouble. What were you thinking? No, never mind that question. You obviously weren't thinking. How can I keep you safe when you keep leaping into dangerous situations?"

He obviously wasn't through, but I interrupted. "Jeff, you aren't making any sense. Please sit and start at the beginning. I can tell I've done something to upset you, but I have no idea what you're talking about."

Actually, I had some idea where he was headed, but I wanted him to calm down and tell me the whole story. After my statement, he stared at me a few more minutes and then sighed and sat. After a couple more sighs he said, "Okay, here it is in a nutshell. Today in town you approached Frank, the man in the antique store, about buying and selling Egyptian items. It's obvious you suspected him of being the fence for the items you'd seen in Building Six. Don't you see that two people have already been killed, and those deaths are very likely connected to those artifacts? If Frank had been the real deal, he might have decided to do the same to you."

"You've made a bunch of suppositions there, but I'll start by asking who and what Frank is and why he has a phony antique shop in town."

"Phony? I'll have you know those are some of the best antiques around. I hear you didn't hesitate to buy a few."

"Look, we can go on like this, but it isn't getting us anywhere. Obviously, you disapprove of my attempt to find out if the shop owner was involved in the Egyptian artifact mess. What was I supposed to do, when twice I've seen you skulking around his shop? I've trusted you with all the information I've found out, but you have either been lying to me or holding a lot of information back. Either way, you can't expect me not to try and find out what's going on. Also, it is not your job to protect me. I have been taking care of myself for some time."

A couple more sighs and he said, "My reason for being here isn't something I'm supposed to talk about, but I'm going to explain anyway. It may be the only way to keep you from jumping to wild conclusions. I'm not actually a police detective. I work for a government organization that deals with international antiquity theft. I was sent here because we had information that illegal items, stolen from Egypt, were being held and sold in this area. Frank is here for the same reason. We are hoping the real thieves contact him. Today he thought you were that contact. The local police are cooperating with my agency."

He leaned over and handed me a very official-looking document validating what he'd said. It might have been forged, but I chose to take him at his word. We talked for at least an hour more as we asked questions and exchanged information. Now that he'd been honest with me, I was tempted to tell him about the clock and three-tiered bottle, but it was late and I knew explaining them would be time consuming. I decided to wait for another opportunity. If I were completely honest with myself, I had to admit I was still very worried about how Jeff would respond to my revelation. It wouldn't be an easy thing for him to fit into his worldview.

I was still sleepy when morning arrived, so I decided on coffee and a donut before starting work. It also gave me an opportunity to assure Laudine that Jeff and I were fine. I knew Jeff probably meant me to keep quiet about his real reason for being here, but I gave the main facts to Laudine anyway. I trusted her completely and knew she would never let on that she knew.

Nineteen

The next few days, while I worked on the jewelry catalog and waited for the reliquary expert to arrive, were quiet. Leroy did mention that the body we'd found in the wall hadn't been identified, and because it was so old it was not a top priority. The authorities had told him they might never find out who she had been. I didn't see a lot of Jeff and assumed he was busy. In one of our brief encounters, he did tell me no one had contacted Frank about fencing the stolen items, but to his surprise, the antique store was getting a reputation and was becoming very busy. If it kept getting so many customers, they were going to have to request more inventory. He didn't know if his agency would comply, or decide it was a waste of time and close it down.

~ * ~

Father Timmon arrived on a Sunday afternoon, so there was time to get him settled and show him around the school before we started work Monday morning. I was glad he would have a little time before dinner, because he looked tired. He wasn't a young man, but it didn't seem like he was old enough for the trip to Druthmar to have completely worn him out. I would need to keep a close eye on him to be sure he was up to this job. Articles I had read about him had given me the impression he was only in his early fifties. Leroy had given him a room across the hall from the one Laudine and I shared. He hadn't brought much, so his settling in didn't take long. After a short walk around campus and an explanation about the buildings, I was ready to take him down to the workroom. I couldn't wait to see the expression on his face when he saw the windows for the first time. Thinking you are underground and then seeing windows to the outside was amazing for me, and I wondered what he would think.

Father Timmon's reaction to the view was everything I could have hoped for, but his first view of the reliquaries excited him even more. He just couldn't seem to credit what he was seeing. After several moments of shock, he said, "Alicia, this is astounding! I have studied religious artifacts all over the world and never seen anything like this. I don't think anyone knows a collection like this exists."

"I was shocked too, Father, but I'm not an expert. I knew one was needed if the catalog on these reliquaries was to be believed."

"I'm still not sure anyone will believe what they read until they see for themselves, but when these go up for sale, it should cause quite a stir.

"You know, if we're going to be working together you need to call me Jonathan, or better yet John. Father Timmon is going to get cumbersome, and Jonathan is almost as bad."

We chatted a while longer before the priest went to rest until dinner. We would begin actually working with the reliquaries first thing the following morning.

At dinner, I introduced Father Timmon. Everyone seemed happy to have him as one of the groups, and it wasn't long until he and Claude were having an in-depth discussion about religious art. Like everyone, the priest raved about Laudine's cooking, but I couldn't help but notice he ate very little. When I went upstairs, he and Claude were still talking. I interrupted long enough to arrange to knock on his door at eight in the morning to help him find his way down to the workroom, and said goodnight.

The next few days settled into a work routine quickly, and to my surprise the priest didn't seem to have any trouble learning the route down to Sub C. He was extremely knowledgeable and was working his way through the items efficiently and quickly. By the third day, I was no longer stopping by his room in the mornings. He often went down early enough to join the staff at breakfast. I would either run into him there or he'd already be hard at work when I arrived. By the end of the week, we had settled into a routine of sorts. Then, on Friday, I didn't see him at breakfast, and when I got to the workroom, he wasn't at his usual spot bent over the table examining one of the items. I just assumed he'd slept in for once, but the minute I walked through the cage door, I saw him sprawled out on the floor. He wasn't moving and with all that happened recently, I was afraid he had been murdered. When I got closer, I was relieved to see he was alive but unconscious. I quickly picked up the house phone and called Alex. He answered almost immediately and I asked him to call for an ambulance. The priest seemed to be breathing okay and he had a heartbeat, so I just sat by his side waiting until the paramedics arrived. Fortunately, they came quickly. Even more quickly, they loaded him into the ambulance and took off to the small local hospital in Canajoharie.

The ambulance drove away, leaving me unsure what I should do next. I wanted to go directly to the hospital, but decided I'd wait to find out the seriousness of the problem. If they kept him overnight, I'd go to see him in the morning. I realized I needed to let Leroy know what had happened. He immediately called the hospital to make sure the priest was suffering with a medical problem as I'd thought. He was concerned it might have been another attempted murder. Naturally they wouldn't give him any information. Next, he called Jeff, assuming he could find out. He promised to let me know when he got any news.

While I waited, I sat at the worktable and began reading through the priest's notes on the reliquary he'd been working on. It was only moments until the detailed notes captured my full attention.

Even without looking at the actual item, Father Timmon's description was so detailed I could picture the reliquary in my mind. It read, "As with all of the reliquaries examined so far, this one is of Christian origin. It is in the shape of a foot, which is not a particularly unusual shape used for this purpose. This one is a philatory, which means it has a transparent window in order to view the encased relic. Next to the window is the undamaged seal of a Catholic bishop. The relic inside is a male finger bone purported to be from Saint Francis of Assisi. All indications point to it having been constructed in the early 19th century. The foot measures fifteen inches long and is eight inches tall. The material used is bronze. Where a normal foot would extend into the leg, the reliquary is capped with a carved ivory plate. There is an ornate pattern of spun gold around the viewing window and down onto the toes. A large number and variety of gemstones are inset in the bronze. Although not one of the most expensive items in the collection, it is an exquisite work of art. I would value this item at \$5,700."

Coming back to the present, I went off to find Leroy. I hadn't had any word from him so I suspected he didn't have any news, but I wanted to let him know I was going to go to the hospital and see what I could find out there. I found him still in his office. His door was open and there was no secretary in sight. I said, "I see you are still on your own. Are you looking for a new secretary?"

"I am. In fact, I have two women coming in to interview this afternoon. Also, you will be happy to know the police picked up Leonard's wife last night. She's being charged along with her husband. They've confessed to stealing from the college, but they are denying any knowledge about the murders."

"Their capture is good news, and we're due for a little good news. I'm guessing you haven't heard anything more about Father Timmon?"

"No, not yet. The priest seems like a nice guy. I hope whatever is going on is nothing serious."

"Me too. Besides being a nice guy, he is really knowledgeable."

"I promise I'll call you if I hear anything. You do the same if you learn anything at the hospital. Oh, by the way, our book expert will be arriving tomorrow. I know you hoped to meet him while he was here."

From Leroy's office I went to find Laudine. I explained my restlessness and told her that I was going to drive to the hospital rather than wait for answers. She didn't argue with my decision, because she knew I wouldn't rest until I knew what had happened. When I arrived, the receptionist's behavior seemed a little strange, but she directed me to where I could find Father Timmon. This surprised me, as I expected him to be having tests or supervision that would prevent visitors. I found him, but I was more confused than surprised, because the priest was still in a cubicle in the emergency room and was fully dressed and walking around. I said, "Father, shouldn't you be in bed? What are the doctors saying?"

"Ah, Alicia, your arrival couldn't have been better timed. I needed a ride back to the college and here you are. Staying here isn't going to help me. I can see by the look you're giving me you're confused and I don't blame you. I promise I will explain on the ride back to Druthmar."

As soon as we were in the car and had driven out of the hospital parking lot, I said, "Okay, let's hear this promised explanation."

"Before I begin, let me say that I hope you will keep what I tell you between the two of us, although I know you can't make that decision until you hear what I have to say. There is no easy way to say this, so I'll come right to the point. I have cancer. The doctors tell me it's somewhere between stage three and four. They are not sure, but think it may have started in my lungs, but now it's spread pretty well through my whole body. They believe I have one to two years left. I knew this when I took the job here and should have told you, but working with this collection is a dream come true for me, and I wanted to do one last meaningful job. Today was the first time I've passed out, and I think if I'm careful, it shouldn't happen again while I'm here. I'd like to finish what we've started, since I think it can be completed in about two months, but I will abide by whatever you decide."

"I am so sorry. You should have told me sooner. You scared me to death today. I even thought you might have been attacked by the killer I told you about. Still, I don't see any reason why we can't finish evaluating the collection. However, I will have to tell Leroy, in case there is some type of liability, or other administrative requirements I'm unaware of. If you're agreeable, I suggest we go directly to his office when we get back. Once we've talked to him, we'll know what comes next."

"That's more than fair. I really am sorry to have worried you."

Leroy was in his office when we arrived. He had the priest sign a document I assumed freed the college of liability should his health deteriorate during his time working there, but he had no problem with him staying to finish the job. Mostly he seemed distracted while we were in his office. I assumed he was thinking about his upcoming interviews with prospective secretaries.

I told John we would take the rest of the day off and begin fresh in the morning. He thanked me for my help and chose to skip lunch in order to rest until dinner. As he turned to leave, his cell phone rang. He looked at it, but put it back in his pocket without answering. It was that same sound I had confused with Claude's cough. It didn't sound as much like a cough to me now, but it certainly didn't sound musical either. I said, "Does everyone with your brand of phone have that same ringtone? I keep hearing it a lot."

Father Timmon said, "I think it must be the default tone. I'm sure I haven't ever changed it."

I was disappointed to realize the sound wasn't going to help identify our killer. It was just too common to narrow the field of suspects.

The priest entered the elevator, and I was once again at loose ends and unsure what to do next. The jewelry catalog was ready and would be sent to the printer when the reliquary one was done. I could work on that using the items completed so far, but at the moment I was sure my thoughts were too scattered. I finally decided having that cup of coffee while I told Laudine what I knew might settle me down.

I began by explaining about the priest's condition. She said, "It seems like such a shame. I feel very sorry for Father Timmon. He is such a nice man."

"I agree, but I have to confess I'm relieved this wasn't another move by the killer. I seem to be holding my breath, waiting for whatever is going to happen next. It feels like we are biding our time waiting for the killer to make a move. I want to keep that from happening, but we can't seem to find a way to do that."

"I understand, for sure, and I think to one degree or another, everyone on campus has that same feeling. Have you talked to Detective Crown lately? I keep hoping he'll find something useful."

"I haven't really talked to him for a couple of days. He did mention this morning that he was coming by for dinner tonight and we could compare notes then. We'll just have to hope he knows something new."

It was lunchtime and dinner seemed a long way off, so I ate a small piece of spinach quiche with the staff. Leroy came by the dining room and asked me if I had time to stop by his office.

I had no idea why he'd asked. He surprised me by saying, "I hate to add to your workload, but I wonder if you'd have time to look over the inventory list for Building Six? If you could just flag a few of the more valuable items, I could have Alex check to see if any of them are missing. There is way too much over there to check each entry, but hopefully if anything has been stolen, the thief would have gone for the valuable items. I know I'm not qualified to figure out what those might be, and no one else here seems to be either. You are the only one with enough knowledge."

"I'm not sure if my qualifications are exactly right either, but I'd be happy to try. Right now, I'm mainly writing up the catalog entries after Father Timmon examines an item, and I can do that a lot faster than the evaluation takes, so I have some free time. If you have the inventory ready, I can get started right away."

"I can't thank you enough, Alicia. The college will compensate you for the extra work."

"Nonsense. I was just wishing for something proactive to do, and now you've provided it. I should be thanking you."

I left the president's office lugging the inventory books and wondering what I'd gotten myself into. Each of the books was the size of a large ledger and fatter than I would have thought possible. I hoped I could skim through them and anything of value would catch my eye. Then I could make a list of the valuable items as well as their locations.

I spent the afternoon and evening skimming the first inventory book and listing names and locations of fifteen items I considered the most valuable, but I suspected my efforts were going to be a waste of time. I had begun by looking up the location where I'd seen the crate of Egyptian artifacts and discovered that the inventory claimed that spot had been occupied by a carton of old hymn books from the late eighteen-hundreds. If whoever had stored the artifacts had used the same method for any other stolen items, there was no way the inventory could help. I believed when Leroy had someone check to see if the valuable items were where the inventory claimed, he would find they were all there. It seemed to me someone was using the storage building as a place to hide, and sell items stolen elsewhere. I doubted they had stolen anything from the actual inventory because they wouldn't want to compromise their ability to store and sell items from the convenient storage building. I knew some collectors would pay fantastic sums for artifacts they couldn't only obtain legally.

I did manage to catch up with Jeff after dinner, but he had no new information to share. I told him about Leroy's request. He seemed to agree it probably wouldn't yield any new information, but it would still be worth doing to be sure the college wasn't missing valuable assets.

I'd planned to give Leroy the partial list I'd compiled in the morning. I thought the school could use it to begin making sure nothing had been stolen from their storage. If all those items were where they belonged, it would help support my theory that whoever had hidden the Egyptian antiquities wasn't stealing from the college, but was instead using it for a front to fence illegal artifacts.

During the night I had spent some sleepless hours trying to come up with some way to identify the thieves I was sure were also killers.

By the time I'd finally fallen asleep, I had decided that before I gave Leroy the list, I would make another trip to Building 6 and check it out myself. The danger in doing so seemed minimal.

I didn't think the Egyptian artifacts were hidden in with the stored items any longer, so there would be no reason for the killer to be watching for intruders. I was also fairly sure I'd figured out the meaning of the list of numbers I'd found in the picture frame in Castille's office. I was convinced the numbers corresponded with the storage sites Castille had used to hide the crates of artifacts he'd stolen until he was able to sell them. I could check that out while I was up there tomorrow. It wouldn't solve anything at this point, but it would confirm Castille's guilt.

Twenty

I began cataloging the reliquaries the Father had waiting for me early the following morning. I wanted to get my work done before I made the trip to Building 6. I also warned Laudine about what I had planned. I thought someone should know where I was going. She seemed to agree that checking out the list shouldn't be overly dangerous.

I finished the cataloging around ten-thirty and decided I had time to skim the second inventory book and still make the trip up the hill before lunchtime. When I looked up from the last page of Book Two of the large inventory books, I noticed the workroom seemed dark. I checked the clock, wondering if I'd worked longer than I had planned, but it was only eleven. Looking out the windows, I saw that clouds had rolled in and it looked like it might rain or even snow any time. Even so, I decided to risk making the trip, but did take the precaution of grabbing an umbrella on my way out.

I bypassed Building 5 partially because I knew nothing was stored there and partially because its run-down condition and my previous unpleasant experience there gave me no reason to want to see the place again.

I'd been wandering around checking out my list for about fifteen minutes, but so far hadn't found anything missing. I had discovered that the two storage spots we were sure had contained stolen artifacts did correspond with two of the numbers on Castillo's list. It was enough to convince me that was the right explanation for the numbers.

As I stood deciding where to look next, some noise outside the room I was in caught my attention and I realized I wasn't alone in the old building. Not wanting anyone to know I was spot checking the storage inventory, I slipped through a closed door at the side of the room. It was the only door in the room other than the way I had entered. I felt sure the noise had come from the hall outside the door I'd left open when I'd entered.

Clear back when I'd first heard about it, I'd consciously decided not to explore the ancient underground tunnel running from Building 6 down to the main building, and now I was pretty sure that was where I was anyway. The darkness surrounding me was complete, but the scents of damp earth and stale air were strong clues. I had begun feeling along the wall for a light switch, sure that I was hoping for the impossible, when my hand made contact. I pushed the switch up and the tunnel lit before me as far as I could see. The light wasn't bright, but after the complete darkness it seemed heaven-sent.

It had obviously been added fairly recently, because it consisted of uncovered wire running along the ceiling with naked light bulbs attached at intervals. The bulbs were spaced so the distance between them caused the light to fade and then brighten again as I walked, but nowhere was completely dark. Looking as far ahead as I could without seeing anything that looked like structural damage, and not knowing who waited behind me, I decided to proceed along the tunnel as long as it seemed safe.

I'd walked what I surmised to be about a third of the distance back toward the main building without seeing anything but the single long passage before me. I felt sure this tunnel was man-made and marveled at how long the construction must have taken and how difficult it must have been. I resolved to come back when I had the free time and look around outside to see if I could find any trace of what the builders had done with the rock and dirt they had removed.

I had paused briefly, wondering what purpose the tunnel had originally served, when I heard a noise somewhere ahead of me. Now I was sure I'd been congratulating myself on finding no rats way too soon. Forcefully bolstering my courage, I gritted my teeth and again began walking. Not much further along, there were some large niches carved into the tunnel sides. I thought they must have originally been designed to hold some form of decoration, possibly statues. It was spooky being encased inside such a long expanse, so maybe the builders had needed a religious icon or two for protection. There was nothing here now to explain their original purpose. From time to time, I heard more furtive noises but no rats had materialized.

A little past where I'd seen the series of niches, I came upon the first exception to all the walls being rock. Inset in the rock on my right was a thick wooden door. The wood was dark and discolored, with a door handle shaped like a large snake that was both green and corroded by time and moisture. I didn't see any type of locking mechanism, and since I was there, I thought I should take a look inside. As I got closer, I could see that the door had once been closed off with large boards. I thought they must have been removed recently, as the wood where they had been was lighter and less weathered. I gave the handle a strong pull. Some of the crud encasing it crumbled off in my hand but the brass underneath felt strong. My tug had caused the top part of the door to move, but the bottom half was wedged somehow and didn't budge. I used my shoe to remove the dirt that had accumulated in front of the door and tried another pull. This time the door swung open easily. It rotated so smoothly and silently I knew it had been oiled recently.

Initially, the dim light shining in from the passage gave me quite a start, as it made what I was seeing look like a room filled with people. I stood frozen in place, but when my eyes began to adjust to the diminished light and I saw no movement in the room, I realized I was seeing eleven or twelve life-size statues. They had to be what had originally adorned the niches I'd passed in the hall. Scattered among the statues were six wooden crates. Even before I opened the first box, I was sure I'd found the missing Egyptian artifacts.

As soon as I lifted the lid on the closest box, my suspicions were confirmed. Now my only thought was to get out of the tunnel and back to the college so I could report to Jeff what I'd found. I didn't want to be discovered by whomever was using that room.

Hurrying forward, at about halfway through the snakelike cavern, I came upon the first turn of the passage. I rounded it quickly only to come to a screeching halt when I came face to face with Claude, who was pointing a gun straight at my face.

I said, "Oh, geez, thank goodness it's you. I hope you won't need the gun, but I'm very glad you're here. I have discovered the missing artifacts, and we need to get back to the main building as soon as possible so I can call the police."

My voice had been a little high and shaky and I was talking way too fast, but I knew immediately he had understood me and that I wouldn't be thankful he was there after all. The passing looks, first of regret followed by one of all-out anger, were self-explanatory. I had not only found the artifacts but most likely also the killer. The odds didn't look too good that I'd live to tell anyone.

Instantly he reached out, grabbed my arm, and pushed me in front of him, with his gun pressing against my back. When he said "walk," I began walking. I had a dozen questions running around my mind, but for the first few minutes I couldn't get my thoughts organized enough to ask them.

We hadn't gone very far when the passageway made another turn. This one brought it back to the original direction. I could only assume the jog had been necessary to avoid some natural obstacle. We'd only gone about ten steps past the turn when Jeff stepped out of a side niche. He had his gun out, and I'd never heard anything so wonderful as the sound of his voice.

He said, "Give it up, Claude. Alex discovered your secret earlier today when he accidentally intercepted a phone call that was meant for you."

I couldn't imagine how Jeff managed to be there, but I heaved a sigh of relief and was ready to run to his side when I felt the gun momentarily leave my back, heard the shot, and saw Jeff fall. Claude hadn't said a word. I started to move to Jeff's side to see how badly he'd been hurt, when once again I felt the pressure of the gun and my captor said, "Keep moving or I'll kill you right here."

With one last look at Jeff and the blood pooling beside him, I moved. I'd never be able to help him if I were dead. I also knew he needed help quickly if he were going to make it, and was busy weighing my options, when I heard a thud and the gun once more disappeared from my back.

I whirled around to find Claude and Kenneth wrestling on the ground. Claude's gun was also on the ground a couple of yards away from the fighting men. As I bent to pick it up so he wouldn't be able to use it if he got free, Claude kicked Kenneth hard enough to break free, scrambled to his feet, and took off running toward the entrance to the main building. I managed to fire one shot at his fleeing back, but my aim was way off the mark and only managed to chip the side wall.

Kenneth said, "You are going to have to follow him. It is the closest possible way to get to where cell service picks up. Call the police and an ambulance as quickly as possible. I have a little medical knowledge from my time in the service, so I'll go back and see if I can help Jeff."

I was so overwhelmed from all that had happened, I didn't seem able to speak, so I just nodded and took off running.

With every step, I expected Claude to step out from somewhere and grab me; but even so I kept running. We had been farther from campus than I'd thought, and it seemed like I had been running forever when I stumbled through the door and into the hall on the main floor where the business offices were located. There were two people unconscious on the floor, but I didn't see any blood so I sprinted straight for Leroy's office. Since my cell phone was upstairs in my room, it seemed the closest place to find a phone. The outer room was empty so I assumed there was no new secretary yet. At the same time that I collapsed into the desk chair, I was grabbing the phone.

As quickly as possible I explained to the 911 operator what was needed. My breath was ragged and the operator had a problem understanding at first. I gulped a few deep breaths in order to make myself clear. While I was explaining the situation, Leroy came out of his office to see what was happening. He looked haggard, and I regretted adding this new burden to all the problems he was already having with the administration.

As soon as I made myself clear about what was happening, he said, "You go wait out front so you can direct the medics to Jeff. I'll call the on-duty security police and begin looking for Claude."

I could already hear sirens in the distance, so without hesitation I once again started running. Emergency vehicles were on the long drive up to the school when I reached the porch. I was literally hopping from one foot to the other by the time the ambulance pulled up and the EMTs jumped out. The next few minutes were a blur as I again dashed through the tunnel, this time willing Jeff to hold on until we arrived rather than worrying about being attacked by Claude.

When at long last we reached Kenneth, he jumped up and began explaining what he'd done to try and stop the bleeding, so I knew Jeff was still alive, but both my mind and body refused to handle anything else. I slid down the closest wall and sat there, unaware of my surroundings except for the unresponsive look on Jeff's face. I don't know how much later it was before Kenneth pulled me to my feet, but Jeff was already on a stretcher being carefully walked down the passageway.

Kenneth said, "You definitely need a break. There is nothing we can do at the hospital for a few hours. I think we should bring Leroy up to date and find you some coffee or maybe a stiff drink."

Now that the necessary emergency action was over for the moment, I was beginning to feel somewhat better. The experts were handling things, and I was glad. Even so, I couldn't help expressing my relief and gratitude, so I threw my arms around Kenneth and through a few tears thanked him for turning up when he did.

Our first stop outside the tunnel was Leroy's office, but he wasn't there. I assumed he was still working with security, so we decided our next stop should be the kitchen. Laudine took one look at us and rushed us to chairs at the wooden table by the side of the room. For the first time, I realized Kenneth's hands and shirt were bloody. I looked down and saw that I wasn't much better after the hug I'd given him.

If we'd had the energy, we might have gone off for showers and clean clothes then; but instead we opted for washing up at the deep kitchen sink and letting Laudine bring us coffee, laced with something from an amber bottle she had on a high shelf, and a fresh-baked apricot danish. We'd only finished half of the first pastry when I felt up to telling her what had happened.

Kenneth picked up the story, "I got involved kind of by accident. I had been curious about Building Six since Alicia first began talking about it, and today I had some free time and decided to explore. I was wandering around looking at all the old supplies that had been saved over the years when I heard a noise and saw Ali slip through a door at the side of the room.

I wanted to join her, but by the time I'd worked my way through all the stacked crates and opened the door, she was already out of sight. Since the passage seemed to be one long, straight opening, I thought I could just follow it until I caught up with her. It wasn't long until I heard a shot. I had no doubt it was gunfire. After being in the service, it's a sound I will never forget. Immediately I took off running, trying to be as silent as possible. When I saw Jeff on the ground bleeding and Claude up ahead pushing Ali along, I had no choice but to jump him from behind. Fortunately, the surprise attack caused him to drop the gun. The rest, you know."

Laudine said, "My God! I can't let either one of you out of my sight for a minute without one or both of you getting into trouble."

We both grinned kind of sheepishly while she shook her head and said, "I guess the next question is what do we do now? For all we know, Claude is still on campus."

I looked at Kenneth and said, "It's possible, but there are police everywhere, and Leroy and the security guards might have caught up with him even before the police arrived. After one more cup of coffee, I guess we'd better go find Leroy and see where things stand."

Kenneth nodded in agreement while Laudine poured more coffee for all of us, but I noticed that this time she didn't add anything from the amber bottle that had disappeared back into the pantry shelf. She'd just finished filling the last cup when Alex Walsh burst through the door. His eyes darted madly around the room until he spotted us. He wasn't quite to the table when he demanded to know what in the world was going on.

"First I passed Leroy actually running through the hall. When I tried to question him, he didn't even slow down, just yelled over his shoulder something about another murder. Then I couldn't find Jeff or you guys, so I decided to come here. By the time I got down here, the building was swarming with police. Now I find you covered in blood. Can someone please explain?"

Kenneth and I looked at each other, hating the thought of having to go through the whole story again so soon. Laudine sighed and said, "You two just relax and I'll bring Alex up to date." Kenneth must have been as grateful as I was, because we nodded our agreement at the same time and then leaned back in our chairs. After she had related the whole story, I said, "I'm not really sure what we should do now.

"According to Alex, Leroy is still out hunting for Claude. I suppose Kenneth and I better go find the policeman who's in charge. Someone has to have taken over for Jeff. Then I plan to go to the hospital and wait for news about Jeff's condition."

Laudine said, "The staff has today's meals well in hand in case anyone wants to eat, so I'll be going to the hospital with you. I'm not leaving you alone for a moment until that monster is caught."

"I think Claude will be too busy trying to escape to cause any trouble, but I will appreciate the company. I'll come back and get you once I've talked to the police and changed clothes."

I dragged myself out of the chair, hugged Kenneth one more time, smiled at Alex, and left the kitchen to go find the police. I was surprised how shaky my legs were as I made for the door. I was very grateful when Kenneth took my arm and said, "I'm sure the police will need to talk to us both, so we might as well go find them together."

We didn't have to go far. As soon as we walked out of the kitchen into the dining room, we came face to face with a large gray-haired man. He didn't look at all happy when he pointed at us and said, "I think you are the two I need to talk to. Here is as good as anywhere, so let's sit down and have a little chat."

My first thought was how much I dreaded going through the whole story again, but I knew it couldn't be helped, so we sat and explained. The detective, who we learned was Luke Chambers, wasn't local. He was from Jeff's unit and only in town to find out how Jeff was doing on the artifact thefts and to make some decisions about the antique store in town.

I was glad he was there, because even though he wasn't friendly, he seemed capable. He asked all the right questions and grasped the whole situation quickly. As it turned out, Laudine didn't go to the hospital with me. The detective requested she stay to be sure the kitchen could handle feeding the policemen as well as the staff. She agreed when Kenneth volunteered to accompany me because she knew I'd be safe. Within thirty minutes, he and I were off to the hospital and Detective Chambers was searching for Leroy. I appreciated his optimism, because when we left, he said, "Be sure and tell Jeff I said hello when you see him."

I have always hated hospitals. None of my experiences connected with them has ever turned out well. I made a strong plea to the universe as we walked through the door that this time would be different. I followed quietly behind Kenneth as he asked all the right questions and finally led us to the door of Jeff's room.

There was a policeman stationed outside, but he waved us on through, so we must have been on some list of who was and wasn't allowed to visit. As Kenneth pushed open the door, I took a deep breath as I mentally prepared myself for whatever we might find inside. At least we knew he was still alive, but that was all the information we had been able to find out so far.

For just a moment once we'd entered, I thought we must be in the wrong room. There were no tubes, no piles of bloody clothes, no attached machines. A bag on a pole was attached to his left arm by a clear tube. Otherwise, he could have been dead or sleeping peacefully. I'd never seen Jeff when he wasn't vigorous and active; his face was so peaceful he looked like a little boy. Kenneth walked up next to the bed and sat, but I just stood in the door staring. I don't know how long we stayed like that before Jeff opened his eyes and said, "How long have you guys been here? You should have woken me. I seem to sleep pretty much non-stop. I suspect some sort of drugs are involved."

I still couldn't seem to speak, and a wave of relief flooded over me so strongly I momentarily felt dizzy. I was saved from embarrassment by a nurse who bustled in right at that moment. Young, crisp, and seemingly efficient, she said, "Oh good, you're awake. I thought maybe you were going to sleep all day."

Jeff, sounding alert but a little weak, said, "Don't blame me. I'm sure the cause is whatever you put in my saline drip."

She laughed good-naturedly. "Oh no, you can't explain your laziness that way. There is nothing in there except nutrients your body needs. Don't feel bad, though. The body often takes the rest it needs to heal."

Their banter ended when a man entered the room. The nurse turned to him and said, "Good morning, Dr. Menlow. Your patient is awake for once."

The doctor smiled. "Okay, everyone, give me a few minutes alone with this guy, and then if he can stay awake, you can have a good visit."

Kenneth and I moved out into the hall. He said, "Wow, it seems like things aren't as bad as we feared. I can't wait to hear what the doctor has to say."

We didn't have long to wait. Dr. Menlow joined us in the hall in about ten minutes. Even so, it had seemed like hours, and I couldn't wait any longer, so without even a greeting or introduction I said, "Doctor, what can you tell us about Jeff...Detective Crown's condition?"

He smiled as though familiar with impatient worried family and friends. "Normally I couldn't tell you much, but the detective has given me permission to tell you the details of his recent injury. Let me start by saying he is a very lucky man."

Looking at Kenneth he said, "The ambulance crew told me you administered first aid at the scene of the shooting. If so, he has you to thank for saving his life. The bullet went straight through but managed to break a rib and nick a major vessel. There should be no lasting damage, but if you hadn't slowed the bleeding, he would have bled to death before help arrived. As it is, he's lost a lot of blood, but in a couple of days he should be fine except for plenty of discomfort from the broken rib. It should heal just fine but will be painful while it heals." He'd barely finished speaking before it became obvious he was anxious to move on to the next patient, so we thanked him profusely and let him go.

Kenneth said, "Good news! The detective must lead a charmed life."

"If so, at the moment you must be the charm."

He gave me a funny look and then finally a big grin. Once we were allowed back into the room, we spent the next half hour bringing Jeff up to date and learning he would be allowed to go home the following day, but would have to stay away from work for another week. He seemed disappointed that he couldn't get right back to work, but assured us Detective Chambers was very good at his job and urged us to be careful until Claude was captured.

When we could tell he was getting sleepy again, we promised we'd be back the following day to take him home and took our leave. Outside, the policeman at the door said, "I've radioed the station and updated them on Jeff's condition. The guys at the station have gotten pretty close to him since he's been here, and there has been a steady stream of local cops coming by for information."

We thanked him for his thoughtfulness. I took a deep breath as I sank into the seat of the car. It was a relief to be back out in the sunshine.

Kenneth said, "Man, I hate hospitals. It's always such a relief to leave."

It was already three in the afternoon when we arrived back at Druthmar. With much of our worry alleviated, food seemed like a good idea, so we once again set a course for the kitchen. We were barely inside the door before Laudine was ushering us to the side table and hauling food. So far, I'd spotted fried chicken, potato salad, and a bowl of mixed fruit. Neither of us hesitated before filling heaping plates. I wanted to ask Laudine to tell us what had happened while we were gone, but I had a mouth full of food. Before I could speak, she demanded that we tell her all about Jeff's condition. Between bites, we told her what the doctor had said.

"That's excellent news. There isn't much going on here to report. The police have once again searched the whole campus, but no one suspicious has turned up. There is still no sign of Claude. He is either completely off campus or has somewhere to hide we haven't discovered. The police are working under the theory that Claude does indeed have a partner in the thefts, and the partner is probably the boss and the murderer. They think if they could find Claude, he would lead them to the partner, who probably is the one who has been dealing in stolen artifacts."

Still talking between bites, I asked, "Do they have any idea who the partner is?"

Laudine sighed. "They don't know yet, which is why they want Claude so badly, but Leroy has been missing since he supposedly went looking for the security team, and suspicion is beginning to lean strongly in his direction."

I nearly choked on my current mouthful of food. Kenneth and I looked at each other and pushed our plates away. The thought of one more friend being involved in murder had killed our appetites.

Kenneth said, "I certainly didn't see that coming. I know Leroy had problems with the board because of his sister's situation, but I honestly thought he loved this place and had its best interest at heart."

I didn't entirely agree with him. I wasn't willing to convict Leroy until the police had concrete evidence of his involvement.

Surprisingly, the next week passed almost normally. Jeff was back hanging around the college almost immediately, and I was sure he was there before the doctors wanted him to be. He looked thinner and paler, but refused to admit to any weakness.

Detective Chambers disappeared the day after Jeff returned, and I got hints he was probably Jeff's boss and didn't usually work in the field anymore, but no real explanation for his departure was ever given.

The college board sent one of their members to handle Leroy's duties until he was either found or replaced. They had also managed to find a replacement to take over Claude's classes. I had to admit Mr. Gilroy was an improvement and made the classes much more interesting, but I hadn't gotten to know him very well because he lived off campus and was never around except at class time.

During that week, I finally got a chance to go to the formerly empty library room and meet Dr. Loomis. From what I could tell, the books were in good hands, but the man himself wasn't especially friendly, so after a brief introduction I left him to his work. The books weren't part of my job, but I was glad they were being handled professionally.

The college and I both missed Leroy. The college seemed like a ship adrift, and I'd come to consider him a friend. Every day I hoped they would find him and get the situation straightened out one way or another, but according to Jeff, they weren't making much progress.

Jeff...what to say about him? He was still friendly, and we continued to discuss all things pertaining to the murders, but since he'd returned to duty, his behavior had held no hint of anything more than casual friendship. I had to admit to myself that I was hurt, and I spent more time than I should have wondering what had caused the change. Maybe eventually I would get the courage to ask him.

We'd kind of skipped over Thanksgiving because of all the turmoil, and it wasn't long until it would be Christmas, and then the end of the semester. The new atmosphere without Claude and Leroy, together with the changes in Jeff, left me feeling somewhat depressed, and I was considering going home at the end of the semester. I would be through with the collection by then, so I wouldn't feel like I hadn't fulfilled my contract. I needed to see how Laudine would feel about the idea, and intended to talk to her soon. They were so happy with her work she could easily stay if she wanted to, even if I left.

I decided it was time to see if the three-tiered bottle had any new wisdom for me. It hadn't volunteered so much as a flicker of color for days, so I picked it up and held it in my lap to see if I could force the issue. There were a couple of brief wisps of the lavender color I was used to seeing and then nothing. I sat still for quite some time, wondering if the bottle was losing its power or if something was off with me.

As I was about to set it back on the nightstand, I realized all three globes were swirling with, not the benign lavender, but with an almost black purple. I couldn't stop staring at the beautiful but angry-appearing patterns. Finally, I asked what it was trying to tell me. Again there was a long pause. When the bottle finally spoke, I was shocked. I don't know what I'd been expecting, but the disembodied voice certainly wasn't it.

It said, "Find Leroy! Find him now." I sat for a long time with the bottle in my lap trying to understand why I'd been given that message and hoping there would be more, but the deep purple disappeared as fast as the words and I received nothing else.

That evening after dinner I discussed the message with Laudine, but she didn't understand it any more than I did. She said, "It seems like if that darned bottle is going to give orders, at the very least it could also give some idea of why and how."

I understood her frustration, but said, "I agree that would be nice, but we know the bottle has its limitations. Maybe it gave me all it knew. I decided some time ago to trust what it told me. Now doesn't seem like the time to rethink that. There is no possible way I can think of to find Leroy, unless he's still somewhere at the college. I guess tomorrow I'll explore around some. I know the police have looked, but another pair of eyes can't hurt."

Laudine frowned, but all she said was, "You be careful. Bad things keep happening around here. If he is the murderer, he isn't going to be happy to be found."

By morning I was even more convinced that hunting for the college director was a waste of time, but I had extra time these days, so I would follow the bottle's instruction. I was determined that, if I were going to look, I would do the best job I could. By then, I had become very familiar with the college and had poked around most of the rooms and all the tunnels that had been discovered. The only place I hadn't explored was Sub A because it was supposedly unused due to water damage. I had poked my head into Sub B, but it really was just one big area with no place to hide.

Since my work space was in Sub C, I'd explored it thoroughly. Most of it was unused. I decided to start my search in Sub A if the water damage wasn't bad enough to make the place dangerous. It was the only area I could think of that might not have already been thoroughly searched.

I followed the hall until I came to the heavy wooden door to Sub A. I'd suspected it would be locked, so I had come prepared. I'd brought my set of lockpicks. I was no expert with them, but I had been practicing and thought I might be able to deal with the old locks down there. As it turned out, I didn't need either one. There was a sign on the door that warned everyone to stay out due to structural damage from water seepage, but the door was unlocked. That seemed strange, but made my access easier.

As I entered, I moved quietly and carefully. Until I discovered how bad the damage was, I intended to be cautious, and if Leroy were hiding down there, I didn't know how he would react if I found him. I was hoping to find some sign he'd been there so I could leave and send the police to investigate. I wasn't at all comfortable with the dank atmosphere and the smell of decay.

I couldn't risk turning on lights and didn't know if the electricity even worked, so I clicked on my flashlight. I checked the nearby walls and ceiling first. The water damage, though extensive, didn't yet seem to have compromised the structure. The walls were badly stained, appeared damp, and there was a pervasive smell of rot, but everything seemed solid. The atmosphere was creepy, but otherwise, so far so good. The layout here seemed to be identical to Sub C. I decided to tackle the furthest hall first, so I walked down to the turn, opening every door as I went. I took the hall all the way to the end and checked each room.

By the time I'd finished, I'd been there an hour and a half with nothing to show for it but a slight headache from the smell. I considered coming back the following day to explore the other long hallway. However, the thought of having to come back down there again convinced me to get it all over with today. Next, I wandered down the second hall, where the rooms were as empty and silent as the ones on the other side of the building. I found nothing interesting.

Eventually I reached the room that was located in the same place on this floor as the once-empty library room on Sub C where I'd found the tunnel behind the bookcase. I decided it deserved a closer look. Attached to the door I found a brand-new shiny hasp screwed to the frame. Through the loop there was a large screwdriver.

The only purpose for putting this on the door would be to keep something or someone inside. As quietly as possible, I pulled out the screwdriver, lifted the hasp, and opened the door. I could tell there were no bookshelves there, but I couldn't tell much else as the flashlight was getting dim. Without much hope it would work, I flicked the light switch and was surprised when the room lit up brightly. I walked a full circuit around the room, feeling the walls, but nothing seemed out of place. The floor was too wet to see footprints even if there had been any. Finally, I stood in the middle of the room looking each direction. On my third full circle, I thought maybe I could see a faint pattern on the wall that resembled the door on Sub C. I walked closer and traced the faint pattern with my hand. Feeling around somewhere in the middle of the pattern produced a distinct click.

Encouraged, I traced the rest of the pattern and then pushed on the wall. For a moment nothing happened and, disappointed, I was just turning to leave when a small section in the wall slid back and revealed another tunnel. I knew full well I should not enter. Turning the flashlight back on, I checked around inside the door, but there was no light switch. Standing still and listening intently, I heard nothing. Rationalizing away my fears, I told myself it wouldn't hurt to explore just a little way inside.

Not very far into the tunnel, I found a door. Once more, I calmed my fear with the hope of finding another stash of books or other artifacts inside, and shoved the door open. What the flashlight revealed caused me to make an involuntary noise that may have been considered a small scream.

I snapped off the flashlight and stood perfectly still. When after a few minutes, I didn't hear anything, I began searching around the door for a light switch. Again, I found nothing. Guided by the dim flashlight, I crept to the center of the room where I'd seen an unconscious Leroy tied to a metal chair. I knew that even if I untied him, I wouldn't be able to move him, but his labored, shallow breathing assured me he was alive.

Knowing I had to leave him, I took a moment to check that Leroy and I were alone. I knew I was taking a risk, but I turned and ran as fast as possible back the way I'd come. As soon as I was out of Sub C, I began calling for help. I didn't encounter anyone until I stumbled out of the elevator on the first floor. I must have still been calling out, because the door was barely open before Jeff came flying through the dining room door. I grabbed his arm and yanked him into the elevator, too out of breath to do more than to gasp, "Leroy, come, help."

To his credit, he didn't ask any questions. As the ancient elevator creaked its way down, he held my arm and told me to hush and catch my breath. I leaned against the elevator wall and did exactly that. Finally, we reached the room where I'd seen Leroy. I stepped back and let Jeff enter first. This time when I entered the room, I noticed how musty the air was and how bad it smelled. Jeff had turned on his bright flashlight and, I heard him curse softly.

He immediately pulled out his cell phone and cursed louder when he realized there was no reception down there. I was so relieved he was there to take over I wanted to sink to the floor. I felt both slightly faint and unbelievably tired. I think I actually groaned when Jeff said, "Here, take my phone and go back up until you get a signal and call for an ambulance." Forgetting how I felt, I grabbed the phone and sprinted for the door.

I managed to get a call to go through from Sub-level C, so I grabbed a bottle of water from my office and headed back to Jeff. I didn't know how long a person could live without water and didn't know how much, if any, food and water Leroy had been given, but he had been missing for a week and might be very dehydrated. I didn't see anyone going in either direction. When I dashed back into the room, Jeff had Leroy untied and lying on the floor. He wasn't moving, but I could see a faint movement of his chest so I knew he was still alive. "I brought some water. Do you think it's safe to try and get him to drink a little?"

Jeff glanced up and said, "I'm not sure, but we can wet his lips and try a drop or two to see how it goes."

I handed Jeff the water bottle and said, "I think I better go back up and wait outside for the ambulance. There isn't any way they could find this place without a guide."

"That makes sense, but Ali, don't tell anyone but the ambulance people what you've found or where you're going. Someone did this to Leroy, and they are still here somewhere."

"All right. Hopefully we'll be back here soon, but you be careful as well. It's possible whoever put him here may come back to check on him."

He nodded and gave me a smile before I headed back up to the main floor. It took less than half an hour for the ambulance to arrive, load Leroy, and race for the hospital with sirens blaring. At the time it seemed like hours to me. As soon as they left, Jeff called the station and arranged for a policeman to stand guard over Leroy's room. With that done, he reached out and pulled me close. It felt good to have his strong arms hold me. Without realizing I was going to say anything, I asked, "This feels so right. Why have you been so distant lately?"

He sighed, and I thought he might not answer but he said, "After what happened with Claude, I thought that associating with me was putting you in danger. I failed to keep you safe and I felt so guilty."

"I hope you realize how ridiculous that is. I'm a big girl and can get into plenty of trouble without your help."

That wasn't exactly what I meant to say, but he was smiling when he said, "Boy, isn't that the truth! You just can't keep away from trouble. I've decided instead of keeping my distance I had better just stick close to keep an eye on you."

Normally I would have taken exception to the implication that I couldn't look after myself, but the look on his face made it plain he was teasing me. I decided to accept it was just his way of telling me the distance between us was over.

He said, "Let's go upstairs, have some coffee, talk to Laudine, and decide what we need to do next."

It sounded good to me. I was definitely ready for a chance to sit and regroup. When we reached the kitchen, Laudine took one look at me and quickly led us to the table at the back of the room. In no time there were fresh coffee and danishes she'd baked that morning on the table. I surprised myself by realizing I was hungry. After the first cup of coffee, we revived enough to bring Laudine up to date on the most recent events. She listened to the whole story without interrupting. We swapped back and forth telling the story, and when we finished, she said, "Poor Leroy! All the time he was suffering down there, people have been suspecting him of being the killer."

"I know. It's horrible, and I have to admit, I couldn't help but wonder myself since the timing of his disappearance was so suspicious. Maybe the killer even had that in mind. I hope when he wakes up, he'll be able to tell us who kidnapped him. He may know the killer's identity."

Jeff said, "That would be the best case scenario, but at the moment I need to go to the station, because we need the right people out here to scour that room to see what evidence they can find. I appreciate the pick-me-up, Laudine. I'll talk with you both tonight to compare notes."

Once Jeff left and I had polished off a second danish, I headed upstairs to get cleaned up before taking off for the hospital. A light snow was falling, but nothing heavy was expected, so I wasn't worried about the drive.

Twenty-one

Leroy had been taken to the same hospital where they had treated me, Father Timmon, and Jeff. I asked the nurse manning the desk about his condition. She remembered me and was very friendly, but she couldn't really tell me anything helpful. He was in intensive care and the doctors were still with him. She sent me up to the third floor to the ICU waiting area and promised a doctor would come to talk with me when they finished assessing Leroy.

In the waiting room, there were several other people I didn't know. I was still very tired, even though the coffee and danish had helped, and I sank gratefully into a padded easy chair in the corner. I don't think I actually slept, but I was definitely in a vegetative state, because when the doctor walked through the door and called my name, the room was empty. A glance at my watch told me I'd been there for two and a half hours. I struggled out of my chair and met the doctor in the middle of the room.

He wore a very serious look, but the permanent lines in his face indicated he wore that expression habitually. I cleared my mind, held my breath, and waited for what he had to say. Almost immediately after he started talking, my breath whooshed out and I was flooded with relief. Leroy was dehydrated and tired. His feet would probably give him trouble for a while, but otherwise he was unharmed.

The doctor was optimistic his feet would heal completely, since the blood vessels seemed to be in remarkably good condition. Even the stern doctor gave a slight smile at my obvious relief. Leroy would only have to spend a night in the hospital. I wanted to visit him, but the doctor made it very clear his patient was sedated, needed rest, and would see no one until tomorrow, not even the police. There was nothing more I could do but thank him and promise to return in the morning.

I had just pushed open the door and walked out into the chilly sunshine when Jeff walked up with Tim close on his heels. I knew they wanted to find out what Leroy knew. "I hate to tell you, but the doctor says that no one, including the police, will be allowed to see Leroy until tomorrow."

"I was afraid that might be the case, but I wanted to come by anyway to see how he was doing. If I can't visit him, how about you give me a ride back to the college? I had Tim bring me over and my car is still at Druthmar. You can tell me how Leroy is doing on the way."

"You're more than welcome to the ride, but I think you'd better drive. I seem to be falling asleep on my feet. Hello, Tim. I understand you want to know what Leroy knows as much as anyone, but I'm afraid we're all going to have to wait until tomorrow."

"It looks that way. I hope when we do get to talk to him, he'll have information that will help us move forward."

As we walked off toward my car, I said, "You and Tim are certainly chummy these days. What's up with that?"

"Nothing is up exactly. We've come to a mutual understanding for now."

I couldn't get him to say anything else on the subject of Tim Ashley.

Back at the college, I made my excuses and went straight to my room for a nap. When I woke it was dark. I quickly checked my clock, hoping I hadn't missed dinner. I was starving, since the danish I'd had when we talked to Laudine was the only thing I'd eaten. I was surprised to find it was only five-thirty before I remembered the days were much shorter now that the season had changed, so it was getting dark earlier.

I hurriedly cleaned up and headed down to the dining room. Laudine's people served a fantastic beef stroganoff. Even though it was her recipe, I had to admire how well she had taught them. The flavors were full, rich, and perfectly blended. A light parfait had been created for dessert...I was way too full to even taste it. I hoped there would be a few left over so I could snack on one later. Jeff, Laudine, Kenneth, and I did talk briefly after the meal, but there was no new information to help us understand what was going on. I said, "You know, both professors were killed with a knife. We have only seen Claude use a gun. It will be interesting to hear what Leroy has to say when he wakes up. It seems likely to me there must be two people involved if one uses only a knife and the other's weapon of choice is a gun. Maybe it means nothing, but it is something to think about."

Laudine and I decided to make an early night of it. We weren't going to accomplish anything more tonight, and sleep seemed like a good idea. It was breakfast before I got to discover that last night's parfait had been strawberry-lemon and delicious.

The following morning started out as usual, but around ten-thirty I took a break and drove back to the hospital. I hoped Leroy was awake and remembered his time in captivity. I wasn't the only one who was curious, as I found Jeff and Tim already in the room when I arrived. The head of Leroy's bed was up, giving him the appearance of sitting, and the smile he gave me when I walked in went a long way toward reassuring me. I walked up to the bed and gave him a big hug. "I'm so glad to see you awake and looking more like yourself. We have been so worried."

"I hear I have you to thank for my rescue. I can't tell you how glad I am to be out of that room. You saved my life."

I couldn't say I had put all my energy into the hunt because the three-tiered bottle had told me to, so I said, "I'm just glad I decided to take a look around and that you're going to be fine."

As I stepped back from the bed, Jeff said, "To save Leroy having to go through the whole story again, I'll give you the highlights of what he remembers. Our suspicions were right...it was Claude who kidnapped him and locked him in that room. He took him at gunpoint, and the only person he saw the whole time was Claude. Claude gave him a small bowl of rice and a little water each day, but Leroy still got the impression that Claude was waiting for him to die. Claude had a gun he waved around a lot, but never a knife. None of that helps us much. It seems Claude was totally out of his mind. Leroy says he muttered to himself nearly all the time he was in the room. None of his ramblings made much sense, although a few times he seemed to mention a partner. At one point, he told Leroy he'd better hurry up and die or he was going to have to shoot him because "the boss" was getting impatient. I guess that kind of proves our two-man theory."

"So I take it there was no mention of a name or any hints that would help identify this boss person? I'm also guessing Claude didn't spill where this partner was hiding out?"

This time Leroy answered for himself. "No, there wasn't any information shared. Boy, I wish I could get my hands on that guy and shake some answers out of him.'

Both Jeff and I started to answer at the same time, but he deferred to me. "Leroy, thinking about revenge isn't a good idea. It will just land you in trouble. You need to let the police do their job."

I could see Jeff trying not to laugh, but all he said was, "Good advice." And then more quietly, "Too bad some people don't take their own advice."

I chose to ignore his sarcasm. At that point, the doctor came in and shooed us all out. I gave Leroy one more hug before leaving. He hugged me back and whispered, "Be careful!"

I drove back to the college feeling better. Jeff and Tim were hanging around until the doctor finished with Leroy so they could drive him back to Druthmar.

~ * ~

As the Christmas season continued to descend on the college, my mood picked up some. Jeff was looking more like himself, and things between us had gotten back to normal, or what I'd thought was normal before he'd been injured. The priest and I were nearly finished with the reliquaries. The catalogs were turning out to be both beautiful and informative. Having Leroy back at the helm was an added bonus. He was thinner and sometimes had a strange haunted look in his eyes, but he was there once again doing his job. Even knowing Claude was still out there somewhere, it was hard to stay depressed with all the glittering lights, greenery, and colorful decorations. The huge tree in the dining room looked and smelled fantastic. I knew Alex was responsible for most of the decorating, and he'd done a super job. I made a mental note to tell him so the next time I ran into him. I still hadn't talked to Laudine about leaving, but I'd decided we deserved a shopping trip to Canajoharie. We could pick up a few Christmas presents, and I could bring up my thoughts then.

On the day of our trip to town, Laudine and I were ready to leave early. There was still heavy frost on the ground, but no snow or heavy ice. We'd gotten lucky and the day was sunny with a predicted high of fifty degrees. For upstate New York that time of year, that was considered a balmy day. We were gradually getting used to cold weather, but I can't say either of us really liked it. The few light snows we'd had so far were beautiful coming down, but it wasn't long until what was on the ground was dirty slush or dangerous ice. I much preferred the sparkle of last night's ice storm that lingered this morning. I knew in another hour or two it would be gone.

Laudine and I had been taking pictures for when we were back in the desert. Today we'd captured sun rays shining through the ice-coated bare limbs of a huge tree causing each twig to sparkle. It seemed magical and gave a festive feel to our trip. During our drive we discussed who we wanted to buy gifts for, what they might like, and the best shops to check out. We decided to give separate gifts to Kenneth and Jeff and a joint gift from us both to everyone else. While we were shopping, we would also get our gifts for the people at home and get them in the mail. Laudine had a huge feast planned for Christmas day. Many of the off-campus staff and their families would attend. It would be an unusual Christmas for us, and I knew we would miss the small group of our friends at home that we considered family, but even so, we were looking forward to the celebration. Finally, I brought the conversation around to my thoughts about going home. I listed the pros and cons and then waited. She was quiet for so long I began getting worried. Finally, she said, "To be completely honest, I have been missing home and my work at the restaurant like crazy lately. A full school year seems a lot longer than it sounded when we arranged this trip. I haven't told you, but I'm hoping to buy the restaurant in Scottsdale. The owners want to sell, and I am close to having enough saved to buy it. I've been waiting to bring it up until I was sure it might really happen. If we leave, I can begin putting that plan into action."

"Oh, Laudine, you should have told me, I would love to lend you whatever you still need toward the price."

"I think that's part of the reason I haven't mentioned it. I wanted to prove to myself I could do this on my own. Now that I'm so close, I'm sure that once I own the building, I'll be coming to you for that loan to cover some remodeling and supplies to get up and running."

"This is so exciting and I'm so happy for you! This means we definitely need to get you home ASAP."

"Not really. The owners know my intentions and they want to sell to me. They've owned that restaurant a long time, and they want to be sure someone who loves it will be taking over. They will be as patient as I need them to be. A few more months isn't going to hurt anything. Besides, there are a lot of things I love about this place, and if you end up deciding to stay, I intend to stay with you. If you decide one semester is enough, then I'll be perfectly happy to go home with you. Either way will work out fine."

"Oh, great! Dump the decision on me." I was smiling as I said it and continued by saying, "We have several weeks left before we have to decide what we want to do, so for now, let's put things on hold and see how we feel when the time comes. With all the holiday excitement, there's a lot to enjoy here right now, and besides, I've never had a white Christmas."

"That works for me. I was being completely honest when I said that either way you decide is perfectly fine with me."

Laudine's plans for the future were exciting. Her news pulled me all the way out of the mood I'd been in and got me thinking about my own future. On a new high, we set out to enjoy our day. We managed all our shopping in record time and had another delicious Mexican meal. The only downside of the day was the "going out of business" sign on the door of the strange antique store. Even this had an upside as well, because all the merchandise was marked way down, making it possible for me to buy a ton of new high-quality inventory for Eclectic Treasures. I could only guess Jeff's bosses had realized the store was no longer necessary now that they had found the Egyptian antiquities.

After we ate, Laudine and I separated. I needed time to pick up her present, and I assumed she also wanted to do some private shopping. We agreed to meet at the kitchen store in an hour. I arrived a few minutes early. Laudine was already there, piling items onto the checkout counter. When I raised my eyebrows at the huge pile, she laughed and said, "Don't judge. It's not much worse than what you did at the antique store, and if we do decide to go home, it may be my last chance to pick up the things I want for the restaurant."

I smiled. "No judgment here. I just hope you're having all that shipped home, because I doubt there would be room for it on the plane."

The older woman behind the counter assumed I was seriously concerned and said, "Oh, yes, we're shipping it all to Scottsdale. Your friend has been such a good customer we aren't even charging her."

I was tempted to say, it might be cheaper for you to just hire a truck and drive all her purchases to Arizona, but I wasn't sure she would know I was kidding, so I turned to Laudine and said, "I don't know about you, but I'm worn out. Are you about ready to head back to the college?"

"Yes, yes, I definitely am, but I found the cutest coffee shop around the corner, so let's have a cup before we head home."

We sank into comfortable chairs in the quaint little shop, delighted with the smell of fresh-roasted coffee and baking pastry. It was past lunchtime and before dinner, so there weren't many other customers. Once we had our dark roast coffee and delicious looking cherry tarts, Laudine said, "You know, if we decide to go home at the end of the semester, that means leaving Kenneth and Jeff behind. I know we have to do it sometime, but I'm not looking forward to it. Somehow, though, I think it is going to be harder on you than on me. I like Kenneth and we have fun together, but in the long run I don't think he is the one for me. You and Jeff, on the other hand, seem like a very good match."

"Why don't you think Kenneth is for you? You two seem perfectly matched to me. I'll admit I've never understood why anyone so well-trained and capable has chosen to teach at such a small college, but I'm sure he has his reasons."

"I've never asked him that question directly, but I have wondered. From little things he's said, I think he did some hush-hush work for the government, and had a pretty traumatic experience. I've kind of assumed he's been hiding here while he recovers. That's not why I don't think things will work out long-term for us, though. Mainly I can't see myself wanting a long-distance relationship, and I'm not sure he's ready for city life yet."

"Makes sense, I guess. People say you can work out any problems if it's important enough, but I'm not sure that's true. When it comes to Jeff, I'll admit I like the man a lot, and as you may have noticed, he is very good to look at."

She laughed. "Oh, I've noticed. I imagine every female on campus has noticed."

"Very funny! Like I was about to say, I don't know how it would turn out if we had the time to find out, but like you, I don't think a long-distance relationship would be very rewarding. So if we leave sooner rather than later, it probably won't make any difference. I can't help remembering how my long-distance relationship with Nick worked out."

The following Monday, I had the final class of the semester. Since Claude's attack on me in the tunnel the day he'd shot Jeff, we'd had a substitute teacher. Mr. Gilroy had been the first substitute, but he had only lasted for two classes. I wasn't surprised when our permanent substitute turned out to be Dorothy Penn. That woman seemed to manage to insert herself into everything that happened on campus. What was a surprise was that she turned out to be an excellent teacher, seemed to know her subject matter in depth, and made the classes much more interesting than Claude or Gilroy. Even though I was looking forward to the Christmas break, I would miss the classes. I felt like I'd learned a lot and hoped that proved to be true when I took the final exam the following week.

Alex and Leroy seemed to have activities planned for nearly every day until Christmas. Saturday, a sleigh ride at sunset was scheduled. We were having perfect Christmas weather. It had snowed some every day since Laudine and I had made our trip to town. The snow on the ground wasn't horribly deep, but everything was covered in white. It was my first white Christmas season ever, and I was looking forward to it. It wasn't often that a desert rat got such an opportunity. Jeff and I planned to go, and Laudine had said she and Kenneth were also going.

When the time came to load the sleigh, there were twenty of us waiting at the place where Alex had said he would pick us up. I couldn't imagine how we were all going to fit, but the mystery was solved when Alex pulled up. He was driving a huge four-wheel drive tractor and pulling a sleigh big enough to hold at least half again as many as were in our group. It wasn't the horse-pulled sleigh I'd imagined from pictures I'd seen, but it looked like fun nonetheless.

We all piled in and found seats on the padded bench seating. The seats were arranged so everyone had a great view, and it felt like we were traveling through a fantasyland. We had bundled up so much and were seated close enough to each other that I wasn't even cold. The soon-to-set sun was reflecting off every ice crystal, so the whole world sparkled. It wasn't snowing at the moment, but more was predicted later that night.

We hadn't gone very far before we'd startled several rabbits and one large buck with a huge rack of antlers. I was thinking that even after I returned to Scottsdale, I needed to make the effort to get to Flagstaff a time or two during the winter to take advantage of the wonders a snowy world had to offer. I was totally relaxed and completely immersed in this new experience, and then someone screamed. I never did find out who, but almost before the sound had ended, Jeff was up and leaping over the side of the sleigh. He turned back long enough to holler for everyone to remain seated before sprinting to a nearby clump of trees.

I couldn't understand how he could move so quickly in the deep snow. I was still struggling out of the contentment I'd been feeling. It took a moment or two before my eyes spotted the dark shape staining the snow under the trees. Relaxation fled, and I groaned.

Jeff requested that Tim stay with him and sent the rest of us back to the college. There was no cell service this far out, so he tasked Alex with calling the station to explain what was needed when we got back in cell range. The sun set while we were still in the sleigh, but we never noticed because it was behind us and Alex had the bright lights of the tractor lighting the woods ahead of us. Laudine and I just looked at each other, and I knew we would soon be meeting in the kitchen to discuss tonight's events. I'd already had a good idea what was under the clump of trees, but just before the sleigh turned and headed back to campus, Jeff had leaned over and whispered, "It's Claude. You be careful till I get back."

Once we arrived at the college and everyone had gone off to their own spaces, Laudine and I did meet at what was becoming our discussion spot in the kitchen. For once, neither of us was hungry, but it wasn't long until we were warming our hands with cups of hot coffee. I told Laudine what Jeff had told me, but she was no more surprised than I'd been. She said, "I was afraid this would happen. Claude was obviously cracking under the strain of it all and if he had a partner as we thought, his partner couldn't take a chance on his being caught and spilling what he knew."

I agreed with her completely, but was frustrated that we were no closer than ever to figuring out who his partner might be. "Claude was willing to kill if he had to, but mostly it seemed like he got in over his head when the thefts began coming to light. Whoever his partner is had to be running things from the beginning, and he seems to have no problem committing murder. I have to say that if it is someone we know, he or she doesn't let their true character show. I find it impossible to imagine that anyone we know could be guilty, but even more impossible to think a stranger has been lurking around and has gone undiscovered all this time."

With nothing new to add to what we knew, we sat lost in our thoughts as we waited for Jeff to return. I don't know what Laudine was thinking, but I was hoping that this time the killer had left some evidence behind.

It was ten-thirty when Jeff and Tim joined us in the kitchen. They were both covered with snow that had started coming down wet and heavy about an hour before. We got them settled with towels and something hot to drink before asking them to bring us up to date. I still didn't trust Tim completely. I knew the least about him and his motives of anyone involved, but Jeff seemed to trust him completely. He made no objection to Tim remaining as he passed on what he knew so far. "There really isn't much to tell. We didn't find anything at the scene to help us identify the killer. I'm hoping the forensic boys will have better luck, but the killer has been too thorough to leave trace evidence behind in the past, and this new snow will complicate things."

Jeff and Tim agreed with our assessment of why Claude had been killed, but otherwise he seemed as frustrated as we were. They also looked exhausted, and it wasn't long before we all went our separate ways to try and get some sleep.

During the next few days, we found it hard to grieve for Claude after all the harm he'd caused, so as the days crept closer and closer to Christmas, the mood on campus once again returned to something resembling normal. Now and then I felt guilty enjoying the holiday festivities with the murders unsolved, but I reminded myself that I couldn't change the past. It was three days after Claude's death before we found out that, once again, no useful evidence had been left at the crime scene. A few hairs had been found, giving the lab a good DNA sample that might help identify the killer if we had a suspect, but we didn't, and no match was found in any database. At dinner that night, Jeff asked if we would all be willing to give a DNA sample to see if a match was found. Everyone was more than willing, but when the tests were done, none of us was a match.

Twenty-two

A few days before the date of my final exam in art history, Father John and I put the final touches on the reliquary catalog. I was able to send it and the one on the mourning jewelry off to an editor friend I knew would catch any grammatical errors we might have made. Father Timmon was planning to leave that same afternoon. During our last conversation, when I was thanking him for his help, he surprised me by saying he'd gotten a look at the statues that had been in the niches in the lower hall. The surprise wasn't that he'd seen them, but that it was his opinion I should get an expert to look at them, because he thought they seemed quite old and probably valuable. How valuable would depend on who had created them. I was shocked that I hadn't thought of that already. Had the thief and murderer thought of it yet? Maybe I could think of some way to use them to set a trap.

The next couple of days, I was busy reviewing for my test and didn't give much thought to anything else. When test day came, I felt fully prepared, and when it was over, I was cautiously optimistic that I had done well. It would be some time before I knew for sure, because the grades wouldn't be posted until after the Christmas break.

With my class ending and my job here completing, I knew I wanted to return to Scottsdale around the first of January. I didn't think I would be happy with just one class to attend. I hated to leave before the killer was caught, but there didn't seem to be much I could do to help anyway. Now that I'd made that decision, I made the time to explain my decision to Jeff. He understood how I felt, and admitted that as soon as the killer was found, he would be reassigned somewhere else. We agreed we wanted to keep in touch to see where our friendship led, but couldn't help being worried about a long-distance relationship. I knew that soon Laudine would be having the same conversation with Kenneth.

The night after the final, I began to relax and realized how tired I was. I had just crawled into bed early, anticipating a long peaceful night, when I noticed the dark purple, swirling clouds in the bottle. I dragged myself into a sitting position and picked it up from the nightstand. I almost dropped it when it began speaking immediately. Recently I'd gotten used to long pauses before anything happened. Once I had it safely in my lap, I caught up to what it was saying mid-sentence. "...and anything that valuable is bound to tempt the thief and murderer that still lurks around the college. I see danger for you and others connected to those statues. You need to be sure to use extreme caution during the remainder of your time at Druthmar."

I asked a few questions, but the bottle had nothing else to tell me, and as I set it back on the nightstand, there was no trace of the swirling purple mist. As I finally drifted off to sleep, my last thought was, first the priest and now the bottle. I definitely needed to give those statues some thought.

I began to form a plan for one last chance to unmask the murderer before returning home.

Once I was sure going home was the right decision, I called Barry to let him know Laudine and I would be returning. He seemed both relieved and happy. I'd been calling him fairly regularly to keep him up-to-date on my activities. Even though I had downplayed the events that had occurred, he had never come to terms with us being both so close to danger and so far away from home. Once more I tried to reassure him, wished him and Susan Merry Christmas, and promised to see him soon.

Next, I told Laudine of my plan to leave the first week of January. She seemed happy with the decision and promised she would be packed and ready. I didn't tell her about the plan I was contemplating. I knew if I did, one of two things would happen. Either she would do her best to talk me out of it, or even possibly tell Jeff, or she would insist on helping me. I wasn't willing to risk it either way. I could resist Barry's voice in the back of my head telling me not to put myself in danger, but I wasn't willing to put Laudine in harm's way.

I had a feeling the killer was one of the people living on campus. I didn't have any real proof to support this, but I trusted my instincts. In spite of the DNA tests, which I suspected could be altered or faked somehow, the killer knew too many things that people not there full-time didn't know. I was banking on the fact that the killer had been so busy concentrating on the Egyptian antiquities and the items stolen from the college they hadn't realized the statues might be valuable. I knew it was possible because I had done it myself. My idea was to wait until after Christmas, somewhere around the twenty-seventh, then pick a time when everyone was present at dinner and announce that the next afternoon, I was going to spend a few hours studying the statues to determine their value. I would hint strongly that I thought they might be worth a great deal of money. Then all I would have to do was watch the statues and see who came snooping around. Any one of the group might be curious, but only one would want to move them somewhere hidden. I would keep this plan to myself until I found out who tried to steal them. I didn't know how Jeff would react if I told him what I planned to do, but I knew he would help once I had some proof. Until then, I had a few days to work out exactly how to proceed.

The next couple of days passed in a whirl of holiday gatherings. There were parties most nights, and Leroy held afternoon open houses for different groups like the college alumni, all the professors and assistants, and even one for students who remained on campus through the holidays. They were all catered, with added goodies from Laudine and her staff, and I was sure I was gaining weight at an alarming rate. Then, almost before I was ready, it was the last night before our big Christmas Eve celebration and then a sumptuous Christmas Day dinner.

Since there would be a ton of people attending the Christmas Eve party from both on and off campus, we decided to wait until Christmas morning to exchange gifts. The dinner that day would just be for the people who lived or worked at the college. I was eager to give Laudine her present. I felt sure the symbolism between the gift and her new status as a restaurant owner would please her. I was a little less sure about the gift I'd chosen for Jeff. It was hard to choose a gift for a man you had feelings for but hadn't known very long. I'd have to wait until Christmas morning to see if he liked it. Ironically, Laudine had chosen an antique book about mathematics for Kenneth, and I had gotten a "how to" authentic Mexican cookbook for Jeff. I knew he loved to cook when he got the chance and remembered him mentioning how he loved Mexican food but didn't understand its preparation. They weren't typical gifts, but I thought they would both like their books.

Christmas Eve I spent the day helping Laudine and her staff prepare for that night's party. This time she had insisted there be no catering. She was determined to do all the food herself. Since we were leaving in early January, she wanted to do one last thing for the friends and colleagues she had made there.

The party that night was a huge success. I knew there would be a crowd, but more people showed up than I'd ever imagined. I think everyone had a great time. We all probably drank a wee bit more than we should have, which may have contributed to all the dancing, singing, and all-around merriment. Laudine had prepared plenty of goodies of varying types, and I was sure everyone found something they found delicious to eat. I think we were all glad of a chance to celebrate after all the awful things that had happened during the semester.

Christmas morning started at eight with Laudine's special pastries, coffee, and gift giving. I had gotten Laudine an antique whimsical chatelaine. It was fourteen karat gold with a decorative sterling silver spoon, fork, and ornate wine-tasting cup attached by short, intricate chains to the jeweled belt clip. I watched her opening the package, hoping my friend would like my choice. The best gift I received that morning was the way her eyes lit up when she saw it. She was watching just as closely as I opened her gift to me. I couldn't believe my eyes when I saw the perfect pair of antique lusters she'd gotten me. I had been looking for just the right ones for my fireplace mantel for a long time. These were twelve inches tall with a double ring of crystals on a bronze base. When I lifted one out of the box, it immediately caught the light and reflected colored sparkles around the room. They were exactly what I'd been looking for. She must have known how thrilled I was, because when I looked over at her she was smiling. I couldn't resist hurrying over to give her a big hug along with my heartfelt thank you.

This smaller group of just the people living on campus had come to be like a family. Even though I missed the people from home, I was happy to be there. Everyone seemed thrilled with the gifts they'd received, and I was especially glad to see Jeff smiling as he leafed carefully through his book. Laudine and I were both surprised and pleased by the thoughtful gifts we received. Kenneth had gotten Laudine a beautiful embroidered chef's apron. The workmanship was superb, and the whole apron looked like a spring garden. Jeff had gotten me a rare first edition book on the earliest American Indian antiques. I knew I would enjoy reading it in detail at my first opportunity.

There are really no words to describe the meal Laudine and her staff had prepared for us. I knew there was no one at the table that would ever forget that Christmas dinner. For meat we had goose, turkey, and prime rib. There wasn't a single side dish I could think of that wasn't on the table, and there were plenty more that were new to me. The huge variety of desserts was beautiful, but I don't think anyone found out how amazing they tasted until later in the day when they finally managed to make enough room to try them. Once we'd eaten, everyone pitched in to clean up, and we refused to allow Laudine to do a single thing. As we packed up the mountains of leftovers, I asked her what would happen to them if we couldn't eat them all. She just laughed and said, "You aren't going to get the chance to eat any of them. This afternoon Alex is delivering them to the Eastgate Nursing Home facility in town. It will be their evening meal."

They had no idea what a treat they had in store. When we had her kitchen shipshape once more, I'm pretty sure I wasn't the only one who opted for a nap.

It was almost eight before I woke. I wasn't starving, but I knew it would be some time before I could sleep again, so I made my way down to the kitchen to see what everyone was up to. I wasn't surprised to find Leroy, Alex, Jeff, Kenneth and Laudine gathered around our usual table at the back of the kitchen. The table was loaded with food, and each person was munching on something different. I had planned to skip supper, but couldn't resist a prime rib sandwich slathered with stout homemade horseradish. That with a small spoon of sweet potato casserole and a few plump green olives was all I could handle. Well, that and a piece of pumpkin pie with sweet whipped cream. While we nibbled, Laudine and I explained that we would be returning to Scottsdale the second week of January. I think they were genuinely sorry to hear we were leaving, but seemed to understand when Laudine told them about her restaurant plans. We must have just talked for three hours or so, and for once we talked about everything but murder. Things like our pasts, our futures, and our lives away from the college. These were good people and I would miss them. I made sure they all knew if they were ever out west, I expected them to spend as much time as they could with me. Laudine extended the same invitation. When I finally got to bed around midnight, I surprised myself by going right to sleep.

The next day we were all pretty lazy and I don't think much got accomplished. The following day, things began going back to normal. The mail brought me a sample copy of both the mourning jewelry and reliquary catalogs so I could proofread them one last time before printing. I spent the day working on that and also began to compile a list of people to mail the finished catalogs to that I hoped would be interested in making purchases. The college planned to take advance sales for a month and then auction off what was left.

Twenty-three

By December 27th, the campus still twinkled and glittered with the Christmas decorations, as they wouldn't come down until after the new year, but otherwise seemed very peaceful. The bulk of the students were still out on break. With no classes being taught, many of the professors weren't around either. Only our small group that lived on campus was still maintaining a daily routine. Even we were very laid back compared to normal. That night when everyone turned up for dinner seemed like a perfect time for me to put my plan into action. Ten or so minutes into the meal, I said, "You know, Leroy, I've been thinking. We haven't paid much attention to the statues that were discovered in the tunnel. Too much else has been going on, but I have a feeling they are very old and possibly very valuable."

Glancing around the table, I saw I had everyone's attention, so I continued. "I think it would be a good idea for me to go down there, look them over well, and take some pictures. Once I have pictures, I can do more research and send the pictures around for some expert opinions. I'm tied up with the catalogs for the next two days, but then I would have plenty of time to take a look. What do you think?"

When I finished, Laudine and Jeff were giving me an are-you-nuts look, but Leroy's reaction was just what I expected. He smiled and said, "I should have thought of that sooner. With all that's been going on, I haven't been as sharp as I should be. It would be great to find out who made those statues and what they're worth. If you have the time, I would greatly appreciate your taking a look. The one time I saw them, I remember thinking how detailed they were. If nothing else, they should be in our small museum in the archaeology building. I'll look forward to hearing what you think."

I tried to avoid Laudine and Jeff on the way to my room, but they weren't about to let me escape so easily. When I walked into the creaky elevator, they both walked in directly behind me. Laudine said, "Trying to run away, are you? I think the three of us need to have a little chat up in our room."

I couldn't help laughing. "I knew you guys would catch up with me eventually, but I was hoping to buy a little time for you to cool down."

Neither of them laughed, but I could see that Laudine, at least, was fighting hard not to smile.

We were silent the rest of the ride, but were no sooner in the room with the door closed before Jeff said, "What is the matter with you? Do you like having people shoot at you?"

"Now you're exaggerating. Besides, so far the killer has only ever used a knife."

"Now you're just being ridiculous!"

"Okay, try to withhold your judgment for a moment while I explain what I have in mind. I really have no desire to tangle with a killer, but I have a plan that should avoid that."

I needed to explain my plan in a way that would satisfy my friends about my safety. Without their cooperation, I didn't think I would be able to pull it off. I took a deep steadying breath and said, "I know we all want this killer caught. This is probably the only chance for that to happen before Laudine and I head for home. We know the killer is also a thief, so it seems reasonable that he or she would want to know if the statues are valuable. We should be able to set up cameras to record the area around the statues. Anyone here might be curious enough to poke around, but the thief would want to evaluate them and decide if there were a market for them. They would probably try to hide them away until they could sell them. Anyone showing a real interest should generate enough suspicion to allow the police to see if they match any or all of the forensic evidence that's been collected at the crime scenes. I can monitor the cameras from the safety of my own office and call Jeff and the police if anyone shows up. What do you think?"

Jeff said, "Two things. This is the first time you have mentioned the possibility that the killer could be a woman. Do you really think that's a possibility?"

"No, but stranger things have happened. I don't want to limit our expectations in any way."

"Okay, second thing. If we were to agree that your plan might work, why not bring in the police and let them monitor the cameras? That way they would already be on-site when they were needed."

"I thought of that, but so far the killer has always been one step ahead of everyone. I'm sure any extra police on campus would alert him to the fact that something was up. After all that's happened, I can't see him taking any chances unless he feels completely safe in doing so."

Laudine said, "It all sounds pretty safe to me. Even Ali should be safe since the killer has two days to check out the statues before she plans to examine them. Jeff, you should be able to get the cameras we need. They need to be small enough that we can hide them. If the killer is going to take the bait, he should act in the next two days. We can all take turns monitoring the cameras so Ali isn't stuck watching them twenty-four-seven."

We spent another hour discussing the plan, but in the end, they turned my plan into a joint effort, which hadn't been my original plan. I had to admit that once the plan became a reality, I was glad my friends were going to help. Jeff surprised us by admitting he already had three cameras on hand. They were ones that had been in the antique store before they had closed it. He swore they were tiny, and I was sure they would work, because I'd certainly never noticed them in the shop. We decided to set them up immediately in case the killer chose to examine the statues later that night. Jeff would be the one to install the cameras, and Laudine would take the first watch. Jeff could relieve her in the morning and I would take the following night's watch. With just three of us, they were pretty long shifts, but the monitors were set up to ding when the cameras were activated by movement. This way we could at least relax and maybe even doze a little while we were on duty. We all agreed this was a plan to watch only. At the first sign of anyone poking around the statues, we would report to Jeff and he could call in anyone he thought would be needed. We decided to set up the monitors in the empty library room instead of my workshop, since we couldn't be sure who might wander into my workroom to visit.

Jeff left to install the cameras immediately, and Laudine went to change into something comfortable and rest until time to begin. I headed to the kitchen to have coffee and run all the details of our plan through my mind to check for flaws one last time. Those quiet moments were not to be, though, because Leroy, Alex, and Kenneth were already ensconced at what we now thought of as our table. I joined them, happy to spend time with them while I still could. Right away, Leroy wondered where Laudine and Jeff were. I explained that Laudine was tired and had decided on a nap and that I had no idea about Jeff. I implied he probably wasn't even on campus. I felt bad keeping secrets from my friends, but we had promised to tell no one. I knew the fewer people who knew what we planned the better. It seemed impossible any of these people could be a killer, but someone had committed the murders.

Twenty-four

When I got to bed, I fell asleep immediately, but for some unknown reason I woke up at 1 a.m. I didn't think I'd be able to get back to sleep, and I felt bad about the long shift Laudine was spending watching the camera feed. There was no reason I couldn't take over until Jeff began watching in the morning, so I quietly made my way to Sub-level C. Laudine seemed happy to be relieved, and wasted no time in sneaking upstairs for some sleep. No one had shown up on camera during Laudine's time on watch, and my shift was equally quiet. I had hoped to discover the killer's identity the first night and was disappointed, but not yet discouraged.

Jeff was surprised to see me when he showed up for his morning shift but had no problem with us breaking up the shifts into shorter segments.

Jeff had brought coffee and fresh donuts when he arrived, but after my abbreviated sleep I needed something more substantial for breakfast, so I left him to his watching and headed upstairs.

Laudine wasn't in the kitchen when I arrived, but her staff was so well trained by then that meal preparation was running smoothly and on schedule. I filled a plate with two poached eggs, bacon, fresh fruit, and even added a chocolate-frosted donut before sitting at a table with Leroy and Alex. I knew they would probably have questions I couldn't answer, but I couldn't avoid them without raising more awkward questions. Sure enough, I'd just taken my first bite when Alex said, "What, all on your own? No buddies today?

I laughed. "You make us sound like Siamese twins. I was doing a little early work downstairs, but for once I got hungry."

Leroy said, "I wonder where the good detective and our illustrious cook are? They're usually around this time of the morning."

Still smiling I said, "Well, I can answer for Laudine, because I know she was up late grading papers last night and she was still asleep when I left our room. As for the detective, I have no idea. Maybe for once his work kept him from getting here in time for breakfast."

Alex mumbled, "Sounds likely" around a mouthful of bacon. From there, conversation settled down to normal chitchat, and I relaxed and enjoyed the food.

Laudine put in a brief appearance around eleven before going to take over from Jeff so he too could have a shorter session. These shorter times watching the camera were working out better than the longer shifts we had originally established.

I intended to spend the afternoon doing some last-minute work down in the workroom, but I'd only been down there about an hour when I realized I could barely keep my eyes open. If I were going to be any good at tonight's watch, I had to take a nap. I'd barely made it to my bed before I was sound asleep. When I woke, the room was darker than when I'd fallen asleep, but not dead-of-night dark. When I glanced at my tablet to check the time, I saw it was still early. Perfect. I could grab some dinner and then take over for Laudine in time for her to get some supper. It wasn't until I sat up that I noticed that the ominous dark purple color was swirling up the bottle's three tiers. I picked it up, hoping the voice would tell me why it was agitated, but even though I held it for a full ten minutes, nothing happened. Finally, I sighed, put the bottle back on the dresser, and went down to eat.

The meal was as wonderfully prepared as always, but I didn't have much of an appetite. I spent a little time being social, and then went down to relieve Laudine in the old library. I knocked on the room's door in the pattern we'd agreed on, but got no answer. After pounding a few more times, I got worried and went back to the workroom to get my lock picks. I was still learning how to use them and wasn't really good with them yet, but the locks down there were old and uncomplicated. Even so, it took me almost ten minutes to get in. The whole time I worked, I didn't hear any sound from inside, and being so worried for Laudine didn't help me keep my hands steady for lock picking. When I finally got the door open and walked in, I found Laudine with earphones on as she conscientiously watched the monitor and swayed back and forth to whatever music she was listening to. I didn't know whether to hug her or throttle her.

My movement must have caught her eye, because she looked up, removed her ear phones, and said, "Hello. I hope you're here to begin your shift, because I'm starved. Hey, how did you get in here? I'm positive I locked that door when I came in."

In the relief of finding her alive and well, I sank into one of the chairs at the table where she was sitting and said, "I got in by picking the lock."

Laudine gave me a strange look, and I realized I must have sounded harsher than I'd intended. She said, "Why didn't you just knock, or were you just wanting to practice with your picks?"

For some reason, her answer struck me funny, and I laughed and said, "Oh, I knocked, and then I knocked some more. Do you want to see my bruised knuckles as evidence?"

She got a stricken look before saying, "Oh, God! I didn't hear you because of the headphones. I am so sorry. I didn't realize they blocked sound so well."

"Oh, no problem. You only took ten years off my life and gave me a reason for a couple of weeks of nightmares."

She looked like she were about to apologize again, but by then I was laughing so hard she just stared at me for a moment and then burst out laughing herself. When we finally got control of ourselves, she said, "This really isn't all that funny!"

I gave one more chuckle and said, "You're probably right, and yes, I am here to relieve you. If you hurry, you can still get a hot meal. I think Jeff will probably be along sometime between twelve or one, so I'll be back to our room then. Since you haven't called us or the police, I take it there was no activity during your shift."

"Well, actually both Alex and Tim went by and looked at the statues, but they didn't seem very impressed and made no effort to move them. I figure that if nothing more incriminating happens, the police can always talk to them later. We will have the recording from the cameras for evidence. If I'd called the police and they were just curious lookers, it would have alerted the real thief to our plan. Besides, it stands to reason people would be curious."

I had to agree with her reasoning. Once she'd gone, I picked up the headphones to see what she'd been listening to. I was surprised to find her choice had been seventies rock music. At the moment, Credence Clearwater Revival was singing "Proud Mary." No wonder she hadn't heard me knock. Not wanting to be distracted, and thinking I should stay alert for any outside noise, I turned off the music and removed the headphones. Then, settling back, I watched the monitor, and nibbled the almonds I'd brought for a snack. I knew this was the last night for the killer to check out the statues before I'd said I would be looking at them. That alone was enough to keep me on edge and awake. My mind kept running through the preparations we'd made, looking for flaws and hoping we had all the details right.

When several hours had passed and nothing had happened, I began to think our last ditch effort to unmask a killer wasn't going to work. It would only be a couple of hours until Jeff came to take over the watch. If nothing happened on his watch, I didn't think the killer would take our bait. As I was wondering if there was anything else we could do before we left, there was a knock at the door. It was the knock pattern we had agreed on, but I wasn't taking any chances so I asked who was there before unlocking the door. When I heard Laudine's voice, I relaxed and let her in. She was carrying a coffee pot and two cups. "What's up, Laudine?" I asked. "You already did your stint for today."

"I know, but I couldn't sleep wondering what was happening, and I know the last couple of hours of a shift are the worst, so I thought I'd bring some coffee and keep you company."

"Both the coffee and the company are welcome. I was just sitting here thinking that if something didn't happen soon, this whole thing would be a bust. I tried to think of something else we could try before we leave, but I came up completely blank."

"I know how much you must hate to leave a mystery unsolved, but we really are out of time. We're scheduled to leave the college in two days, and I can't think of anything else we could do during such a short time."

I caught myself sighing before saying, "Before I came down here tonight, an ominous purple color was swirling in the bottle. I've gotten the idea that when I see that color it means danger or trouble of some sort. After seeing that, I was sure something would happen tonight, but it hasn't. I'm disappointed we couldn't do more, but I guess we did the best we could."

I'd no more than finished the sentence before we heard a grinding noise and the section of the bookcase hiding the tunnel opened. Leroy stepped into the room closing the opening behind him. I was surprised because he shouldn't have known we were here, but not overly worried, at least not until I saw the gun in his hand. With a confused look, Laudine rose from her seat at the table as I said, "What's going on, Leroy? Has there been some kind of trouble?"

As I took a good look at him, I became more concerned. He was dressed in Levis and a dark sweatshirt. I couldn't remember ever seeing him in casual clothes, but my concern came from the look on his face. His features were twisted into what seemed like regret and determination. When he spoke, he left no doubt we were in serious trouble.

His left eye was twitching and his voice was devoid of expression as he said, "Well, look at this. I have both the troublemakers in one room together, and I have them all to myself."

Without another word, he fired the gun and a deafening boom echoed around the room. I felt no pain and immediately looked over at Laudine. She seemed fine. Looking back at Leroy, I realized the gun was pointed at the wall, not at us.

Leroy said, "That was your only warning. I'm in charge here. Regretfully, I'm going to have to kill you both. I've tried to find a way to avoid that, but you just won't stop meddling. I don't want to shoot you, but even though I have guns, I will if I have to. I can assure you I much prefer a knife."

This seemed like the same Leroy we'd known for months. His tone sounded normal and it seemed impossible he was saying such awful things. I wasn't sure if it was safe to speak or not, but I had questions and if I could keep him talking long enough, maybe Jeff would show up in time to save the day. So I said, "Leroy, tell us why. I was so sure you loved your work and the college. Why the thefts and murders?"

He must have wanted to talk, because the gun drifted down a little and his expression became thoughtful. I'd just begun wondering if I could reach the gun before he could raise it and fire, but even as I had the thought, he steadied the weapon directly on me before saying, "You always think you're so smart. You should have it all figured out by now, but as it turns out, I guess you're not as smart as you think you are."

Without any warning he fired the gun again. I emitted a small scream, and Laudine fell to her knees. Leroy said, "That little wound won't kill her if you keep pressure on it so she doesn't bleed to death. Keeping her alive should keep you occupied while for once someone hears my side of the story."

It was surreal how calm he seemed. Except for what he was saying, he seemed just as he always had. I yanked off the over-sweater I was wearing and hurried to my friend's side. Once I had her stretched out on the floor, I realized he was right. The wound wouldn't kill her unless she bled out. The bullet had passed through the upper part of her left arm and was bleeding profusely. I wrapped the cotton sweater around Laudine's arm and put pressure on both sides.

With a casual smile, he said, "That should keep you busy so I don't have to wonder what you might do next. Oh, and if you're hoping to keep me talking long enough for Jeff to show up, I should tell you he is otherwise occupied with problems of his own."

My hopes of rescue plummeting, I felt panic clawing at my mind. What if he had already killed Jeff? No, I couldn't think about that now. I tried slowing my breathing in order to get control of my emotions. I had to think of some way to keep Laudine safe.

Still in the calm conversational tone, he said, "In answer to your question, I did once love my work at the college. It seemed like the perfect job for me, and I was good at it. In the beginning, I gave it all my attention. Then my sister began showing signs of the disease that would soon take over her life. When the college refused to let me house her here so I could keep an eye on her, I chose to disregard their decision and house her up in Building Five. When her medical expenses began to get out of hand, I asked for a raise. The board turned me down. I didn't know why, because I knew they had plenty of money. It was then to cover the mounting bills that I began taking a few items from Building Six.

"The college received more valuable donations and its investments grew at a fantastic rate, but I still received no raise. It wasn't long after I brought my sister here that her condition worsened to the point that she couldn't take care of herself, and I couldn't always watch her, so I hired Leonard. I quickly realized he was the perfect solution, because he was a great caregiver and also a crook. I watched him begin stealing small items from the things stored in Building Six. He never took a lot, and there was no way for him to get caught unless I reported him, and I didn't care. He would have been a convenient scapegoat if anyone had ever noticed the missing items."

Leroy paused to check his watch, mumbled something about plenty of time before his plane left, and continued his story.

"This kept us afloat for a while, but Leonard's salary, combined with the rising medical costs, soon drove me to want more high-dollar items to sell. The perfect opportunity presented itself when Professor Castille mentioned how much collectors would pay for items, no matter how they were obtained. He was lamenting the fact that he didn't have any Egyptian artifacts to sell them. He swore he knew several collectors that would buy anything. He tried to make it sound like he was kidding, but I knew I could use him. I carefully recruited him to round up the collectors while I went to work setting up a system to find the items and have them shipped to the college. When we had enough valuable items, we would hold an auction. The first one was so successful we kept the system going. While we accumulated enough for an auction, we hid all our items among the stuff stored in Building Six. So you can see I just didn't have any choice. I had to take care of Beth."

Curiosity got the best of me, so I asked, "If Professor Castille was helping you, why did you kill him?"

Leroy frowned at my interruption and I held my breath, but finally he answered. "Greed, of course. When he saw how much we made at the first auction, he wanted a bigger share than we'd agreed on. I'd been letting him stay in one of the unused dorms over the summer so no one would know he was on campus, so when I didn't really need him anymore, it was easy to get rid of him. I had no choice. He forced me to take action by demanding money I wanted for my sister. Then his replacement in the archaeology department complicated things by finding a detailed list of the numbered places where we were hiding the stolen items. Stupid Castille had left it in his desk in the archaeology office. Hillman was smart and the list was very thorough, so he had a pretty good idea what the list meant. Unfortunately, his solution was to do the honorable thing. Right away he came to me with his suspicions. I assured him I would handle it. I hoped that would be the end of it, but of course it wasn't. He kept stopping by my office asking what the police were doing with the list. I could tell he was getting suspicious. When I was sure he was going to go to the cops on his own, I knew I had to kill him. So you see, just like Castille, it wasn't my fault Professor Hillman had to die. He forced me to do it."

Leroy stood quietly for several minutes. I didn't like the look in his eyes that said, 'I'm done talking now and it's time to kill you.'

So I asked, "That explains the first two killings, but why did you kill Claude? It seems like he was helping you."

He laughed and said, "That's right, keep me talking. Keep hoping for that rescue that isn't coming. Oh well, I might as well tell you. I have a few minutes before I need to leave for the airport, and my car is parked right outside, packed and ready to go."

I couldn't believe he still sounded like the Leroy I had known for months. His tone was conversational. He seemed to believe he was just a good guy that had been forced to make bad choices.

"Claude was an idiot! Even knowing Castille had been my partner and I had killed him, he thought I was going to make him rich. He might have lived a little longer if he could have stopped himself from using that stupid noisy gun he had. There is a time and place for a gun. A time like now, but most kills are done much better with a knife. I tried to tell him, but he just couldn't keep a low profile so we could continue to work under the radar. I knew sooner or later he'd be caught, and there was no doubt in my mind he'd give me up to help himself. As soon as I'd proved my innocence with the kidnapping stunt, he had to go. The dumb fool never saw it coming. Once again, I just didn't have any choice. I kept having these decisions forced on me."

While he'd been talking about Claude, I'd seen movement on the far wall. Slowly the bookcase had moved back into the wall, leaving the tunnel wide open. I was scared to death Leroy would notice, but he was too deep in his thoughts and enjoying the sound of his bragging voice telling us how clever he'd been. I held my breath, expecting Jeff to walk into the room at any moment. I hoped he'd hurry because I was pretty sure this time Leroy was through talking.

He proved me right when he said, "Sorry, ladies, that's all the time I have for sharing. I'm off to the airport, but I'm not leaving the two of you alive to tell tales. If you aren't alive to tell them about me, they just might think the killer got me, too. I never wanted to kill anyone, but at this point, two more won't make any difference. It actually does get easier each time, and I've gotten pretty good at it."

It seemed he was going to forego his pleasure with the knife and shoot us after all. He had begun to raise the gun when Alex Walsh walked out of the tunnel and said, "Sorry, Leroy, but I'm afraid you aren't going to be able to make that plane."

Leroy spun around to fire at Alex. I jumped to my feet immediately, thinking that if Alex went down, I would tackle Leroy. He was slightly bigger, but also older. I might have a chance to take him down. I had underestimated Alex, though, because Leroy was only halfway turned when Alex fired. Leroy fell sideways, dropping his gun. I knew he wasn't dead from all the whining he was doing. I quickly kicked the gun out of his reach.

Almost immediately, EMTs began running out of the tunnel entrance. I was nearly overwhelmed by all that had happened, but fear for Laudine was my prime concern and kept me from falling apart. I heard someone say the police would soon arrive. Evidently Alex had only requested an ambulance with his original call. He hadn't given a reason, so the police hadn't been notified until a little later. While the EMTs put Laudine on a stretcher and got her outside to the ambulance, I hugged Alex. I relaxed a little as he whispered that Jeff was okay, but as soon as she was loaded, I climbed into the back of the ambulance and sat next to Laudine. Multiple police cars were arriving as we drove away. It was the following evening back at our usual table in the kitchen before I found out all the details of what had happened after we'd left for the hospital.

~ * ~

When Laudine and I walked in together, the three morose men at the table all jumped up. Jeff, Alex, and Kenneth all began asking questions at once. Laudine held up her arm that wasn't heavily bandaged and said, "Let's all sit down. You have questions, and we definitely have a bunch, too. Before we get started, let's see what the staff has in the way of goodies to munch on." The guys laughed but sobered quickly when Laudine gave them a look and said, "Hey, you guys try eating hospital food for a day before you criticize!"

I said, "Okay, food it is, but this time, Laudine, you sit still and I'll see what's available."

While I gathered up a snack, everyone questioned Laudine about her injury. She happily explained it was just a flesh wound and she was sore but fine. It wasn't long until I had the table stacked with a variety of cheeses, crackers, and fruit, along with a lemon meringue pie. When Laudine was happily munching away, I said, "Alex, why don't you start by bringing us up-to-date on what happened before you arrived on the scene?"

"We'll get to that, but first I should let Jeff tell you what happened to him, since that was the beginning of events."

"Okay, I'll go first, but I hate how lame it makes me look. Knowing it was the last night for the thief to get to the statues, I should have been more prepared. I think I had pretty well decided he wasn't really interested in them and Ali's idea wasn't going to work. Even so, I should have been more prepared. I'd decided to go down to the room a little early to relieve her. Those surveillance sessions got pretty tiresome by the end, and I knew Ali would be glad for company.

"I'd just started down the hall when something hit me from behind. It must have been quite a blow, because I blacked out right away. When I came to, I was tied up in one of the niches we assume were originally made for the statues. I had no idea how I'd gotten there. I was frantic, because I knew the tunnel led right to the room where Ali was, and I didn't have any idea how much time had passed. I was barely awake when Alex found me.

He'd gotten curious about what he called our strange comings and goings. When he saw Leroy go into the tunnel, he decided to follow. Not far inside, he discovered me. Somehow, he'd missed seeing Leroy drag me into the tunnel. When he found me, I was just waking. He untied me, but I was still pretty out of it. Alex sprinted far enough back up the tunnel to call nine-one-one. He returned quickly. It was obvious something bad was going down, so I gave Alex a quick explanation and my gun. I was sure I had a concussion, because I couldn't even stand up straight, let alone go after Leroy. Alex immediately took off running for the old library room. Using the wall for support, I slowly tried to follow. I must have passed out again somewhere along the way, because the next thing I knew, the EMTs were there putting me on a stretcher. The rest of the story is Alex's."

I interrupted, "And what did the doctors at the hospital say?"

"I must have a hard head, because I got off with just a mild concussion and a large goose egg. While I was there, I heard Laudine had been shot, but they wouldn't let me see her, so I came back here to wait for news. Alex arrived back from the police station at about the same time."

Alex picked up the story. "When I left Jeff, I ran all the way down the tunnel to the opening behind the bookcase. I was terrified the noise of opening the door would be heard by anyone inside, but I also knew I couldn't wait. I didn't know what to expect, but Jeff's panic had convinced me there was no time to waste. Fortunately, Ali had Leroy so involved in his story he didn't hear the bookcase move. I overheard just enough of Leroy's story to realize he was the killer. You all know what happened next. The authorities tell us Leroy is alive and will recover physically, but seems to have lost his grip on reality. Mostly he babbles about nothing being his fault, but in the process, he has confessed to everything. I don't know if he'll end up in jail or an institution, but he won't be out where he can cause any more harm."

Kenneth said, "What a time for me to be off campus and miss the whole thing! I'm glad Alex came along when he did." He turned to Alex. "You were certainly the hero of the day, and we all have a lot to thank you for."

We all heartily agreed, and Alex managed to blush bright red.

Twenty-five

Two days later, we said all our tearful goodbyes and drove out the cobblestone driveway for the last time. We'd made some good friends at Druthmar, and we were grateful for all we had learned there, but sincerely hoped the college would have a more peaceful future under a new president.

We spent the next three days exploring New York City. We both loved the city and took full advantage of our time there. The architecture was fantastic, as was the quality and variety of food. I'll even admit we couldn't resist the temptation to do some shopping at all the fantastic stores available. We'd managed to fit in one Broadway show. Neither Laudine nor I could get enough of all the amazing museums. Even so, when we were finally headed down the hall to board our plane, I was excited to be going home.

It would have been a completely relaxed and enjoyable flight if when we walked through the plane's doorway, the bottle, carefully wrapped in a towel and stowed in the bottom of my carry-on, hadn't been mumbling something. It went on for quite a time, and I hoped it wasn't overly important, because I knew I couldn't take it out to listen until the plane landed in Phoenix, where we would have our first chance for privacy. Once we were seated, Laudine and I looked at each other, silently sharing the knowledge that we wouldn't be completely able to relax until we found out what cryptic message our disquieting three-tiered companion had for us. I hoped we would be ready for whatever was coming next.

Meet Eileen Harris

Eileen Harris likes to move and has tried many different areas of the U.S. At present, she is living in the Deep South but believes another move is in her future. Her writing may be set from upstate New York to the Arizona desert, or anywhere in-between. She writes when a book comes along asking to be written. The rest of the time she spends taking advantage of the opportunities and delights of her current locale.

Other Works From The Pen Of

Eileen Harris

__Antique Magic__ - An antique dealer hired to appraise a massive collection of treasure hoarded in a mansion is haunted by her past, a murder, and her future.

__Antique Forgery__ - Magic can't resist making an appearance when antiques, forgery, murder, and betrayal come together in a small Pennsylvania town, putting Alicia and her friends in grave danger.

__Antique Discovery__ - Murder, discovery, and mystery overtake Alicia when she is on vacation at a luxurious dude ranch and spa. The ancient discovery must be protected at all cost.

__Antique Legacy__ - While the castle crumbles, every room must be searched. Each discovery is more horrifying than the last. Murder follows Alicia, and only the large cat seems to offer an answer.

__Desert Shadow__ - An adventurous couple discovers human trafficking and the "Shadow Wolves" while living on the Arizona-Mexico border. Are either connected to the strange object hidden on their property?

__Black Cane__ - One woman refuses to let age render her invisible. Helping a small boy changes her destiny and that of her group of talented friends.

Letter to Our Readers

Enjoy this book?

You can make a difference.

As an independent publisher, Wings ePress, Inc. does not have the financial clout of the large New York publishers. We can't afford large magazine spreads or subway posters to tell people about our quality books.

But we do have something much more effective and powerful than ads. We have a large base of loyal readers.

Honest reviews help bring the attention of new readers to our books.

If you enjoyed this book, we would appreciate it if you would spend a few minutes posting a review on the site where you purchased this book or on the Wings ePress, Inc. webpages at: https://wingsepress.com/

Thank You